Celia Emmeline Gardner

Stolen Waters

Vol. 2

Celia Emmeline Gardner

Stolen Waters
Vol. 2

ISBN/EAN: 9783337408459

Printed in Europe, USA, Canada, Australia, Japan

Cover: Foto ©Andreas Hilbeck / pixelio.de

More available books at **www.hansebooks.com**

Stolen Waters

BY

CELIA E. GARDNER.

"Stolen waters are sweet."
PROVERBS, IX. 17.

NEW YORK:

G. W. Carleton & Co., Publishers.

LONDON: S. LOW, SON & CO.

M.DCCC.LXXI.

TO ONE

WHO HAS PROVED

AT ALL TIMES THAT HE IS

THE DEAREST, THE NOBLEST, THE TRUEST,

I this Dedicate,

WITH THE GRATITUDE, LOVE, AND ESTEEM
OF A HEART THAT HAS YET NEVER KNOWN SWEETER DREAMS
THAN THOSE HE HAS FILLED, AND WHOSE PRAYER IS, WHEN DEATH
SHALL HAVE STILLED OUR HEARTS' CURRENT WITH HIS ICY BREATH,
WE MAY STAND WITH EACH OTHER BEFORE THE WHITE THRONE,
OF HIM UNTO WHOM ALL HEART-SECRETS ARE KNOWN,
WHO, TEMPTED IN ALL POINTS AS WE ARE, LOOKS DOWN
WITH COMPASSION DIVINE, AS HE STUDS OUR BRIGHT CROWNS
WITH A GEM FOR EACH CROSS WE ENDURE, WHILE WE WAIT
FOR THE SUMMONS THAT COMETH TO ALL, SOON OR LATE.
THUS GRATEFUL, AND HOPEFUL, I THIS WORK TO THEE
CONSECRATE! PROUD TO SIGN MYSELF

THINE,

C. E. G.

1871.

PRELUDE.

You who never have loved—you who never were tried,
Lay this volume, without a perusal, aside !
Should you read it, you'd find much to shock preconceived
Ideas of what should and what should not be.
You would find no perfection of character here ;
Only weak human nature—the hopes and the fears
Of a heart, if undisciplined, loving and true ;
Temptations resisted, and yielded unto ;
And the tale of a love far beyond estimation,
All potent, in doubt or in realization.

I claim for my *heroine*, nothing ! except
Her humanity.   Yet from the reader expect
The remembrance that this is a Journal, wherein
She confides all her secrets ; some which would have been
Most carefully, jealously guarded, 'tis plain,
From the world.   For my *hero*, your *honor*, I claim.
For my *work*, ask that your criticism be mild,
Recollecting, in authorship, I'm but a child.

Sev'ral similar cases to this having come
Under my observation, when there has been done
By the world much injustice to those who have proved
In the end, although human, both earnest and true,
Three things it has been my endeavor to show ;

And lest I have failed in portraying them so
That they may be discerned,—like an artist I know,
Who writes o'er the landscape he paints, " These are trees,"
So I o'er my work write the points, which are these :—

First ! That no one can tell what they'll do 'till they're tried,
Must in like circumstances be placed to decide.
That those the most strong in asserting their own
Immaculateness are most often the ones,
Not alone to be tried in that special respect,
But to yield to the offered temptation when met.

Second ! That it is *possible,* for e'en a love
That's forbidden—impassioned and earnest above
All expression, to be not alone true but *pure.*
And that love without marriage not always ensures
Criminality for those who to it succumb.
And that a true love can but act upon one
Beneficially, and a refiner become.

And *third !* That though conscience and principle may
For a time be crushed down, in the end their full sway
They'll resume, and accomplish what naught else could do.
And with this prelude brief, I my work leave with you.

STOLEN WATERS.

PART FIRST.

" Sweet are stolen waters! pleasant is the bread
   In secret eaten."

POLLOCK.

" And thus, unnoticed and apart,
   And more by accident than choice,
   I listened to that single voice,
   Until the chambers of my heart
   Were filled with it by night and day."

LONGFELLOW.

Stolen Waters.

Part First.

NEW YORK.

November 2d, 1862.

SUNDAY.

My dear little Journal! so fresh, white, and new,
I have seated myself for a short chat with you,
And to tell you where I have been passing the eve,
If you will but listen, and give me the leave.
Annie called here to-night, and desired me to go
To the new church but just dedicated; and so
I donned cloak and furs, hat and boots and went forth.
'Twas cold, too! the wind blew direct from the north,
'Twas but a short distance, we soon reached the place,
And passed in with devout hearts and reverent pace.
'Twas lovely! but I am too weary, to-night,
To describe in detail all the music and light,
Soft carpets, rich carving, the Organ so grand,

The tablets containing our Lord's ten commands,
And all that.   But perhaps I may some other time
Describe all to you, even to the bell's chime.
To tell you the truth, my dear Journal, my thoughts
In vain sought to rise above earth, as they ought.
I seemed to be dreaming, or under a spell,
And which one it was I can yet hardly tell;
For a mouth wreathed with smiles I could see but too near,
And a voice full of melody burst on my ear;
For he sang as he smiled, and his dark, lustrous eyes,
Seemed reading my soul; and I found with surprise
That my cheeks burned with blushes, my eyes sought the
        ground,
The blood rushed through my veins with tumultuous bound,
Ev'rything was forgotten—time also, and place;
I heard but one voice, and I saw but one face.
This strange fascination continued complete
Till the service was over, and I in the street,
When the cool, bracing wind fanned my feverish cheek,
Subdued its deep flush, and unnatural heat,
And calmly the blood coursed once more thro' my veins,
And I my own stoical self soon became.
What was it affected me thus, there to-night?
I have heard people talking of " Love at first sight."
Was it love for a stranger that sent such a thrill
Through my frame, 'till my very heart seemed to stand still?
Was it love for a stranger?   No! that cannot be ;
We oft hear of such things, but who'd think it of me?
I, who have so many known—flirted so long,
To yield now, to a voice I've heard only in song?
Think of *my* proud, high spirit subdued by a smile,
A glance from soft eyes.   Call it consummate guile,

Call it music's enchantment, the pressure of light—
Call it sorcery, witchcraft, or aught that you like,
That so deeply impressed me at service to-night,
But *don't* say I'm in love with a man at first sight;
I hope I am not so susceptible, quite !

February 15th, 1863.

SUNDAY.

Well, my father at length has engaged a nice pew
In the handsome new church which is almost in view,
And henceforth, I suppose, we shall worship within
Those walls that were never polluted by sin.
That beautiful temple, so rich, yet so plain,
With large, Gothic windows through whose di'mond panes
The softened light streams with subdued, mellow ray,
O'er the worshippers therein assembled to pray ;
The walls faintly tinted, but unadorned still
By the chisel of sculptor or artist's fine skill;
The seats softly cushioned with green, and the floor
With carpets like Nature's own verdure laid o'er,
The pulpit of chestnut, green-carpeted stairs,
Rich books, velvet cushions, and sofa, and chairs,
Just below it the table, on which there is spread,
On the first of each month the wine holy and bread,
On service of silver ; and in the background
Stands their beautiful organ, from which such sweet sounds
Of melody float, you might fancy, almost,
That you were surrounded by Heav'n's shining host,

And think you were list'ning to harps of the blest,
Whose strings by the hands of bright angels are pressed,
So rich, so sublime, so mellifluous, sweet,
Now far off, low and faint, and then nearer and deep,
'Till its thunders arouse from its lethargic sleep
My ravished, entranced soul.   Then, at the right hand,
Gothic tablets, engraved with our Lord's ten commands;
At the left is the choir; a small, Gothic alcove,
Its darkness dispelled by dim lights from above,
While in the background, 'graved in letters of gold,
Are extracts from the Psalms of King David of old.
Our seat's near the choir—O! I must not forget
To tell you, my Journal, the choir's a quartette.
Well! in that lovely place we have worshipped to-day,
Arose when they sang, bowed the head when they prayed.
There I saw, too, a face I had seen once before,
Heard the same voice, with melody sweet gushing o'er,
Saw the lips, too, enwreathed with the same witching smile,
The eyes, merry glances thrown downward the while.
But his glances and smiles were all powerless, to-day,
I looked at him coldly, turned calmly away,
My heart beat no faster, no flush dyed my cheek,
But his voice!—oh, it was, indeed, wondrously sweet,
And I eagerly listened, as under a spell
As each note on my ravished ear then rose and fell.
The singers were all good, but *he* was sublime.
But 'twas the soft witch'ry of music, this time:
The charm which e'er dwells in harmonious sound,
Not love for the man which now held me spell-bound.
Indeed! as to-day I looked into his eyes,
I could not but think with a wondering surprise
Of the spell he cast over me, when our eyes met

A few weeks ago, for the first time ; and yet,
It *was* passing strange what o'ercame me that night,
Unless 'twas the heat and the strong press of light.
Whatever it was, I am firmly convinced
He had nothing at all to do with it !   And, since
It was not what I feared that it *might* be, that night,
I will have no more faith in this " love at first sight."

———

March 1st, 1863.

SUNDAY.

When I drew up the blind, somewhat early this morn,
I found there had been quite a heavy snow-storm,
And when it was church time, I hardly could tell
If 'twas best to go out or to stay at home.   Well!
Did not much like remaining within doors, all day,
So I donned rubber-boots, and we started away;
And when we soon after arrived at the church
Mr. Tenor was standing right there in the porch.
His glances at me were quite earnest, and I
Looked closely at him, too, while passing him by.
So you see, my dear Journal, I had a fair view
Of this wonderful (?) man, and this fine singer, too.
I suppose you would like a description of him,
I have told you so much of him.   Well! to begin,
He was not very formidable after all!
He is neither quite short, nor is he very tall.
His shoulders are wide, and you'd feel you could rest
Safe sheltered from harm on his broad, manly breast.

Dark hair, soft, dark eyes, and a mouth passing sweet,
Soft mustaches and whiskers shade both lip and cheek.
Hands white and well-shaped, moderately small feet,
You have now, my Journal, his picture complete.
Now if this noble gentleman only just knew
What a flatt'ring description I've given to you,
Of his exquisite singing, his fine manly grace,
His smiles and his glances, his form and his face,
What *would* he say to it ?   But that ne'er will be !
I can say what I please, my dear Journal, to " thee,"
Tell you all of my secrets, and ne'er have a fear
That you'll ever disclose aught that I whisper here
But, dear me ! what a soft little goosey I am,
To be thinking so much of a quite unknown man !
But I told you about him, upon that first night
When I " fell in love (?)" with him, you know, at first sight ;
I mean, therefore, to tell you henceforth all I know
Of him who's of late interested me so.
But to tell you the truth, perhaps I've over-drawn
My fair picture of him ; for a calm looker-on
Might not, perhaps, call strictly handsome his face ;
But his smile, and his grand, indescribable grace,
Which once made me forgetful of both time and place,
Are more charming by far than mere beauty of face.

March 22d, 1863.

SUNDAY.

Well! another brief week has passed swiftly along,
And another sweet Sabbath is now nearly gone.
And to service of course I again went to-day—
'Twould take strong inducements to keep me away,
For a Sunday at home I can never endure—
A stormy one even—and so I am sure
There's nothing that scarcely could tempt me to stay
From church upon such a magnificent day
As this one has been.   It *was* lovely as one
Could desire to behold ; for the glorious sun,
In unrivalled splendor, shone all the day through ;
The sky was one vast arch of unclouded blue ;
Each twig, bush, and tree were a-glitter with ice,
And the pavement as well, which was not quite so nice,
For many unlucky pedestrians met
A fall on the sidewalk so slipp'ry and wet.
The new-fallen snow, with a pure, dazzling sheet
Of white, covered tree-top, and house-top, and street ;
And sleigh after sleigh-load dashed swiftly along,
And before one could fairly behold them, were gone ;
And the tinkle of bells on the listening ear,
Fell with musical murmur so merry and clear.
The whole scene was charming ! but soon we passed in
From the splendor without to the beauty within.
Already, the organ's deep, exquisite notes,
All through the vast edifice solemnly floats.

The whole congregation is silent as death,
And I listen entranced, and almost catch my breath,
As the tones of the singers, so thrillingly sweet,
Join the organ's, and render the charm quite complete.
What, think you, cared I then that a bright smiling face
Was beaming on me from the usual place,
And a pair of soft eyes looking into my own?
I saw nothing, heard naught but the musical tones
Of the voices I've learned to, of late, love so well,
And that ever bewitch me more than I can tell.
But when next they arose the enchantment was o'er,
And I then could look into his fine face once more;
But he so intently gazed into my eyes,
That, in spite of myself, I could feel the blood rise
To my face, and I knew he had found he could call
A warm flush to my cheek, notwithstanding, too, all
My cold looks, and his glances indiff'rently met,
And the smiles that are haunting me, too, even yet.

July 5th, 1863.

SUNDAY.

Well! yesterday was the grand "Fourth of July,"
Our national holiday.   Gertrude and I
Went out to my brother's, and spent the whole day
In the cool, verdant country, so quiet; away
From the heat of the city, the dust and the din
Which prevails from the time that the "Fourth's" ushered in,
By the booming salute in the sweet early morn,
'Till the hour of midnight proclaims the day gone.

We passed the day quietly, pleasantly, then
At evening came back to the city again.
I felt this A.M. just a little fatigued,
But to church went as usual, my " Unknown " to see.
I saw *him*, and the smiles, too, that brightened his face,
As I my seat took in the usual place.
Oh, dear! I would much like to know what's his name,
But yet, what is the use? 'Tis of course all the same,
The gentleman nothing at all is to me,
And what is more still, never will, or can be.
I presume, did I know him quite intimately,
I'd think no more of him than of others I see;
'Tis the myst'ry that charms me, and if that was o'er
I'm convinced I should think of the man never more,
I know 'tis a mere passing fancy, and yet
It seems to be one I'm not like to forget,
At least very soon,—while I sit in the seat
Which I now do in church.

         'Twould be gladness complete,
It sometimes seems to me, if I only could rest
For one single moment upon his broad breast,
Could but around me have the clasp of his arm,
And know that he'd shield me from every harm.
But what am I thinking of?   How could I write
Such words as these *I've* written herein to-night?
Yet I read in a fine modern author, to-day,
"There is not a *true woman* but what longs to lay
Her head on the fond loving breast of a man,
And see in his eyes the one look that he can
Give to no one else in the whole world."   And so, why,
If the man truth was speaking, oh! then, why should I,

As I sit here this evening, in silence, alone,
Hesitate to write what not an eye but my own
Does now or will ever behold?　Why, I say,
If that be the case, should I blush to obey
The wise laws of nature, which prove me to be
A true woman according to *his* theory?
But I'm weary, and sleepy as well; and the light
Flickers so that I scarcely can see now to write.
The gas must be poor!—Well! I'm thro' for to-night.

———

August 9th, 1863.

SUNDAY.

How swiftly, indeed, time does hasten along!
Two whole months of summer are already gone,
The middle of August is now very near,
And ere we're aware of it, winter'll be here.
But yet, notwithstanding time passes away
So exceedingly fast, and that day follows day
In such rapid succession that one hardly leaves
Their bed in the morn ere it comes dewy eve,
Yet the same old story 'tis over and o'er,
The same weary routine gone through with once more,
The same dull monotony day after day;
Now a trifle of work, then a small bit of play,
A book that's absorbing, a brilliant day-dream,
Or a bright, flashing ray from hope's glittering beam,
A walk now and then on a clear moonlight night,
A letter received, or perchance one to write;

A call from a friend, or a brief visit paid,
An engagement fulfilled, or some promises made,
Sometimes a fine drive, an occasional song,
And thus, the long, warm, summer days pass along.
I am heartily tired of these trivial things!
I *would* like a change, now, whatever it brings ;
Something wonderful, startling, or thrillingly strange,
Something new, something grand, *anything* for a change !
I almost had said I would rather it be
Even grief than this sameness so irksome to me.
It is true we receive startling news every day
From the army, but that's such a distance away,
And no one is out there for whom aught I care,
With exception, it may be, of Colonel Allair.
Nor do I know why I should care for him much,
Though I think him a friend, and I like him as such ;
But then my acquaintance with him was but slight,
And yet I did think he would certainly write.
He did not, 'tis true, *say* he would, but I thought
He intended to do so, but that matters not ;
I was thinking, perhaps, that it possibly might
Have been some variation, although it were slight,
To the usual round that of late marks each day.
But there, let him pass ! I have something to say
About the events of the day nearly gone.

I went out to service as usual this morn,
But not as in general saw I the face
Of my charming "unknown" in his usual place ;
For a stranger, to-day, occupied his old seat
In the choir, and thus rendered their number complete.

Mr. S. gave to us a war-sermon this morn,
Which I of course listened to only with scorn.
I cannot at any time hardly submit
Under one of his ultra war-sermons to sit,
But think I was annoyed and disgusted still more
This morning than ever I have been before.
The discourse provoked me, was tediously long;
The music was harsh, and there seemed something wrong,
Something wanting, in all of the service to-day,
But what it might be I pretend not to say,
And I only can tell that, as over and o'er
I turned toward the choir, that I missed indeed more
Than I like to acknowledge, I think, e'en, to you,
My dear Journal, a face that I've been wont to view,   .
A voice I have listened to gushing in song,
And smiles that have beamed on me now for so long.
I wonder where *he* could have been all to-day,
And what could have kept him from service away.
By the way, my dear Journal, I'll say in this place,
That I heard a few days since his last name was " Chase,"
And that 'tis his intent to be married soon, too,
And then I should like to know what I'm to do!
For she will get all of his smiles if she's there,
And he will for me, then, have not one to spare.
Such a fate *would* be terrible(?).   And, by the way,
Perhaps that is why he was absent to-day,
And when next I see him, perchance by his side
I shall then see a beautiful, sweet, " blushing bride."
But there! I should really like to know who
The " fair ladye " may be if the story is true.
And I wonder if he will then give up his place
In the choir, if that should be the state of the case.

I hope not; I do not believe they will find
His peer very soon, not, at least, to my mind.
Perhaps, though, that *I* may be partial somewhat;
But then, who that ever has heard him is not!
By all I believe he's acknowledged to be
" Ne plus ultra " in singing, at least!   But, dear me!
I am too tired to think, and I'm too tired to write,
And presume I have said quite enough for to-night.

August 23d, 1863.

SUNDAY.

I have not been to church since the last time I wrote,
But have had of the service each day a report,
And each Sabbath they've politics had o'er and o'er;
And I thought I would not go to church any more
Until there's a change, for I cannot endure
Politics in the pulpit, and think, I am sure,
We hear quite enough of them during the week,
Without going to church and there hear a man speak
Of nothing at all beside slavery and war.
Now, I do not believe but that *I* do abhor
The system of slavery as much as does he,
Am just as desirous the slaves should be free.
But I own I don't think that the end justifies
The means; nor to me does it seem hardly wise
Our country to plunge into this civil war—
Which every nation should always abhor—
And our fair land to cover with unnumbered graves,
For the possible issue of freeing the slaves.

I think that if there had been made a decree
That every child henceforth born should be free
That it better, far better would been in the end,
For all would, of course, educated been, then,
For freedom; been qualified thereby to do
Their share in this life's hard, stern battle. And, too,
In a few fleeting years slavery would have been o'er,
And the "cry of the oppressed" would be heard never
    more—
All chains would be broken, all slaves would be free.
And then, too, how many fond hearts there will be
Left sad, and how desolate! *I* don't pretend
To be so patriotic. I never would send
Any dear friend of mine, to lose limb, perhaps life,
In this fratricide war, in this unholy strife.
I am not patriotic enough, yet, to bind
The sword to the side of a loved friend of mine,
And to bid him "God speed," with a clear, tearless eye;
Bid him go forth to battle, perchance, too, to die,
All alone and forlorn, with not one dear friend nigh
To catch the last word, or last, tremulous sigh;
Or, in a rude hospital, sick and unfriended,
To lie moaning with pain, yet unwatched and untended;
Or what would be worse still, in prison to be,
Unfed and unclothed, sick for sweet liberty.
Had this cruel war been with some other nation,
We could have endured our fair land's desolation—
Our broken home-circles, our firesides so drear,
The hush of the voices that once were so dear.
So fearfully hard it would not be to see
Our loved ones torn from us. Yes, it would, indeed,

Be different far if 'twas strife with another
Land or power; but brothers against their own brothers!
'Tis too horrid to think of, or speak of, or write!
And I think, too, that I have already said quite
Enough on the subject; I did not intend
To do the same thing which I just now condemned,
And preach a " war-sermon," my Journal, to you.
And perhaps, just as ultra this one has been, too,
As those Mr. S. writes, which I can't endure.
But I'm not in the pulpit, and I am assured
That my congregation is not a mixed one,
So I think there is not any great mischief done.

It has been pretty stormy the whole day, and so
I did not this morn go to church; and although
I expected, as usual, they'd have war to-day,
And that our Mr. Tenor remained yet away,
I was somewhat mistaken on both points, I find,
For the sermon this morn was exceedingly fine—
Father told me (he went out this morning alone),
And the music of course was, because " my Unknown"
His usual seat in the choir filled this morn;
And of course I regretted that I had not gone.
I would like to see him, and find out if I can,
If of him I must think as a lost, married man.
And I might have been able to tell if I'd gone
To church. But, it's being so stormy this morn,
She would not have been out very probably, so
I presume it's as well now that I did not go.
But I *would* like to know if he's married or not—
I, indeed, scarcely think that he is. I forgot

2

That I had the gentleman's name ascertained;
I *should* call him by it.   Yet it's all the same!
To me he's the " Unknown," beside, I'm not quite
Assured that the name to me given was right.

As father thought he would go down town to-night,
And as it was stormy, and dark, too, about
Half-past seven, to service none of us went out.
But next Sunday morning, I think I shall go,
And try to find out if he's married or no ;
And then, my dear Journal, I'll let you know, too,
And until then I think I must bid you adieu.

———

September 9th, 1863.

WEDNESDAY.

Again over two weeks have flown swiftly past,
And two Sabbaths have flitted by since I wrote last.
I service attended two Sundays ago,
And saw Mr. Tenor, but still do not know
Any better, in fact, than I did the last time
I wrote of him here in this journal of mine,
If he's married or not; I indeed only know
That as usual he sat in the choir ; know, also,
That no lady was with him that morning, and, too,
He looked and appeared just as he used to do.
I might, therefore, as well still believe him to be,
Until I know better, " heart-whole, fancy-free ! "

I went out to Tarrytown last Saturday,
Remaining 'till Monday, and so was away
From service on last Sunday morn.   Nothing new
Has occurred since that time. Yes, indeed ! there has, too !
The carrier called yesterday afternoon,
My Journal, and brought me a letter ; from whom
I could not imagine at first, as the hand
Was quite unfamiliar ; but when I began
A perusal of it, and had looked to see where
It was dated, inferred 'twas from Colonel Allair ;
And, on turning to look for the name at the close,
I found it to be just as I had supposed.
'Twas indeed a nice letter, but only just such
As I knew he would write, and it did please me much.
'Twas dated at Vicksburg, the twentieth day
Of last month ; and informed me that he'd been away
On service detached, for some little time past ;
But had now been sent back to the army, at last.
That at the surrender of V. he was there ;
But on the day following, Colonel Allair
Was detailed to convey to his far Western home
The mortal remains of a friend of his own,
His regiment's Major.   And that was why he
Had postponed for so long, this, his letter to me.
But hoped I'd excuse his unwilling delay,
And very soon write him a few lines to say
He still might regard me a friend.   That 'twas not
Because for a moment that me he forgot,
But feared that ere this I'd ceased thinking of him,
But hoped not, and trusted, though that might have been
The case before now, this would serve to remind
Me sufficiently of him to send him a line.

I said to him once, I was fearful that we
On certain points possibly might disagree.
So he writes :   .

            " My dear friend, why suppose that we do ?
I do not imagine we'd quarrel, do you ?
I believe, certainly, every one has a right
Their own free opinions to hold.   Though they might
Differ widely from others, I never should think
That they much moral courage possessed, should they shrink
From freely expressing the same.   And although
I am likely to say what I think, am also
Willing others should do just the same.   So think we
Shall not, my dear friend, *very much* disagree."
Then in speaking soon after of what he well knew
To be my opinions on war and peace, too,
He says :

            " I imagine, from what you have said,
That *your* ' love of union ' is too limited.
I think that, if I understand you aright,
That your love of union must ever be quite
In abeyance unto your wishes for peace,
To your earnest desire that the war should soon cease.
Now *my* love of ' union with peace ' is strong, too,
But when it is necessary to subdue
Rebellions like this, I say, ' union with war.'
But there are more unions that I've a love for.
' A union of States, and a union of lands,
A union of hearts, and a union of hands.'
And a union of man to the woman he loves,
Providing, of course, that both parties approve."
Then he adds farther down,

"But I yet do not know,
Of the passion of love, anything at all! So,
If any peculiar sensations are felt,
I own I am ignorant of their effect;
Nor do I intend, now, to make any such
Proposals to you, unless I very much
Change my mind on the subject. But hope now and then,
For some flashes of wit from your bright, lively pen,
That, for sweet friendship's sake, you'll sometimes send to me
A few lines, the monotony thus to relieve
Of my dreary war-path; and as far, too, as lies
In my power to do so, I ever shall try
To render it pleasant to you."
                                        That's about
All he wrote! But my light is so fast going out,
I must shut up my book, I suppose, for this time,
And go down-stairs. But, hark! the bell's ringing for nine,
So the gas in my dressing-room think I will light,
Read an hour or two, and not go down to-night.

———

September 27th, 1863.

SUNDAY.

My dear little Journal! I come here once more,
To have a nice chat, as so often before
We've chatted together in this tiny room,
At sunrise, at sunset, at midnight, and noon.
Under all circumstances as well as all times,
Right here, in this little dear "Sanctum" of mine,

This place all so quiet, where no one intrudes,
The spot where I always may find solitude,
1 sit here when the morning sun's glorious beams
Through the deep, arching window so dazzlingly streams,
And gilds with a radiance almost sublime
Every object in this dear apartment of mine—
The easy-chair here in this curtained recess,
The table beside it with wide-open desk,
The papers, engravings, and late magazines,
And touches again with its radiant beams
Every favorite book in the cases, and all
The familiar dear pictures which hang on the wall.
I love the spot, then.   When the deep glowing noon
Makes oppressive the heat, then I come to this room,
And I draw down the curtains to soften the light,
If a book I've to read, or have letters to write.
Then I love to sit here when the gathering twilight
Proclaims day is rapidly yielding to night,
Watch the swift-fading hues of the far sunset sky,
The stars glimmer out in the blue vault on high,
And trying to count them, as fast, one by one,
They dot the wide circle of Heaven's arching dome.
Then I love to come here in the night's silent noon,
When from high, spangled throne the fair, pale " lady Moon"
Serenely looks down on the still, sleeping world,
With its armies at rest, and its banners all furled,
Its doors barred, windows blinded, and storehouses closed,
And everything sleeping in perfect repose.
But though on the world she looks coldly, and me,
She floods with pure silver each leaf, bud, and tree,
And my " Sanctum " she fills with a weird, mystic light.
Oh, who can help loving a clear, moonlight night?

Then I sit in the window and rear in the air
Castles gorgeously grand, and surpassingly fair !
And give myself up for the time to bright dreams,
And imagine that all things are just what they seem ;
That all that doth glitter is pure, unalloyed gold,
That the world is not heartless, and cruel, and cold,
That friends never are false, nor our loved ones untrue,
No lost hopes to mourn, and no errors to rue,
That all is sweet harmony, purity, love,
No sorrow below, and no dark clouds above.
But when wishing to sleep, give me then a dark room,
No gas-light, no star-light, no light of the moon,
Let the curtain droop low, and draw down the blind tight,
And bid to things earthly a silent good-night.

   Well ! my brother each Saturday's been up for me
To go for the Sabbath with him up to T.
Since the last time I wrote, and of course, too, I went—
I had no excuse, there was naught to prevent,
And so I have not been to church 'till to-day,
Although I disliked much remaining away.
And it did seem so pleasant to be there once more,
And to hear the grand organ's exquisite notes pour
All through the vast temple, and hear once again
The tones of the choir with the organ's notes blend.
'Twas nice, just to sit in my usual place,
And see there above me the same smiling face.
I went out to service this eve, too, again,
It is *so* pleasant there in the evening ; and then
I like my " Unknown " to observe best at night,
Though he looks quite as well by day as by gas-light.

He's splendid in all places, and at all times;
And I *do* like him ever so much, too, in fine!
By the way, I believe I at last have found out
His name; and this time, too, without any doubt.
I never, in fact, believed really yet
My former intelligence very correct
In regard to the matter; nor could I have called
Him by that; but his name is not pretty at all,
The first or the last; but I think I'll not tell
You, my Journal, what 'tis—think 'twill be just as well
That you should not know it.   Suffice it to say
That his first name is "John," and a name, by the way,
That I never did like; although 'tis, it is true,
Quite a family name with us.   Then I have, too,
More friends by that name than by any beside,
Its Colonel Allair's, too!   My Journal, good-night.

————

November 3d, 1863.

TUESDAY.

   To-day is my birth-day!   I'm nineteen to-day,
Can another whole year have so soon slipped away?
And can it be possible that I have seen
Of girlhood's sweet birthdays the last in my teens?
It seems, when I look back, almost like a dream,
The years that have passed since I entered my teens,
And thought it would seem such a very long time
Before I was out of them!   But, Journal mine,
The long years have flown very quickly away,
And my nineteenth birthday I welcome to-day.

The weather to-day rather stormy has been,
But cleared off quite pleasant before evening;
The sun sank to rest in the beautiful west,
In his rich-tinted robes just as gorgeously dressed,
As if he'd not hidden almost the whole day
His glorious head behind dark clouds of gray,
And only emerged for a parting good-night
Ere leaving our world with his life-giving light.
Well! as it had cleared off so wondrously fair,
I thought I'd go out for a breath of fresh air.
And so, dressing, I went down to Ed Vamey's store,
For some pond-lily, pens, one or two trifles more.
He seemed, as in general, glad to see me.
What a singular man he to me seems to be!
Like Lord Byron's " bird with cerulean wings,"
Whose song ever " seemed saying a thousand sweet things,"
So his eyes and his tones do speak volumes sometimes,
As he touches my hand, or his glances meet mine.
His every word is almost a caress,
And his manner, in truth, seems at times scarcely less.
He's a rather fine-looking man, and—let me see!
His age I should think is about thirty-three.
I wonder sometimes if he seems just the same
To *all* lady friends, or e'en some I could name;
I presume that he does, though, but such looks and tones
I could give to no one I've as yet ever known,
And though I'm disposed very often to flirt
He seems too much in earnest, and fear I might hurt
His feelings far more than I'd gratify mine,
And for such a flirtation I now have no time.
With letters so often from Colonel Allair,
And my " Unknown " to think about, too, do not care
  2*

Another flirtation just now to begin,
At least with Ed Varney.   Enough, though, of him !
Let him pass for the present.

       And, oh, by the way,
I learned the address of " my Unknown " to-day,
His residence, his place of business, and all !
Next time I go down town I think I will call
At the store ; and if *he* should then chance to be in,
And I am so fortunate as to see him,
I shall know I am right ; then I'll send him a note.
Just the sweetest one also that I ever wrote.

And now, as the hours are fast taking their flight,
My birth-day I'll bid a regretful good-night !

———

November 9th, 1863.

MONDAY.

I of course went to church morn and eve, yesterday,
It has been quite a time now, since I've staid away.
Saw my charming " Unknown," and I heard once again
His exquisite voice in the solemn refrain,
And met the soft glance of his splendid dark eye,
And saw the same smile, as in days now gone by,
Such " perilous glances," " bewildering smiles,"
I very much fear this poor heart will beguile,
'Till I yield me a captive to love's rosy hand,
While he binds me quite fast with his glittering band,
And unlike " Ellen Douglass " and " Malcolm Graeme,"
His hand 'll hold the clasp, while *my* neck wears the chain !

Went down town this P.M. my friend Annie, and I.
So I stopped in the store as I chanced to pass by;
I purchased a magazine, at the same time
Looking 'round for the owner, that "Unknown" of mine.
And I looked not in vain! for, apart from the rest,
He sat, calm, serene, at a low private desk
Swiftly writing—oh, would that it had been to me
He was tracing those lines, graceful, careless, and free,
Intent on his task, never once raised his head,
Nor while I was in there a single word said.
He did look so handsome, so splendid, so grand,
Sublimely unconscious, that so near at hand
Was a girl just sufficiently foolish to let
His mild, handsome face haunt her thoughts even yet.

But enough! let him pass! I have seen him, and when
I get ready a note I will send him, and then
Perhaps he will sit in the very same place,
And over my letter bend his handsome face.

November 15th, 1863.

SUNDAY.

The last week passed quietly, calmly away,
With nothing important to mark its brief stay.
My sister came home from the East, Thursday morn,
And the next day a note from my friend, "Colonel John."
That is all, I believe, that is worthy of note,
Except that one evening a few lines I wrote,

Intending to send it off to my " Unknown,"
But my heart having failed me, I left it alone,
And its in my writing desk, still incomplete,
But I think I will finish it during this week.

It rained this A.M., so we all staid at home,
And father and I went this evening alone.
We were rather late, also, and when we went in,
The choir were just taking their places to sing.
My " Unknown " was there in his usual place,
Smiles adding their charm to his fine, manly face ;
And as the rich light with its radiance warm,
Beautifying and brilliant, streamed over his form,
To his strange fascinations quite captive once more,
I thought him more pleasing than ever before.
What is there about him bewitches me so ?
I am sure that I *would* very much like to know.
It is not his face, for although it *is* fine,
And I've praised it so highly, too, time after time,
Yet I've seen a great many far handsomer men.
There's Colonel Allair, to begin with, and then
Charlie Darling, and Morrill, and Gus, and—oh dear !
A great many more that I can't mention here.
It must be his manner, if 'tis not his face,
His sweet smiles, witching glances, his fine, manly grace,
His exquisite voice ever charming me so ;
And I think, more than all else, the fact that I know
So little of him, and not like to know more,
And am sure if I did that the spell would be o'er.
Acquaintance would break the enchantment, I'm sure,
And of my girlish folly effect a full cure.

Well! the service soon ended as all things must do,
And here I sit talking, my Journal, to you,
And showing, you see, just how foolish I am,
To waste so many thoughts on a quite unknown man.
But there! not a single word more will I write!
So I bid you, my Journal, once more a good-night.

———

November 18th, 1863.

WEDNESDAY.

Well! the deed is accomplished, the die has been cast,
And I've sent to my " Unknown " a letter, at last!
I wrote it last evening, despatched it to-day,
He'll receive it to-morrow, if there's no delay.
I'm impatient to know what its destiny 'll be;
If he'll deign to send a nice answer to me,
In " charity " written, with kindly words fraught,
Or cast it aside as unworthy a thought—
Misconstruing the motive with which it was sent,
Alone on its author bestow his contempt.
My letter ran nearly as follows, I guess,
First, the usual form of the date and address:
Date—   " New York, November 18th, '63.
Address—   " My dear Sir :
                              " I trust you'll pardon me,
And not deem me bold if I send you a line,
You a stranger!   Thus laying aside, for a time,
All etiquette rules; hoping you'll not refuse
To freely forgive me; and for my excuse,

Pleading int'rest in you, and my hopes you will send
A few lines in answer to your unknown friend.

I saw you at first, if I recollect right,
Over one year ago, and in church, Sabbath night.
What drew my attention at once, by the by,
I know not, unless 'twas the glance of your eye,
The smile on your lips, merry, careless, and free,
And your exquisite voice ever charming to me.
Since that time I've seen you again and again,
And each time I have liked you more, even, than then;
And although it is possible I have no skill
In reading correctly one's character, still
I think I may say you're not one to object
To a little flirtation, if *innocent*—yet
If I *am* mistaken I wonder if I
Could not reach your *vanity* if I should try.
Is it nothing to win an emotion from one
Who yields to the charm of your presence alone?
A passing emotion to win from the heart
Of one who has never been 'pierced by love's dart'?
Whose pulse other men have no power to thrill,
Who is queen of herself—and *intends* to be still?
You will think this is strange—so do I!—but you know
There are many strange things in this poor world of woe;
And I must repeat my sole motive to be,
My desire from your hand a few lines to receive—
There! I might have delayed a month longer, or so,
And then for my reason had 'Leap Year' you know;
Why did I forget it? But 'tis all the same.
Now 'tis not my intention to tell you my name,

Or aught of myself, and am sure 'twill be vain
For you to attempt any knowledge to gain
Of your correspondent, and it is alone
A future acquaintance to you'll make me known.
But here let me tell you, *en passant*, my friend,
That though to a stranger this letter I send,
That though ' to thee only e'er turns my fond heart,
And life is all lonely except where thou art,'
Though I sometimes ' long for a glimpse of your face,
With hopeless heart-achings for one dear embrace,'
Yet your wife—if you have one—is not, by the by,
Notwithstanding all this, any purer than I,
And the friendship I now entertain for you, too,
Is as disinterested, as sincere, and true,
As the most nice, fastidious person could wish.
I presume that I need not ask you to keep this
Strictly private ; a man of your age can but know
That it is for your *own* interest to do so,
Even more than for mine.   And, indeed, I may say,
That it matters but little to me, either way,
For you are acquainted with no one that knows
The hand which I write.   So you see, I suppose,
You can know naught of me, except what I propose
This time or in future to you to disclose.

"Now in closing my note, I ask—*will* you not send
A few lines in answer to your unknown friend?
And if, in the mean time, you *should* regard this
With favor sufficient to grant me my wish,
Will you not oblige me by wearing your ring
On your *left* hand, the next Sabbath morn, when you sing?
Not so ignorant am I of what we all call
The ' world,' not to fancy with readiness all

You may think of the one who this note sends to you.
But judge me with *charity*, as is my due,
And some time you *may* have occasion to change
Your opinion of me !—'twould be naught very strange !
Now, hoping to hear from you during the week,
I am,

   " With sincerity,

     " Yours.

       " ' Bitter-Sweet.' "

That, except my address, is the whole, I believe.
I may have an answer by Saturday eve,
But probably not 'till the following week. .
I am glad I have finished—I'm almost asleep.

November 22d, 1863.

SUNDAY.

One more holy Sabbath has vanished among
The things that have been ! And once more I am come
For a few moments' chat, my dear Journal, with you ;
As there's now nothing else I'm desirous to do,
And as I don't care to retire either, yet,
Though I ought to before very long, I expect,
For it's nearly eleven now, I must admit.
I *don't* like to go to bed early one bit !

I meant, as I said the last time that I wrote,
To have gone yesterday, to find out if a note
At the office was waiting, in answer to mine
I despatched to my unknown friend " once on a time."

But when I was dressed, and had stepped out the door,
I perceived what I'd quite failed to notice before,
That 'twas then raining fast; so I thought I'd delay
My walk to another and pleasanter day.
I did not, in fact, care about getting wet,
And 'twas doubtful, beside, if he'd written me yet.

Well! I've been out to church morn and evening again,
As a matter of course, my dear Journal! and when .
The choir were come forward the first time to sing,
Of course my first glance was for *his* diamond ring.
And my first thought for him ! And as then from my book
I raised my eyes slowly, my first quiet look
Was rewarded by seeing him standing up there,
And looking as merry, as gay, free from care,
As handsome, as smiling, as splendidly grand,
As ever before. And there on his *left* hand,
And taking especial pains to have it seen,
Was, as I expected, his elegant ring.
To-morrow some time I'll be certain to go
To see if he's sent me a letter or no.
Or if he was playing when carrying out
The request I in mine made his fine ring about.

My brother and sister were in town to-night,
And went to church with us.
My " Unknown " was quite
Amused about something, but *I* do not know,
Of course, what it was. But—I think that, although
With the same laughing glance he looked into my eyes,
Betraying therein no unusual surprise,
No curious wonder, yet he does not dream
That I'm his unknown correspondent, I ween.

His ring still remained on his left hand to-night,
And I saw it, of course! but he did not make quite
So much effort to hold it in such a way, then,
That it might be observed—as he did this A.M.
Sometimes 'twas behind him, as often he stands,
And sometimes his hymn-book was held in that hand.
But here I've sat dreaming and writing of him
And events of the day 'till my eyes are quite dim,
So my book I will shut up this instant, and write
Not one other line in my journal to-night.

November 26th, 1863.

THURSDAY.

To-day is "Thanksgiving!" But first let me write
What has happened to me since the last Sunday night—
That is, the result of my venture last week,
The kind of reception my letter did meet,
With all that pertains to the same!
                                   You must know
The morning hours, Monday, dragged tediously slow,
While the tasks which employed both my hands and my
        time,
Helped but little to quell such impatience as mine—
Provoking impatience! my most common sin!
Which makes in my heart such perpetual din,
Which ruffles my temper, and oft clouds my brow,
Unstrings every nerve, 'till I'm ready to vow
That life is a burden I fain would lay down,
And yield with the cross all my hopes of the crown;

That life is a battle the strongest must win,
Be they powers of good, be they powers of sin.
So much for impatience ! which, last Monday morn,
An unwelcome guest, which refused to be gone,
With hand on my heart-strings, kept close at my side,
And made the slow hours e'en more tardily glide.

Well ! the afternoon really did come at last,
And about two o'clock, or a few minutes past,
I was dressed, and had started for Brooklyn, to see
If there was at the office a letter for me.
'(I directed, my Journal, his answer should be
Sent to Brooklyn Post Office, in order that he
Might the less reason have for suspicions of me ;
For I, of course, do not intend he shall know
Who I am, either now or hereafter, and so
I must take all precautions lest he should find out,
As he would be glad to do, I've not a doubt!)
Well ! when the detestable clerk there had eyed
Both me and my letter till quite satisfied,
And quizzed me 'till patience was vanishing fast,
The much wished for letter he gave me at last.
With it safe in my hand I left there in great haste,
And for New York I started at once with quick pace,
And once more to impatience succumbing, you see,
And regardless of what etiquette's rules might be
On the point, I at once broke the seal of my note,
And in the street read what my unknown friend wrote ;
But glanced through it so swiftly, I really knew
Little more of my letter when I had got through
Than when I began ; but I hastened back home,
As fast as I could, and when once more alone

I read the nice note to my heart's full content
Which he to his new friend so kindly had sent.
He writes an uncommonly nice, handsome hand,
Especially so for a true business man,
Full and round, smoothly flowing as well as quite plain,
And the well-expressed sentiments, pleasing, the same;
On "Carson's Congress" it was written, enclosed
In a plain buff envelope; the same, I suppose,
Which he keeps in his office for use when he writes
To his business friends.   That, too, is just what I like !
Whenever a man sends a letter to me
I like that the note should a *manly* one be,
In paper, envelopes, and handwriting, too,
As well as its contents both honest and true.
But whenever a lady a note sends to me,
I don't care how dainty the billet may be.

To return to his letter again! Journal, dear,
I suppose you would like me to give to you here
A copy of it, as I have done of mine,
And I think I will, too, though I hardly have time;
It was not very long, or at least the one sheet
Was not nearly filled.   It commenced—
   " ' Bitter Sweet ! '

               " Your note of the 18th to me came
         to-day,
And I truly can do nothing less than to say,
That, as well as surprised, I of course could but be
Somewhat pleased at its contents ! But you must per-
      ceive
That you have indeed the advantage of me,
And I am of course very curious to see

And know you ; altho' you need have not a fear
I will take any means not quite open and clear,
And every way hon'rable, to ascertain
What would give me much pleasure to have you explain,—
That is, who is taking such int'rest in me,
And who my unknown correspondent may be.

" What a fine, pretty hand you are writing ! and so,
Of course, young and fresh it must be.   Do you know
What Don Cæsar Bazan exclaims to the veiled bride,
As he takes her white hand upon reaching her side ?
' It's tol'rably soft, and I'm curious to know,
With such a small hand, if a wrinkled face goes.'
Now that is just what is the trouble with me,
And I wonder if I could your hand just once see,
I could of your face judge, as *you* seem to trace—
Or affect to at least—by a glance at my face,
My character social.   But, let me ask ' who
Hath made thee a judge ' as between me and you ?
Who has said I objected to what you have called
An ' innocent flirtation ? '   Oh, no ! not at all!
And as to the ' vanity,' I have my share.
King Solomon seems to have had some to spare,
If we judge by his words.
                    " But there ! I cannot write.
To you, except 'tis with some vagueness, to-night,
As I do not know who you may be—man or woman,
A spirit or goblin, Divine or quite human.
And do you remember what ' Sam Weller ' says
(Of course you read Dickens ; all do in these days),
' Weal pies wery good is, when one knows as what
They are made of.'   But who *you* may be I know not,

Though the writing does look quite familiar, 'tis true ;
I never was good at conundrums ! Are you ?
If your wish is to see me, why, you can do so !
I'll not eat you, no cannibal am I, you know.
I think up to Carleton's I'll go, by the by,
And a copy of ' Bitter Sweet ' purchase—shall I ?
Do you mean to some fun have at my sole expense ?
I've a poem that's better than what you have sent,
Or *quoted* from, rather, but think it will keep
Until I know more of my friend ' Bitter Sweet ! '
I shall think in the meantime, believe me, of you,
With only the ' *charity* which is your due '—
All of my nature's charity, which I believe
I may say, too, is much.

> " Now in closing, receive
My kindest regards, and believe me to be,
Now and ever, indeed,

> > " Truly yours,

> > > " ' Antony.' "

> " To ' Bitter Sweet ! ' (wormwood and sugar.)"

> > > > And that

Was the end and was all.   Can it be 'tis in fact
A note from my " Unknown " I hold in my hand ?
Am I dreaming, or is it a truth, that the man
Whose eyes have so often of late sought my own,
And whose every motion familiar has grown,
To whose voice I have listened again and again,
In solo, or chorus, or solemn refrain,
Has over this letter bent *his* handsome face,
That *his* hand held the pen which these kind words have
    traced,

That his heart or his brain has dictated this note,
A pleasing reply to the one which I wrote?
I cannot the fact realize.

By the way!

I saw at an artist's rooms lately, one day,
A picture exactly like my "Antony."
(En passant, he seemed to adopt readily,
The fanciful name which I signed to my note,
And instead of his using his own when he wrote,
He too took a fancy one! mine ought to be
"Cleopatra," to match well with his "Antony!")
To return to the picture! And whose it might be,
Or if it was his, I was anxious to see.
The resemblance was striking, the painting, too, fine.
I gazed at its details for quite a long time.
I was sure it was him, or that if it was not,
Whoever it was, he had certainly caught
His smile and expression! and not only that,
The poise and contour of the head were exact.
The features were like, and the beard worn the same,
And in all points the likeness was perfectly plain.
His name of the artist I presently asked.
What was it? let's see! I believe it has passed
Wholly out of my mind. But it matters not, though;
He resides up at Harlem is all that I know.
It was not my "Antony."

Oh, by the way,

Had I gone to the office on last Saturday
His note I should probably found, as the date
Was November 19th. But it's getting quite late,
I must haste with what else I'm intending to write.

The first thing I did, of course, last Monday night,
Was to sit myself down at my desk, to indite
A reply to my note.   And I asked him to send
His next though to Brooklyn, in care of a friend,
My cousin Lorette.   She was over to-day,
And I told her about it ere going away.
And charged her to keep it quite safely for me
Did the letter arrive before *I* was there.   She
Thought it was romantic, yet hardly approved.
She thinks that the world and its people should move
In the one self-same channel forever and aye.
But I tire of the same events, day after day,
A change like sometimes, and the stranger the better.
Oh dear, I will try and get back to my letter.
I don't know what ails me! somehow I can't keep
To-night on one subject.   I am not asleep,
I believe.   But then! I've been so blue all the day,
Though there is no reason for it, I must say;
I believe that I am not like other girls quite.
A houseful of friends we have had here to-night,
In fact, have all day, and all friends near and dear,
But somehow the day has been lonely and drear.
To to-day, though, I have not arrived yet; my thoughts
Seem to be anywhere else except where they ought.
Once more to my letter!
                    The first thing I wrote
Was but to acknowledge receiving his note,
With thanks for the favor; and as to the rest,
'Twas less sentimental than saucy, I guess.
I began with affectionate warmth, it is true,
And there was an undertone of it all through,
But yet it could hardly be called sentiment.
As the frail wood anemone's delicate scent

Is too fresh and too faint to be named a perfume,
So this was too faint and too pure.

                To resume !
I thanked him, of course, for replying so soon,
And fulfilling my wish in regard to the ring,
Was exceedingly glad to find, I assured him,
By the letter which I that p.m. had received,
That he in that point at least had not deceived
His friend yet unknown, howe'er treacherous he
Might in the dim future himself prove to be.
I gave him in answer to what he would know
Of me and my name the quotation below:
   " I know a girl with sunny curls,
      And shoulders white as snow ;
     She lives—ah, well ! I must not tell,
      But *wouldn't* you like to know ?
     She has a name, the sweetest name
      That mortal can bestow.
    'Twould break the spell if I should tell,
      But *wouldn't* you like to know ? "
Somewhat tantalizing he'll think it, I fear,
The best I can do for him now, though, howe'er
Desirous he may be to know more of me.
Then I said—
         " So you fancy that if you could see
My hand you could judge of my face ! I will try
And send you a photograph of it. Shall I ?
Of course you can't guess who I am ! I did not
Suppose that you could ! but I know all about
You and yours ! and not only that, but I've be;—
In your business place, and you were writing, too, but
But it was not to me.
   3

                    " Don't you like, my dear friend,
My nom-de-plume ?   Why! I am sure that the end
Is *sweet* if the rest is not ; possibly, you
Will find, if I'm *sweet*, I am *bitter* some, too.
Its language is ' *truth.*'   I believe I am true !
I think the name pertinent all ways ! don't you?"
I spoke of attending the service to-day,
If nothing prevented, and went on to say
That I never could see him at all, where I sit,
Except during singing, and if he saw fit
To sit farther forward, just so he could see
The preacher, he at the same time would please **me**.
And added,
            " I *do* ' wish to see you,' and do
Quite often, but hardly dare trust myself *too*
Near to you for the present, at least.   I can you
At a safe distance see, but if you would please send
Your picture to your, though unknown, yet true friend
'Twould indeed please her much."
                            Then I asked him if he
Did not like my poetry ; and—saucily—
" Now I thought you would think it was flattering, quite;
I defy you to find any better.   You might,
Though, send me the piece you referred to, and I
Expect it will come to me with your reply."
I wrote somewhat more, but we'll let the rest go.
It rained very hard all day Tuesday, and so
I found it impossible quite to get out
To mail it that day, so I very much doubt
His having received it as yet, though it might
Just possibly come to his hands late last night.

To-day is " Thanksgiving "—I said so before—
And I'm heartily glad that the day is now o'er.
The morning was pleasant, but cold. I must own
'Twas not with reluctance I went out alone
To church this A.M. No one else was inclined
To go out, or in fact seemed to have enough time
To spare for the purpose. And though it is true
We should have a political sermon, I knew,
Yet I had my " Antony " told I should go,
And I mean to do just as I promise, you know!
The sermon, if possible, seemed rather more
Triumphantly ultra than ever before.
The reverend man never energy lacks
When he's preaching of war, or of freeing the blacks.
I did not, however, expect on this day
To hear aught but that; but endeavored to pay
As little attention to it as I could,
Though I could but acknowledge that some points were good
For instance, he quoted in *his* matchless way,
A poem from Whittier, which, I must say,
Was not only pertinent, in itself fine,
But rendered exquisitely.
                                        In the meantime,
I thought of my Antony, who, I well knew
Was right there before me, though hidden from view.
When the service was over, and we going home,
He walked right in front of me, he, too, alone!
How little he knew that his friend " Bitter Sweet "
Was so near at hand as he turned at his street.
How I wished that the spell were dissolved that must keep
Us forever apart; that at one mighty sweep

I might break all the bands with which Custom doth bind
Our acts, though we still keep unfettered our minds.
Well! he passed down the street, and soon entered his door,
And between us there then rose one barrier more.
I, too, hastened home! As I said once before,
We've a houseful of visitors had here all day;
I might have enjoyed it if I had been gay,
As I am sometimes. Hark! the clock's striking one,
I am *so* tired, and glad that at last I have done!

November 29th, 1863.

SUNDAY.

Another week's rapidly flitted away;
Again it is Sunday! I went yesterday
To make a short call on my cousin Lorette,
With hopes that I also a letter might get.
And she *is* true as steel, if she did not approve
My romantic and somewhat unusual move.
I knew I could trust her. We soon went upstairs
To her own little "Sanctum Sanctorum," and where
She placed me at once in her favorite chair,
And gave me my letter, all safe, smooth, and fair.
Not long was I breaking the seal of my note,
Or reading the kind words my Antony wrote.
As I thought, he did not, it appears, receive mine
Until Friday A.M. And his letter *was* fine,
Much nicer I think than the other he sent,
And gave me much pleasure, I own! It commenced

" To my sweetest Bitter, and bitterest Sweet ! "
A form of address I thought rather unique,
Yet characteristic of him, I believed.
And then wrote as follows :
        " Your note I received
In this morning's mail, and of course I was pleased
At hearing from you. But you'll please recollect
That Thanksgiving came yesterday, therefore expect
From a quite torpid brain not much brilliance to-day,
In reply to your letter. And here let me say
I believe that I am not afflicted at all
With a certain disease which is commonly called
' Cacoëthes Scribendi.' "
        And then he went on
To ask if I went to church Thanksgiving morn,
And heard the " political sermon." He thought,
As regards abolition and war, that it ought
To content the most ultra—I'd written in mine
That I was exceedingly fond of that kind.—
He was pleased that his letter was gladly received,
And hoped I'd enough " charity " to believe
It to be on his part but a mere oversight
That he failed in his other to ask me to write.
Says—
        " I ask who you are, and you give me a bit
Of a poem in answer. Now I will admit
Poetry is indeed very good in its place,
But don't answer questions—at least in this case.
Of course I should much ' like to know ' who you are,
My far-off, unknown, ' bright particular star ! '
Do not send me a photograph, though, of your hand;
If you do I'll not have it, indeed ! but you can

The thing itself place in my own, then I'd know
I was holding in mine something more than shadow;
But one of your face you can send me. How, though,
Should I send mine to one I as yet do not know?
I've not lost my reason, or caution, and still
You can have a good chance to exchange if you will,
When I've aught to exchange with."

                       How much I would like
His fine pictured face! How I wish that I might
Comply with the terms, if in no other way
I might have it. Although, it is needless to say,
That's out of the question, of course. He'd know me
As soon as he saw it, and that must not be.
Who his " Bitter Sweet " is I cannot let him know,
Or now, or henceforth; but I don't tell him so.
He fondly imagines he'll know me some time.
I don't undeceive him. Dream on, friend of mine!
Hope is good for the soul, and " an anchor both sure
And steadfast," 'tis said. Though we find it a lure
Too often, I fear, to the bitter despair
Of grim disappointment. Hope promises fair,
And leaves us to find, in reward for our faith,
In our grasp but a phantom, a flickering wraith—
A shadow delusive, as fleeting as sweet,
Yet by all mankind followed with swift, eager feet,
Who will never be warned by another's sad fate
But press madly forward, nor pause 'till, too late,
They find themselves in disappointment's broad lake.
She tells us without her our fond hearts will break,
Then leaves us to sicken with faint " hope deferred."
I have a dear friend whom I often have heard

Declare she has been disappointed in naught,
Because she ne'er hopes.   She had certainly ought
To be indeed happy!   At least, *I* think so.
I envy her more than all persons I know.
But I'm not like her; I have less self-control,
A more turbulent heart, and more intense soul;
Have less calmness of nerve, and less coolness of brain.
Less firmness, more impulse; in short, it is plain
We are cast in two moulds which are very unlike,
Or made of materials different quite.
But if I *could* crush out all hope from my heart,
And in my acts give the " fair siren " no part,
·List not to her calls, shut my eyes to her smiles,
And yield nevermore to her dangerous wiles,
Feel free from her temptings both now and alway,
I would have nothing more to desire!   I could say,
" Howl, wind of November, rough, wrathful, and chilly,
As loud as you please, and I'll not take it illy,
For here in my chamber all's comfort and ease,
All's peace and delight, all is pleasure and glee,
For I'm happy to-night as a mortal can be! "
But " Dum spiro spero " 's my fate, and should be
My motto!
             Well! back to his note—let me see!
How far had I written?   The picture—and then
The next thing he wrote was, I think, near the end—
" Your quotation—I surely no fault found with it,
For 'twas good, and if true was of course better yet.
But then, I am sure it was merely ideal,
And I send you my own, and imagine it real.
This scrawl please excuse, and believe me
                    " Your own
                         " Antony.

" To my ' Bitter-Sweet.' "

This was the poem :

" You kissed me ! my head had dropped low on your
        breast,
With a feeling of shelter and infinite rest,
While the holy emotion my tongue dared not speak
Flashed up like a flame from my heart to my cheek.
Your arms held me fast ! and your arms were so bold,
Heart beat against heart in that rapturous fold,
Your glances seemed drawing my soul through my eyes,
As the sun draws the mist from the sea to the skies.
And your lips clung to mine 'till I prayed, in my bliss,
They might never unclasp from that rapturous kiss.

" You kissed me ! my heart and my breath and my will
In delirious joy for the moment stood still.
Life had for me then no temptations, no charms,
No vista of pleasure outside of your arms.
And were I this instant an angel, possessed
Of the glory and peace that is given the blest,
I would throw my white robes unrepiningly down,
And tear from my forehead its beautiful crown,
To nestle once more in that haven of rest,
With your lips upon mine and my head on your breast.

" You kissed me ! my soul in a bliss so divine
Reeled and swooned, like a drunken man foolish with wine.
And I thought 'twere delicious to die then, if death
Would come while my mouth was yet moist with your breath.
'Twere delicious to die if my heart might grow cold
While your arms wrapped me round in that passionate fold.

And these are the questions I ask day and night:
Must my soul taste but once such exquisite delight?
Would you care if your breast was my shelter as then,
And if you were here would you kiss me again?"

    I think it exquisitely fine. And of course
Seems doubly expressive to come from that source.
Impassioned and sweet, yet refreshingly pure,
No fault I can have to find with it, I'm sure.
But to come to to-day! and to hasten it, too,
For as ever 'tis late, I must quickly get through.
To church morn and eve I of course went to-day,
Saw my "Antony," too, just as handsome and gay—
He does have such an easy and nonchalant way,
As if nothing could ruffle him, let others say
Or do what they might. And his temper is sweet,
I am certain, as well as his manner just meet
To match with his face, so serene, true, and kind.
His soft, laughing, passionate eye still meets mine,
Persistently, sweetly as ever, and yet
I've not the least reason to think he suspects
That I am his Bitter-Sweet! never a trace
Since sending my first have I seen in his face
Of bewilderment, doubt, curiosity, aught
Of inquisitive wonder. 'Tis strange he does not
Have any suspicions, not only of me
But of no one beside. There are many that he
Might with very good reason imagine to be
His unknown correspondent.
                  Oh well, let it pass!
I sent him an answer to-day to his last.
    3*

He'll receive it to-morrow !   And oh, by the way,
He sat not in front as I asked him, to-day ;
I suppose that he thinks he's not anxious to be
Closely scrutinized all the time, even by me,
His " own Bitter-Sweet ! "   That 'tis sufficient that he
Is constantly conscious that some one unknown
Is watching each motion and look of his own
When he sings.   So he sat in his usual seat
In the " corner " this morning, and so Bitter-Sweet's
Request was unheeded.   I asked what he did,
In my letter to-day, when he sat safely hid
From sight in the " *corner*."

                 'Tis late, and in bed
I must hasten to pillow my quite wearied head.

December 2d, 1863.

WEDNESDAY.

Oh, how perfect the night !   I've been sitting upstairs
The whole evening, nearly.   My great easy chair
And my table drawn close to the bright glowing grate,
I have written and dreamed 'till it's getting quite late,
With my journal unopened before me.   The night,
With its undreamed-of beauty all hidden from sight,
By the low-drooping shade, and the tightly-closed blind.
Unheeding the voice of December's chill wind,
Its soft calls for entrance at casement and door,
I have, as I said, sat the bright fire before,
Slow yielding to Fancy's magnetic advance,
Her airy bright dreams, heart-bewildering trance.

At intervals writing, when not in the power
Of the lovely enchantress, 'till hour after hour
Have rolled their swift round, to return never more
From the vanishing past, from Eternity's shore.
" Like a song that is sung, and a tale that is told,"
They have now passed away, and the day waxes old.
Midnight softly approaches, and swift, one by one,
The minutes glide onward, and—*this* day is done !
The clock's striking twelve, my watch ticks a response,
And silence and midnight are now, for the nonce,
Of our city twin-monarchs unquestioned.   The bell
Slowly tolls for the hour just departed, and swells
Softly deep on the clear, frosty air.   Now the last
Stroke is dying—farewell to to-day !
       I had passed
To the casement a short time ago, and I drew
Up the shade to look out on the night.   And a view
Before me was spread I've no words to describe.
My seat I resumed, but I left open wide
Every blind in the room, that the full lustrous tide
Of the night's perfect beauty might entrance gain here,
While I sit here and write.
      And the picture spreads clear
And sweetly before me ! The city lies calm
In night's silent embrace; and a lullaby psalm
Is sung by the wind, though it tranquilly sleeps
And heeds not the clasp or the music which sweeps
So fitfully, tenderly o'er it.   Its spires,
Gleaming white in the moonlight, now seem to point higher
Than ever before to the home of the blest.
All with eloquence speaks of sweet quiet and rest.

So much for the background!   And now in the fore
The park lies all silent, the trees festooned o'er
With creamy white snow-wreaths, and ice-pendants, too,
Which glitter like diamonds, or morning's clear dew,
As over the whole streams the moonlight.   The street
Is deserted! and hark! I can hear my heart beat,
So profound is the hush.   The long, deep shadows meet,
Intertwining and tracing, too, figures unique,
Graceful, fanciful, varied, oft shifting, too,
As the fickle wind flits the white tree-branches through.
And then over all is the arched azure sky,
Deeply blue and unclouded.   The moon's riding high
On her grand throne of state, and her radiance bright
Sweeps over all points of the picture, and lights
With a brilliance sublime the whole view.   And the stars,
Scintillescent, unnumbered, and lovelier far,
To my eye, than all in the picture beside,
Glow softly and purely ; and spangle in bright
And boundless profusion the vast vault above,
A glorious array !   And the bright star of love
Still more lovely than any shines soft from afar—
Sweet Venus, our beautiful " Evening star."

Farewell to the night! let me now turn away
From its beautiful self, while I come to to-day—
The day just departed.
                    I went this A. M.
To Brooklyn to look for a letter again,
And I went not in vain, though I fancied I should
All the way over there.   He's indeed very good!
I said in my last I'd a long way to go,
And hoped he would not disappoint me ; and so

His letter was promptly dispatched.   He replied
As follows to that part :
                    " You do not reside
In Brooklyn, my Bitter-Sweet ?   Well ! it is true
I hardly supposed that you did ; nor did you
Even *say* that you did : but you only implied
It in your first letter."
                    The city is wide,
He cannot locate me.   Poor boy ! 'tis too bad
I can't tell him the whole.   I am sure I'd be glad
To do so at once, if I thought 'twould be best.
Think of that, though, I *must* not !   And now for the re:
And hastily too, of my Antony's letter ;
It was not very long, began—" My Sweet Tormentor ! "
He acknowledged at first the receipt of my note,
Praising me for the promptness with which I last wrote,
Saying I would an excellent post-mistress be,
And then—
                " But don't bother my life out of me,
Keeping me for so long in suspense, like a fish
With a hook in his gills ! "
                        So my gentleman is
Getting rather impatient, I see ; nor can I
Wonder at it, indeed ; but I can't gratify
My dear friend in this point, though I made in reply
Promise fair of acquaintance with me by and by.
He was glad I was pleased with the poem he sent,
And how could I help it ?   *'twas* fine, and he meant
When some better he found to at once let me know.
He sent me with this note another also.
Then he said,—

" In regard to the ' corner ' I read,
Sometimes ' *snooze* ' a little, don't talk much, indeed,
But a great deal of thinking I do.　How should I
For a sight perch myself up? although, by the by,
If 1 knew where you sat, might perhaps get a glimpse
Of you once in a while."
　　　　　　　　　　I remember now, since
Receiving his letter, that I in my last,
Criticising the poem " You Kissed Me," had passed
To say, I supposed every one's heart to be
On the *left* side.　In that case, of course he must see
A position in which a " heart beats against heart,"
At least, must be awkward extremely.　That part
He replies to as follows:
　　　　　　　　　　" Now as to the heart,
Of course every one's is expected to be
On the *left* side! but then, did you never yet see
Or hear of a person that had not a heart?
I have, at least, many, I think, for my part."
Wrote a page or so more, then abruptly he says,
I am going away to be gone a few days,
Shall return Friday morning, expecting to find
A letter from fair Bitter-Sweet.
　　　　　　　　　　" Ever thine,
　　　　　　　　　　　　　" Antony."
　　　　　　　So a note I have written this eve
In reply to his last, and which he will receive,
I trust, as he wished, Friday morn.　A last look
At the beautiful night while I'm closing my book.

December 6th, 1863.

Twilight finds me again in my nice cosey room,
Sitting close by the window; the gathering gloom
Slowly filling my sanctum with weird shadows grim,
While without distant objects now swiftly grow dim.
Fading are the rich hues from the far western sky,
The first star shines out in the blue arch on high,
And the short winter twilight is o'er.   I must light
The gas in my sanctum if wishing to write.
I've sat here a long time, my eyes on the grand
Sunset clouds in the west, with my cheek in my hand,
Unopened the book in my lap.   A tumult
Of vague troubled thoughts in my mind, the result
Of to-day's observation and last night's event.
I'll tell you about it !
    'Twas late when I went
To B. yesterday for my letter.   The day
Had been, oh, *so long!*   Failed in getting away
'Till late in the afternoon; then it to me
Seemed an endless long way from here over to B.
All day I had scarcely dared think I should find
Any letter awaiting me there, and my mind
And nerves were so wrought up with hope, doubt, and fear,
Being anxious to go, and yet forced to stay here,
That I've been somewhat irritable all the day,
Nervous, too, and—well, " *cross,*" I once heard Gertrude say.

And when I at length was *en route* for Lorette's,
As I said just above, the way seemed longer yet
Than ever before.   When I reached there at last,
The sun had long set and 'twas growing dark fast.
My cousin I found entertaining some friends,
And I thought, I am sure, their call *never* would end.
Lorette guessed the question my first glance implied,
And by one just as eloquent quickly replied.
And then softly whispered, while kissing my cheek,
" I've a letter upstairs for my dear ' Bitter-Sweet.' "
I was forced to *seem* calm, although inly I chafed,
While they talked of all things, and of nothings ! and raved
About this one's fine mustache, and that one's sweet face,
Of Miss A.'s last new dress, of Miss B.'s lovely lace,
The next ball, last night's party, and so, on and on,
'Till politeness and patience were both nearly gone.
I turned to the window in silence, and found
It was growing yet darker each moment.   The sound
Of their farewells at length reached my ear ; and then I,
With a smile *not* all feigned, turned to bid them good-by.
Lorette shut the door on her callers, and ran
Upstairs for my letter.   'Twas soon in my hand,
And I went to the window to catch the few last
Faint gleams of daylight, while she lighted the gas.
I turned from the casement at length, with a cheek
A-flush with both pleasure and pain—turned to speak
To Lorette, but the dear girl had gone out the room
That I might be alone with my letter.   She soon,
However, returned, in her sweet, pretty way
Did her best to induce me in Brooklyn to stay
Until Monday A.M. ; but I sent her instead
To her room for a hat for her dear little head,

And her home dress to change for her walking attire.
Her toilet was made with a speed I admire
Very much, but somehow never *can* emulate,
And homeward we started at once, at quick rate.
She returned home this morning.

                       And now for his letter !
I think that he never has sent me a better.
And yet, as I said once before, or implied,
It gave me some pain if much pleasure.   Each vied
With the other for conquest.   But still, of the two,
I think the most pleasure remains.   Though 'tis true
I scarcely can tell which is yet most complete,
But if pleasure, my name it is like, *bitter-sweet!*
In order to make plain some parts of his note,
I'm obliged to refer to some things which I wrote
In my last one to him.   And first, some time ago,
In one of my letters, and when he was so
Very curious as to who B. S. might be,
I told him he need not be looking for me
Among *black-eyed* ladies in church.   And I this
Said because, though I did not assuredly wish
Him to think me his new correspondent, I yet
Did not care, I think, either, that he should suspect
Any one else *but* me.   And to this he has never
Made any reply 'till this very last letter.
Then in answer to what he about the P.M.
In his other had said, I replied—

                       " When I spent
Some time in the country, a few years ago,
I had a dear friend who was post-mistress.   So
I thought it fine fun to assist her, you know !

Nothing new would it be to me, therefore, you see,
To be a ' P.M.' do you not, Antony ?
I think I'd not care to hold office, although,
Under ' Abraham First.' " Then I told him, below,
In regard to desiring to see me, that I
Was going down town to have made, by and by,
A hair ring, which a dear friend in dying gave me,
And then it was possible, too, he might see
His own " Bitter-Sweet." Promises doubtful somewhat,
And I fancy that *he*, too, will think they are not
Extremely reliable. Then I said, too,
Concerning the picture—

                    " I cannot send you
One of mine, I believe, for you'd certainly know
At the very first glance who was ' Bitter-Sweet.' So
If on no other terms you will send yours to me,
Contented without it suppose I must be."

    I come now to his letter, of which I intend
A copy to give from beginning to end,
To you, and to you, my dear Journal, alone.
First, as usual, the date, then—

                   " My 'Antony's own ! '
I received yours this morning, and find you are still
Most punctual in your correspondence ; and will
You be in your *promises* also ?

                   " How came
That thought of the post-mistress into my brain ?
Was it a coincidence, do you surmise,
Or was it pathetism ? say, my Blue Eyes !
And so *you* do not like ' Abraham the First.' Well,
I can't say that *I* do a great deal myself,

Although I doubt not there are yet many men
That are, in some points, worse than he is.   But then
We will let, as a mantle, our 'charity' cover
Their sins of omission and commission over.
Well! I'm just as inquisitive, curious, too,
Now as ever before.   Yours are not 'eyes of blue'
When I'm singing at church I so frequently meet
Upturned to my own, are they, my Bitter-Sweet?
What do you suppose in the 'corner' I read?
'Words, words, words,' but I think not a little indeed
Of late, and of whom?   aye! my friend, that's the question!
Can you guess, or in truth make the slightest suggestion
As to who it might be?   Do we not, it is clear,
Attend service the preacher's fine sermons to hear,
And of what he discourses to *think*?

        " I suppose
When you have your ring made I shall see it; who knows
But I am a judge of the article, too?
Do you really think I should recognize you
If your picture I saw?   Well! and what if I do?
Are you so ill-looking that you are afraid
To be looked at, my B. S.?

       " Quite likely you may
Have before seen the poem, and possibly, too,
The first.   Both were good! I think *this* is, don't you?
 'For the pillow of down where you rest your head,
  I'll pillow my own on your breast instead,
  For love can soften the hardest bed.
   And I know that I love you!
  And when you grow tired of your marble halls,
  Of your weary life and its gilded thralls,
  Come where the voice of true love calls,
   And see how I love you!'

' La patience et amère, mais son fruit est doux ! '
Your whole name is there.   When am I to see you,
No longer to draw on the imagination
Of

      " Your

         " Antony ? "

                    With full realization
That he at last knew me, I went out, to-day,
To service as usual.   Although I must say
My heart faster beat, as I entered the porch,
And also the whole time that I was in church,
Until its pulsations almost made me faint,
And colored my cheek with a crimson not *paint*,
And made me self-vexed at my want of control
Of my heart and my face.   The vexation of soul
Did not better it much.   And then, not only that,
But in front all the A.M. my " Antony " sat,
And by his frequent glances, his witching, and wise,
Conscious look, and soft smiles, too, whenever his eyes
Met my own, very plainly told me, if before
I had doubted, that all mystery was now o'er,
In his mind, at the least, and was certain he knew
His Bitter-Sweet now.   *I* would like to know, too,
After such a long time how he came to suspect
Me to be his unknown correspondent.   And yet,
I wonder, as I've said before, he has not
Read the riddle ere this, and discerned the whole plot.
He sat with his back to the preacher, so I
Could not, if I would, fail to understand why
He sat in the front of the choir this A.M.,
And glanced so persistently at me.   But then,

Although, as I said once before, in his look
There was consciousness plain, even that I could brook,
As long as no triumph blent with it.   And I
Must acknowledge I could not, indeed, should I try,
Take the slightest offence at his actions, or feel
That any desire I need have to conceal
My identity longer from him.   For if pleased
And conscious he looked, and convinced, yet, at least,
There was nothing but sweetness expressed in his face—
And of triumph or sarcasm never a trace.

   This was last night's " event," and was also a part
Of to-day's " observation," which rendered my heart
And thoughts much more troubled than ever before.
" Never singly misfortunes do come."   I was more
Annoyed at his guessing than I have expressed,
And ere I to that became reconciled, pressed
On my heart was another and far deeper cause
For trouble, vexation, regret!   And this was—
But first, I must go back a very short time,
To a trifling occurrence, which made on my mind
At the moment no sort of impression, I think,
And yet, has, it seems, proved to be the first link
In the chain of events which first made me suspect
What now I am sure of.   I don't recollect
Exactly how long, but a few weeks ago,
My Sabbath-school teacher was absent, and so,
With exception of one or two, all of the class,
And the superintendent to me came to ask
If I would a class please to teach for the session?
He'd take no refusal, so I took possession

Of a small class of boys near my own. They were lads,
I think, of about twelve or thirteen. I had
In marking the class-book, to ask them their names—
There were two little boys there whose names were the
     same
That my Antony's is; and then, not alone that,
But they on the same street resided, in fact,
Or one of them, rather, the other boy being
A cousin from out of town; both, though agreeing
Sufficient in manner and look to be brothers;
Were attentive and quiet, while all of the others
Were restless extremely and vexing. They, too,
Were very intelligent, and, it is true,
I took quite a fancy to both, and yet, I
Never dreamed that they *could* be related to my
Antony, notwithstanding that both street and name
Were alike. Still, I think this will not seem so strange,
When I say there are several more of the same
Name in church. And since then I have seen many times
The same boy in the seat abreast nearly of mine,
With a fresh, fair-faced lady appearing to be
His mother; though very young-looking is she,
To claim such a large boy as son.

                    Well, now I
Have heard, more than one time of late, by the by,
That my friend Antony was a married man; yet
The report I have never considered correct,
For various reasons. And first, as the source
From which it had come was not trusty, of course
I could not a story believe which was told
With vagueness and doubt. To be sure he is old

Enough to have been some years married; but then
One never can judge of the age of such men
As he is.   To look at his face, one would say
It was one that would never grow old, and to-day
He might be twenty-five, and from there all the way
To forty, or forty-five, even.   Beside
All this, too, although to the same church have I
Every Sabbath been, nearly a whole year or more,
I have never seen with him, not either before
Or after the service, one lady.   And so
'Tis no wonder I doubted his marriage, I know.

I was early this morn, and I reached there before
My Antony did; but the vestibule door
By some chance was left open; and when he came in
The boy I have spoken about was with him.
The door being directly in front, too, of me,
Of course when they entered, I could not but see
Them both very plainly.   Alike, *much*, forsooth,
In form, not in face, were those two, man and youth.
At my first glance at them, the entire bitter truth
Flashed over my mind in a trice.   This and that
Put together had quickly resolved into fact
What I'd given no thought to before.   I then knew
How thoroughly blind I'd been all the way through.

You must know, my dear Journal, the sermon to-day
May have been Greek or Hebrew, for all *I* can say—
That not much of it entered my mind.   Howe'er well
It may have been written or rendered, it fell
In my case on unheeding ears.   Take all that,
With the just acquired knowledge that he was in fact

At length satisfied who was his Bitter-Sweet;
And not this alone, but within a few feet
He was sitting, his handsome face, tender and grand,
Sometimes turned to me, sometimes bent on his hand,
In a reverie sweet and profound.   And I could
Not have doubted of whom he then thought, if I would.
Then his soft, tender, smiling, and passionate eye
Constantly sought my own.   Do you wonder that I,
My dear Journal, quite failed in controlling my heart,
Or the flush on my cheek?   That I felt the blood start
Through the swift op'ning valves and pulsate through my
   frame
With rapid and thrilling vibrations, 'till brain
Was reeling, confused, my brow throbbing with pain,
And my thoughts in a tumult which it would be vain
To attempt to describe?

      I was glad to reach home,
And at last find myself in my sanctum alone.
Well! the first thing I did was to sit down and write
A reply to the note I had from him last night.
And in the first place did my best to dispel
His ideas about my identity.   Well,
Told him plainly, in fact, I thought he did not know
Me at all (an excusable falsehood, although,
I am certain); and then, somewhat shortly, I fear—
Couldn't help it, though, actress I'm not, it is clear—
I asked him how he should suppose I could know
If mine were the blue eyes he mentioned, or no,
And presumed there were many a pair, too, that looked
That way, when he sang; but that if on his book
His were placed as they should be, he'd not be aware
How many looked at him.   Then asked him right there,

To make some amends for my crossness, you see,
And also to see what he'd answer—if he
Could a place for a meeting appoint, if a time
I should mention.   And as to that hair ring of mine,
I said he should see it, half promised also
He should help me the pattern select.   He will know
It is all idle words, I presume.   And I then
Asked saucily what he had *read* this A.M.
Now I wanted to introduce, too, in some way,
The discovery which I this morning had made,
Ascertaining thus if my suspicions were true
In regard to it.   And, though I pretty well knew
He would tell me the truth if I asked him outright,
Yet I did not know but it possibly might
Be best to assume that I already know
What indeed I am hardly assured of.   And so
As follows I wrote :

          " Do you think it would be
Safe, entirely—a meeting between you and me ?
Or am I mistaken in thinking that you
Are a ' *Benedict* ' Antony?   Please tell me true.
But I'm certain I'm not—think I know, too, by sight,
Your wife and your boy—and I'm sure I am right.
Does *she* know of our correspondence ?   To-day
I fancied a little she did.   Does she ?   Say ! "

   I don't recollect what besides this I wrote ;
Nothing more, I presume, that is worthy of note.
What a day this has been !   Looking back now it seems
Like a long, ever-changing, a vague, troubled dream.
And my mind is yet quite too confused to resolve,
Into aught that's like order, the thoughts that revolve,

4

In such entire chaos through it, and restraint ·
Or control 'twould be vain to attempt.   I've **a faint**
Sense of feeling regret that I ever had sent
My first letter to him, and that ever I went
To service at that church, or ever saw him,
And some indignation that I had not been
Informed of all this weeks ago.   And then, too,
There's a slight thread of deep disappointment runs **through**
The whole warp and woof of my mind and my thoughts—
Disappointment in both; in myself, that I sought
Any method to know him that custom denied.
Disappointment in him, that he ever replied
To the first note I sent him.   And yet, there are few
Men in this age who would not, I fancy.   And, too,
He supposed certainly from the first that I knew
All there was to be told.   As I boastingly wrote
That I knew all about him, in my second note;
And so, he is not much to blame, after all,
And 'tis useless to mourn what I cannot recall.

   No service this evening in church; no one went
Out at all, I believe; and, as for me, I have spent
The entire evening here in my room, all alone
With my thoughts and my journal; and though I must **own**
I have not exceedingly happy been here,
More so elsewhere I could not have been.
                          But I fear
My sleep will be broken.   Must stop, and in bed
Try and rest for a while aching heart, weary head.

December 9th, 1863.

WEDNESDAY.

Good evening, my Journal! I come here once more
To my sanctum, with drawn shades and tightly closed doors,
And bright light, and warm fire, with the table before,
With drawings, and papers, and books littered o'er;
And I'll draw up my chair, and will snugly ensconce
Myself in its depths, and forget for the nonce
All the cold world without; will forget all but you,
My dear Journal, my trusty friend, confidante, too,
All but you, and the one I am writing of here—
And events of the last day or two.
                                    First, my dear,
You must know that my cousin and I yesterday
Went a visit to pay, and one which, by the way,
Has been promised for long.   'Twas to Jersey we went,
To spend the whole day, although with the intent
Of coming back home before night.   We'd a gay,
Pleasant time.   Left for home rather late, on the way
Passed my Antony's store, and saw *he* was not in,
And we did not enter.   Well! I had not been
At home very long ere some young people called
From over the way, and were here nearly all
Of the rest of the eve.
                        Lorette came home with me,
Stayed all night, and to-day I went over to B.
With her for my letter.   I felt rather more
Impatient to have it than ever before,

As a matter of course.   I have more than a few
Correspondents, both ladies and gentlemen, too ;
But somehow, I think that no letters I ever
From others received could afford half the pleasure
That *his* have ; I'm sure, though I cannot tell why.
The Colonel's are quite as well written, and I
No reason can see why his should be so much
More pleasing than others, unless 'tis the touch
Of strangeness and mischief, and mystery, too,
That gives them their charm.

                      It has been, it is true,
Very fine amusement for me all the way through,
To receive all these letters, and know just the source
They came from, while certain that he knew, of course,
Of me nothing at all.   And then church to attend,
From Sabbath to Sabbath, to watch him, and then
Be sure that he could not, however much he
Should desire to know who his unknown friend might be ;
That however he might have examined the face
Of each lady in church in her relative place,
That out of so many he could not select
The one who was in all his thoughts, I suspect,
Whether singing, or sitting so quiet within
The alcove's far " *corner* " secluded and dim.
As I said, I believe that I never have been
More desirous of having a letter from him,
More impatient for time to pass rapidly by,
And bring me the anxiously wished-for reply
To my last note to him, and the questions contained
Within it.

            To feel one must carelessness feign

When burning with restless impatience within,
May be, very possibly, good discipline
For the heart and the soul, but makes sad work with temper
And nerves I am certain.   At least I may venture
To say 'tis with *me* thus ; suspense I cannot
And never could calmly endure ; and then, what
Perhaps made me more anxious than ever to get
His letter to-day, was, the tinge of regret
That must linger around all our intercourse, past
Or to come.   That must break all the bonds, first or last,
That now bind us together ; and make us again
What in fact we are yet, and we still must remain—
Strangers, now and forever.   It had, too, one more
Charm—his letter expected—than any before
Have possessed.   The one, too, that all daughters of Eve,
Who the dangerous charm have desired to receive,
Have found, to their cost, its possession replete
With anguish and pain.   " *Stolen waters are sweet.*"
(*Bitter*-Sweet, it should have been), and those who would
          drink
Of the bitter-sweet potion ought never to shrink
From the taste of the dregs they are certain to find
'Neath the sparkle and foam.
                              We left home about nine,
And when Brooklyn we reached found the Carrier had
          been
But a moment before, and a letter from *him*
Lay on the hall-table awaiting B. S.
I was not *very* sorry to find it, I guess,
And 'twas opened and contents perused in a trice.
'Twas not very long, and not nearly as nice

As the last one, I think ; but of course he'd not write
With as much warmth and pleasantness quite, as he might
If I had not written so crossly in mine.
So I've only myself to find fault with, this time.
'Twas written, indeed, with no little discreetness
And prudence—began thus : " Antonian Sweetness !"
And very soon after commencing he wrote—
" The pair of ' blue eyes ' of which lately I spoke
I have met very often upturned to my own,
But more summers than nineteen o'er *that* head has flown,
And I at the time was not singing. Did not
Read at all Sabbath morn ; with my own pleasant thoughts
I communed. I'm indeed very glad I'm to see
The ring when you get it ! You *dare* not let me
Help the pattern select, though."

       And then farther on :
" I believe that my caution is not wholly gone,
But must say I feel *safe* certainly." And again :
" But when I shall realize all the sweet strains
Of poetry sent, I can then *talk* much more
Of safety than I can with ease write before.
You are not mistaken in fancying me
To be married, my Bitter-Sweet ! How could you be,
If the family you know by sight, as you said ?
And farther, the party does not know, as yet,
Anything about this correspondence." Then says,
" If you shall a *time* appoint, I can a place."

 I felt rather vexed that in this he should sent
A poem from Byron. I don't think he meant
Any insult ; 'twas not, though, I fancied, just what
A gentleman should to a lady send—thought

I would write a rebuke in my answer. He'll not
Send me any more like it, I think. But I ought,
As I wrote him, perhaps have expected naught better;
But I did, and I told him *that*, too, in my letter.
'Twas of course, standard, quite, and I doubt not that he
Never thought of offending, by sending to me.
My rebuke, though decided, was gentle, I hope.
At the end of the poem he copied he wrote,
" No farther deponent doth say, at the present.
But like most of our popular stories—and pleasant
Some think, I suppose, as so many read them—
This is also ' continued ' to be !" But yet, send
The rest think he will not. Then writes at the close,
" I shall go the next Sabbath to church, I suppose,
And there in my ' corner ' shall think, think of one
Who is as far from me, because yet unknown,
As the centre is from the circumf'rence—my own !"
Then in closing he says,

     " I suppose you will get
This to-morrow, and then I shall also expect
To hear from B. S. again one of these fine
Days ! And so keep thy counsel and I shall keep mine;
That is ' entre-nous.'
     " Ever thine,

       " ' Antony.' "

 I remained all the rest of the day o'er to B.,
And answered his letter before I came home.
I can't give a copy, because I kept none,
But my note was more pleasing than was the last one.
I said I was sure that I knew who he thought
His Bitter-Sweet was. Then I next asked him what

Was the style of her hat, how she wore her hair dressed,
And why he had chosen one out of the rest
Who was more than nineteen, when I told him before
That that was my age, just nineteen and no more.
Then as follows I wrote :

                   "I *thought* you did not read
Very much the last Sabbath ; but did there, indeed,
Any *bitter* compete with the *sweet* in your thoughts ?
Or were they with unalloyed dulcitude fraught ? "
Then in answer to what he had said of the ring,
And appointment, I wrote,

                   "I *dare* do anything
But meet you, my Antony !   I am not quite
So foolish, I think, if I judge myself right,
As to place myself yet in your power entire ;
And so you can't blame me if I shall inquire
Where the *place* may be, ere I shall mention the *time*,
And then we will ' think of it,' Antony mine !
Should you like me *much* better, think you, my dear friend,
If you knew who I am ?   And would you till the end
Of two months to come be quite willing to wait
Ere you see me, if I solve the mystery great ? "
Then I asked him if tired he was coming to be
Of our correspondence !   And hoped he'd write me
If that was the case.   This I said I believe
Just after the censure I wrote.   Oh ! some leaves—
Fragrant leaves from my cousin's geranium—I
Then gathered ; some dainty white ribbon to tie
With a " true-lover's knot" the sweet leaves, I then sent
Dear Lorette to her room to search for, and she went,
While I wrote in my letter—" I send you some leaves,
And a kiss hid within ! "

And that was, I believe,
About all that I wrote, or at least all that I
Now remember. No comments must I, by the by,
Make this evening—it's getting so late, just as ever;
The next time, my Journal dear, I will endeavor
To be more entertaining. But somehow, to-night,
A task it has been, and an effort to write.

December 13th, 1863.

SUNDAY.

The night is so cold, and is darksome and dreary,
It rains, and the wind seems to never be weary,
The trees toss without, in the bleak wintry blast
Their bare leafless branches. The chill wind sweeps past
Just now with a sigh, low and mournful, and then
With wild sobs, as of anguish, or deep, bitter pain,
Then rises to moans and shrill shrieks of distress,
Which, slowly subsiding, grow fitfully less,
And merge in low sighings once more. And the rain,
Chill, drenching, and pitiless, splashes the panes
And keeps on the balcony just underneath
A restless continual patter. The eve
Breathes but dampness, discomfort, and darkness; within
All is cheerfulness, soft light, and warmth.
                                    I have been
Sitting here in my sanctum a little time past,
And trying to think. But the turbulent blast,

And the sound of the fast-falling rain have dispelled
All my dreams, which were both " sweet and baneful." Oh,
    well!
I'll let them all go, and the gloom of the night,
And, rousing myself, make an effort to write
Of events of the day, and the days that have passed
So fleetly, my Journal, since chatting here last
A few evenings ago.
               Well, last Friday, again,
I took a ride over to Brooklyn; and when
I arrived there I found that Lorette was alone,
And she would not consent to my coming back home,
At least until night; so remained there all day,
And we did have a nice, pleasant time, I must say.
She *is* a dear girl, and I like her so much!
Pretty, graceful, sweet-tempered, with just a slight touch
Of sarcasm and wit in her nature ; as steel
True to those that she loves, whether woe come or weal ;
Obliging, affectionate, cheerful and sweet,
In her nature so placid and calm there are deeps
Of sympathy, passion, and thought only those
Of the friends who best know her have ever supposed
To be hidden within her soft heart.
                     I need not,
I presume, my dear Journal, need I ? mention what
Called me over to Brooklyn again, nor need I
Assure you I went not in vain.   Indeed, I
Can but say that my Antony *is* very kind
To write me so promptly.   The one sent this time
I fancied to be more than usually fine,
And gave me much pleasure.   I'll give here complete
A copy—commencing—
             " My own Bitter-Sweet !

" How exceedingly promptly the mails do arrive,
And bring to us letters most welcome.   And I've
Received yours this morning, with scented sweets fraught—
How fragrant they are !   And what wonder I thought
Them rendered, indeed, *doubly* so, since they've been
With a pair of sweet lips in close contact.   How, then,
Could *I* avoid having a taste of them, too?
And I did so, in fancy at least, it is true,
If not in reality, seeming to find
With the leaves still some lingering sweetness combined.
Of all the sweet plants, the *geranium* give me !
Did I guess who the blue-eyed young lady might be?
I thought that I asked might it be so and so.
Who I thought that you were do you really know?
Well, who, dear B. S.?   You remember you said
That nineteen bright summers had passed o'er your head,
But did not say *only,* or how many more.
I thought from the fact of your saying before
How much you had seen of the world, and then, that
An innocent intrigue's your life—I, in fact,
Supposed you some older.   At what age, indeed,
Do young ladies commence on a life of intrigue ?
I cannot describe how she dresses her hair,
Or what is the style of the hat which she wears.
My Bitter Sweet, how do you think that of these
Trifling things a poor fellow can think, when he sees
A pair of soft, liquid, blue eyes looking through
His very soul—while they appear to read, too,
His innermost thoughts?
                " The ' French ' sentence I sent
Will tell you I think that there *was bitter* blent

With the *sweet* in my thoughts.   And could you, dear B. S.,
Read that in my face ?   For you know you professed
To do that in the very first letter you sent.
' I *dare* anything do but meet you ! '   Well! then
Let me know who you are.   I do *not* suppose you
So foolish, my friend, as to place yourself too
Entire in my power, and therefore on me
You can call, at my own place of business, you see,
In open day, just as all ladies may do,
And be free, too, from any controlling *pow'r.*

                          "You
Mistake in supposing I did not believe
What you wrote in the first letter from you received.
Believe you I did !   but I cannot pass by
That essential, fine quality, *caution,* which I
Am sure, ' my own Bitter-Sweet,' you should admire
In every person in whom you desire
Or choose to confide.

                 " Yes !   *I shall better far*
Like you, my dear friend, when I know who you are.
And if you will tell me, I'll try, with content,
For two months, or longer, to wait your consent
To a meeting between us ; but I would much like
The favor of looking at you, if from quite
A distance.

             " I must assure you, I regret
The poem offended ; and though I have yet
The rest of it written, I'll keep it at home.
When I ' weary of our correspondence ' become
I will tell you at once.   And I shall not offend
You willingly, ever ; and hope to be then

For all past offences forgiven.   I'm not
Perhaps, my B. S., quite so bad as you thought.
And you do me injustice, too, I must protest,
In saying you 'might have expected no less!'
You certainly did not expect it to be—
The poem—original, did you, with me?
I never have had that opinion extreme
Of women that some profess—as will be seen
In Posthumous tirade in Shakspeare's 'Cymbeline,'
And Dryden's translation of Juvenal's Satire
On woman—an author that many admire.
No! my '*charity*''s almost as vast in extent
As the universe; neither would I with intent
Wound your feelings, believe me!   And so I will keep
'To be called for'—the poetry—My Bitter-Sweet,
Or to the Dead-Letter Office will transmit.

" Is it not *bitter* cold to-day?   How *sweet* to sit
Beside a good fire, listing to the chill wind
As it whistles without.   I will not at this time
Inflict on you any words further of mine.
With one good inhalation from *your* fragrant leaves.
Until the next time I trust you will believe
I am still

        " Your own

            " Antony!

                " To Bitter Sweet."

   That was all! and I certainly need not repeat
What I said once before: that not one I've received
Has more pleasure afforded than this.   I believe
There have been not a great many moments to-day
That *he* has been out of my thoughts.

                    I must say

I am pleased at the way he received my reproof,
And perhaps I *did* do him injustice.   In truth,
He has in large measure one virtue most rare
In this weak sinful world, if all else that is fair
And good, he is wanting in.   Sweet *Charity*,
That no evil doth think!   Of the fair, divine three,
The rarest and greatest is sweet Charity!
I guess he is not such a *very* bad boy,
After all!   And so that afternoon was employed,
A part of it, writing an answer to his.
And I mailed it ere I returned home.   But it is
Impossible that I should now recollect
What I wrote in reply to his letter, except
That I gave him some hopes of receiving next time
My name and address.

                 I've not made up my mind
If I'll in reality tell him or not.
I think that I shall—well!   I hardly know what
I *shall* do!   I have not at any time thought
I should tell him at all.   I suppose that I ought
Not have led him to think I would some time disclose
What I firmly believe that he pretty well knows
Even now, were it not my intent to do so.
And it certainly *was not*.   But then—I don't know
But somehow one thing and another has led
Me to say what perhaps I ought never have said,
And promise much more than I meant to fulfil,
Or perhaps than I mean even yet to do.   Still,
It seems hardly fair, or just either, to him,
To cheat him like this; for he's certainly been
Most kind and most generous all the way through,

And *I* want to be quite as hon'rable, too,
So I really scarcely know *what* I will do.
And then, there is still one more motive, more strong,
Perhaps, than all others, which I have been long
Only half-conscious of in my innermost soul,
But which, nevertheless, has through nearly the whole
Of our correspondence so long, been the power
By which I've been led day by day, hour by hour,
'Till I am where I am.   And that strong motive is
A desire just for once to place *my* hand in his,
To listen just once to his soft, tender tones,
In kind words intended for my ear alone.
Just for once, possibly, to be clasped to his breast,
" With a feeling of shelter and infinite rest ! "
Only just for a moment !—Is it *very* wrong ?
'Twould be something to think of through all my life long.
'Twould be, I suppose, hungry heart satisfied
With sweet fruit from the tree that's forbidden, supplied ;
Raging thirst quenched by sweet " *stolen waters*," which
       flow
From a fountain that hides depths most bitter below.
Oh ! one other thing I remember I wrote—
That is, in the answer I sent to his note—
And that was to try the next Sabbath and see
If he could not discover who B. S. might be.
I brought from Lorette's some geranium leaves
To carry to church to-day, morning or eve,
Intending to let him observe them, while I
Should note the effect in his face.   By the by,
I believe he possesses a quite tell-tale face.

Well ! this forenoon found me in my usual place

In church, and he also in his.   I forgot
This morning to carry my leaves, so did not,
Of course, my experiment try.   Mr. S.
Announced this A.M. that by special request
He intended this eve to the sermon repeat
Delivered Thanksgiving day last.   From my seat
I listened, and raised to my Antony's face
My eyes.   At that moment he turned in his place
And looked down at me.   With a glance in which plain
Was a consciousness, neither, I think, could restrain,
Our eyes met, for an instant, then each turned away.
So much for this morning!

      It rained the whole day,
And was gloomy enough.   But I did not stay home
This evening, and father and I went alone.
Just before service opened, my Antony came
To the front, with some music; and then he remained
There for some little time; and I raised from my book,
Where they rested, the leaves to my lips, and then looked
With full, steady glance in the eyes that were bent
That moment on me.   The act told, as I meant
That it *should* do!   The light was quite strong, and the
  space
Between us was short.   From my book to my face
His eyes my hand followed, and as the sweet leaves
Touched my lips, and he saw what I held, I believe
A change more decided, and sudden, and plain,
And transforming, too, o'er a man's face never came
Than at that moment swept over his.   In my eyes
He looked with a full, searching glance.   Slight surprise,
Satisfaction, and wonder, and pleasure, expressed
In the soft, lustrous depths of his own.   While compressed

Were his lips, very slightly, in efforts most vain
To hide the emotion, betrayed yet so plain,
In flushed cheek, and dark, sparkling eye.

> As for me,

I was, I believe, so desirous to see
The effect of my act upon *him*, I did not
My own agitation give one moment's thought,
Or make, then, the slightest attempt to control
My heart or my face.   And I doubt not the whole
Confirmation of all he would know he could read
In my swift-changing cheek, tell-tale eye, and, indeed,
More than all, in the sweet leaves I held.

> It all passed

In a moment, and he turned away, too, at last,
To his seat in the "corner."   And how I would like
To know what he thought, as, with back to the light
He waited the signal to sing.

> Well! to-night,

All during the sermon, he sat quite in front,
And *not* in the "corner" as he has been wont.
But he sat looking toward the preacher, this time,
But frequently glancing from his face to mine.
And during the last prayer abruptly he turned
And looked down full at me.   How my foolish cheek
        burned!
'Neath his glances so earnest, and thrilling, and sweet!
My eyes faltered and drooped, quite unable to meet
The passion in his, as with head on his hand
He sat motionless quite, I thought looking more grand
And handsome than ever before.   The soft light
In his fine speaking eye, now, to me at least, quite,

And smile on his lips, both of which added much
To his ever-fine face, would have given a touch
Of beauty and sweetness to one that was plain,
And his made exquisitely pleasing. 'Twere vain
To think that he was not enlightened.   He knows
His Bitter-Sweet well enough now, I suppose.
I'm impatient to have his next letter, and see
What he'll write about it.

                      I some notes took of the
Fine (?) sermon, this evening, and wrote to him too.
He looked down and saw me !   Will that be a clue,
When he sees how 'tis dated—" In Church, Sunday Eve "?—
To induce him with more firmness still to believe
That I'm his unknown correspondent ?

                            My leaves
I left in my book at church.

                    Hark! it still rains,
And the chill wind still rattles and beats at the panes.
The night slowly wanes, and is " cold, dark, and dreary,"
And of writing and thinking, I am, oh, so weary !

December 15th, 1863.

TUESDAY.

It is evening again, and once more I am here
For a nice little confab with you, Journal dear,
Ere I seek the repose I am conscious I need,
And I ought to do so at this moment, indeed!
My watch I will place very close to the spot
Where my book lies, and when it is twelve I will stop.

To-day we expected from Jersey some friends,
But they failed to appear.   But Lorette this P.M.
Came over and brought me a letter again
From him, my " own Antony."   And I was glad
To get it.   But, somehow, I always am sad
After having a letter from him.   I cannot,
I am sure, give the reason for it.   My first thoughts
Are ever most pleasant and sweet, I must own,
Though the sweet soon dies out, and the bitter alone
Remains of the stolen draught.

                 Notes from him I
Read again and again, besides keeping them by
Me the whole time, each one, till the next one arrives;
Yet, though they are all I desire, all the time
My spirits are very uncertain, I find.
For instance, one day they're remarkably fine
(Most often the day that his notes are received),
And the next even indigo 'd make, I believe,
A white mark upon me.   And, too, this state of mind,
Or temper, or heart, or whatever, in fine,
It deserves to be called, has been constantly mine,
And not only of late, but through all of the time
Very nearly of our correspondence.   I've found
" The heart cannot always control, or *account*
For the feelings which sway it."   And also must own
" That I think, as I swing on the gate here alone,
How the sweetness of horehound will soon all die out,
While the bitter still keeps on and on ! "

                 Well, about
His letter, which lies here this moment by me:
First—" Sunday, December 13th, '63,

In the ' corner,'" was how it was dated.   I thought
It quite a coincidence—and was it not?-—
That he should that morning have written to me
In church, and then I, who of course did not see
Or dream of his having done any such thing,
Should that very same evening have written to him,
And I also, in church.   I can give here to-night
A few extracts alone.   In one place thus he writes :
" What an unpleasant day ! yet it may not be quite
So to those who have hearts that are careless and light.
Where are *you* to-day ?   Why do I not see you here
This morning at service as usual, my dear ? "
(Just as if he had not known so well I was there !
Dissembler ! that I, too, was sitting right where,
Every time that he bent slightly forward, and raised
From his book or his paper his fine eye, my face
Was almost the first thing arresting his gaze.)
And then he went on :

        " We shall have once again
This evening the Thanksgiving sermon, my friend.
And *you* cannot relish that much, I suppose;
But then, if *we* do not, it seems there are those
Who do, as it is by especial request
The rev'rend this evening repeats it."

                The rest
Of that page, and a part of the next, is of no
Especial importance, so let it all go.
Near the end of the third page he writes—

                 " Do not fear

To come in and see me, for if I'm not here
A lady most certainly never need be
At a loss for excuses for entering the

Public stores, and which hundreds habitually
Are visiting.　So there's no reason, you see,
My Bitter-Sweet, why you can't call upon me.
No!　I'm not getting weary, believe me you will,
Of reading your letters, but look for them still
With a great deal of pleasure, and hope and expect
The favor to have of receiving the next
With the knowledge of your entire name."
　　　　　　　　　　　　　Then he says,
" Prayer now has commenced!　I must stop, my B. S.,
You will have difficulty in reading, I guess,
This letter, and find but a little, I fear,
To amuse, or instruct, or to benefit here;
But anticipate one from me, one of these days,
Somewhat better."
　　　　　　　I think I've forgotten to say
This was written in pencil; in ink, then, he writes:
" Monday.—How it does rain!　is it not enough, quite,
To give one the ' blues'?　and the sermon last night
Might perhaps be the means of assisting it, too ;
Might it not, my dear friend?　Or how is it with you?
But I can this morning do nothing but mope,
And writing is out of the question.　I hope
To hear from you soon, and am
　　　　　　　　　　" Ever your own
　　　　　　　　　　　　　　" Antony.
" To my Bitter-Sweet! "
　　　　　　　I might have known
He'd not say a word in this letter of what
He saw Sunday eve, though I know he cannot
Help but be pretty sure who his Bitter-Sweet is.
But he made a slight guess in one letter of his,

And I answered so crossly he thinks he will let
Me tell him the whole, when he knows, I expect.
I wrote him at twilight before Lorette went,
Although rather briefly, but with it I sent
The note I had written in church, Sunday eve,
And which he to-morrow forenoon should receive.
Upstairs I had just come, I wrote him, to find
A pattern; and, stealing a moment of time
(Notwithstanding I'd visitors waiting below),
On the floor of my sanctum was then sitting low,
And, close by the window, was trying to write
A few lines to him by the fast-fading light.
I sent him the wished-for address at the close,
Though I told him above he would not, I supposed,
If I told him my name, know me then any better
Than he would do before the receipt of my letter.
As he said he ne'er knew how a lady was dressed,
I did not see how I could tell him the rest.
And then, just to tease him, I asked him when he
Expected to know who I am—what of me
He thought.   Also wrote that to service I went
On last Sabbath morning as usual; and sent
At the close of the letter my love to my *friend*.
I shall look for his answer on Thursday A.M.
I am glad I have not any longer to go
All the way o'er to B. for his letters, although
He has been very kind indeed, always to write
Just when I requested, and so that I might
Have never to go there in vain.
                              Well, to-night
My brother and wife were in town, and here, too,
To dinner this evening.   Just twelve! I am through.

December 17th, 1863.

THURSDAY.

How stormy a day ! from the earliest dawn
The clouds have bent low, swiftly showering down
The soft, fleecy snow-flakes.   All nature around
Seems just to have donned a fresh mantle of white,
So spotlessly pure, and so downy and light—
So dazzlingly lovely, this " beautiful snow "—
The air filling all, shrouding all things below,
With a soft-falling vesture more dainty and fair
Than any fine lady can e'er hope to wear.
Yet this white, vestal raiment, unsullied by aught
Unlovely or tainting—oh, what a sad thought !
This snow that's " so pure when it falls from the sky,
Must be trampled in mud by the crowd rushing by,
Must be trampled and tracked by the thousands of feet,
'Till it blends with the filth in the horrible street."

This day has been one of sensations, to me
Rather new and peculiar ; have half seemed to be
In a sweet, happy dream all day long.   I presume
My spirits will be at their lowest ebb soon,
Quite likely to-morrow.   There always must be
With them a reaction ; and one day to me
Of light-hearted joyousness, pleasure, and glee,
Is sure to result in depression and gloom ;
And this no exception will be, I presume.
By halves I do nothing ; and when I am gay
No one can be livelier ; and, I must say,

That when I'm depressed, no one ever could be
In the depths of despondency lower than me;
And it takes such a slight, such a small, trifling thing
To make me unhappy, on one hand, or bring
A smile to my lips, and a light to my eye—
Joy and glee to my heart.
　　　　　　　　　Very happy was I
To perceive it to be in the usual clear
And well-known handwriting of Antony dear
The note was addressed which was handed to me,
When I this forenoon the door opened to see
The carrier there in the pitiless storm—
The feathery snow-flakes all over his form
So lavishly showered—he looked almost like
A snow-bank himself.　With unusual delight
I ran in the parlor at once with my note,
To read, all alone, what my Antony wrote.
He's getting impatient, despondent, some, too!
And I cannot wonder much at it, 'tis true.
I have kept him now quite a long time in suspense
Had no little amusement at his sole expense.
But patient he's been, indeed, nevertheless;
Much more so than I should have been, I confess;
And he does well deserve the reward, I must say,
Which he'll get with the letter I wrote him to-day.
But first I've a few words to say of his note;
'Twas not very long, and I fancied he wrote
A little despondingly, as I believe
I have said once before.　First he writes:
　　　　　　　　　　　　"I received
Yours this morning, and your address also with it,
And shall govern myself in accordance therewith."

That is all that he says about that.   Next replies
To some trifling inquiries I made, and then writes
Shortly :
            " How can *I* tell, think you, when I expect
To know you?   To tell you the truth, I suspect
That I *never* shall know you at all, as I do
Not have any means to find out, and as you
Do not choose to inform me.   And then, as to what
I *think* of you—think that you wish—do you not?
To have some amusement, occasionally,
By a few letters writing, perhaps just to see
What answers there may be returned.   Possibly,
That unsatisfactory oft they may be;
But you must remember that I am still quite
In the dark, as to knowing to whom I now write.
To-day I am feeling especially blue,
But the reason for it cannot give ; and *can you?*
I am pleased to find you are so punctual in your
Attendance at church, my B. S., I am sure !
But where do you sit, and what mean you to wear
The next Sabbath morning if you should be there?
I hope that you had an agreeable seat
On the floor of your ' sanctum,' my own Bitter-Sweet,
When writing to me.   How would you, at the time,
Have liked *some one* to lean on? and did you then find
The pattern you sought?   Guess your friends must have
        thought
It took you a long time indeed, did they not? "
And then right after this quite abruptly he writes :
" ' And *these* are the questions I ask day and night,
Must *my* soul *never once* taste such exquisite delight ? ' "
5

Then with sarcasm writes, that he thinks it indeed
Must be most entertaining his letters to read;
But should judge 'twould as much satisfaction bestow
Some to read from an old letter-writer, as those
Most brilliant effusions were never addressed
To any one person, and must be confessed
That his were to *no one*, or what was to him
The same thing, an *unknown*.   And then says in closing:
" But the fact is, that I can to-day nothing do
But growl; and for fear of inflicting on you
More of this, my ill nature, will bid you adieu,
With the kindest regards to my own Bitter-Sweet,
Of
        " Your
                " Antony."
                            Then enclosed were two neat
New Year's cards; and within the small plain space of one
Was " *Antony* " printed, and prettily done;
The other was blank, and on that one I wrote
" *Bitter-Sweet*," and shall send it back with my next note.
I early this afternoon sat down to write
A reply to his last, and intended to-night
To mail it, but it was so stormy all day
'Twas impossible I should go out.
                            I must say
That when I commenced I'd not given one thought
As to whether or not I should tell him of what
He'd become so desirous to know.   I well knew
By the tone of his last that it never would do
To play with him longer; and that I must write
And give him at once the entire truth outright;

Or write him no more. But they've now come to be—
His letters—almost necessary to me.
At least I should miss them, oh! so very much,
If I ceased to receive them. And therefore, with such
A feeling or thought uppermost in my mind,
When to write I began, is it, dear Journal mine,
Any wonder that all scruples were for the time
Swept completely aside, as with fond, eager hand,
I raised to my lips the forbidden draught, and,
While quaffing the waters so sweet at the brim
Of the cup, quite *forgot* that far down, deep within
The dregs, I a bitter might find to be more
Intense than in any glass I had before
Attempted to drain?

        So my Journal, you see,
In the letter which lies on the table by me,
" Signed, sealed," *not* " delivered," my dear friend will find
His suspicions confirmed, and at last have his mind
From all farther doubt and uncertainty free.
How many a thought sent to me there will be
Between the receipt of this note and the time
For service on Sunday forenoon. As to mine—
Oh ! *my* thoughts are constantly with him, to-day,
And all other days, in fact, now and alway.
And I'm more impatient, too, than I can tell
For next Sabbath morning's arrival.

            Oh, well—
The clock's striking ! hark ! can it be it is twelve ?
A few words of my letter, and then I am through.
I wrote at some length, and quite charmingly, too,
I flatter myself ! or I certainly meant
It should be quite as pleasing as any I'd sent.

I told him that I had commenced "just for fun,"
This, our correspondence, some time since begun;
That I'd had no intentions, in fact, any time,
Notwithstanding my various promises fine,
To allow him to have any knowledge of me
He had not already; that is, unless he
Should himself ascertain who his B. S. might be.
I thought hardly fair would it be, though, to him,
To treat him like that, as he'd certainly been
Very kind, and quite hon'rable all the way through;
And so to his honor I'd trust in this, too.
Then I told him what 'twas my intention to wear
The next Sunday morning, and also just where
I should sit—and that is, only one seat ahead
Of Mrs. ——, his wife, at her right hand.   Then said—
" It will, of course, storm the next Sabbath, but I
Shall be there."   And so will he, too, by the by,
I imagine.
                    I wrote I *did* have on the floor
Of my " sanctum " an easy seat, when I before
Wrote to him; but I *would* have indeed greatly liked
To had *some one* to lean upon; but, if it might
Have been that the only one on whom I *care*
To lean for support had been present, that there
No occasion would been for my writing.
                                        Oh, dear!
I'm so very fatigued I must stop now and here,
And leave all the rest until next Sunday night,
When perhaps I may have something pleasant to write.

December 20th, 1863.

SUNDAY.

Sabbath evening once more, and it's now half-past ten.
I've been sitting right here for an hour, with my pen
In my hand, and my journal wide open, upon
The table before me, the day that's just gone
Reviewing, and trying to bring into form
Its events and emotions, in order to write
With coherent distinctness of them here to-night—
Of a day that has been one long dream of delight—
This Sabbath, the *twentieth day of December*,
Eighteen sixty-three!
            But the fast-paling embers
In the grate are now giving me warning, indeed,
My writing to do with all possible speed,
Or be left in the cold. And so I will proceed.

When I wrote here last Thursday, I spoke of the storm
Which was raging without, and the next (Friday) morn
It had not much abated ; but, turning to rain,
Made horrible travelling. I waited in vain,
Almost the whole day, for a pleasanter state
Of weather and walking, until 'twas so late
I feared that if I should much longer delay,
That he would not my letter receive yesterday.
So with rubbers and water-proof nicely equipped,
Regardless of rain or of slush, on my trip
A few blocks farther down at length started to mail
My last letter to him, that he might without fail

Receive it before this A.M.   And as there
Is a post-office box near Ed. Vamey's store, where
I have often deposited letters before,
I thought that to it I would trust just once more.
I went in to see him a moment as I
Wished to purchase some trifles—and passing right by.
I don't like him, though, much, and his manner I think
Is too tender by half, and I always, too, shrink
From the touch of his hand, or the glance of his eye.
And yet I am sure that I cannot tell why.
I rarely shake hands with him, did, though, to-day,
And he held mine so long that I drew it away
Somewhat rudely, I fear, did my errands as soon
As I could and came home.   And he thinks, I presume,
I am haughty and cold; but I cannot help it,
And I *should* like him better, indeed, I admit,
If he treated me somewhat less warmly.   But there!
Let *him* pass!
                    This bright morning was brilliant and fair
As one could desire.   Just a light depth of snow,
Newly-fallen, quite covered the ice formed below,
By the alternate storms of a few days ago,
And gleamed purely white 'neath the warm, ardent glow
Of the bright morning sun; and like huge bridal loaves,
In the Park the large flower-mounds temptingly rose.
While the boughs overhead drooped beneath the soft weight
Of their dainty, translucent, and glittering freight.
Not a cloud to be seen in the whole arch of blue
Rendered perfect an otherwise exquisite view.

Of course I was promptly at church this A.M.,
And my Antony.   Gertrude went also, and when

From the rack she had taken a hymn-book, I then
Discovered what I had not noticed before—
And then not until she was looking it o'er—
A small piece of paper inserted between
The leaves of the book.   In a moment, I ween,
It flashed o'er my mind what it was; and I knew
Very well that my Antony placed it there.   Drew
It forth, and I found my suspicions confirmed,
For on one side I read " *Bitter-Sweet*," and then turned
And the same on the other side found written, too,
Placed there at rehearsal last eve, I conclude.
I think 'twas indeed scarcely marked by Gertrude :
At least she said nothing about it.
                                        I placed
The paper at once in my muff, at his face
Glancing up, and he, too, was then looking at me,
But at once turned away, so I know not if he
Had noticed my finding the paper or not.
He sat at the front to-day, just as I thought
And expected he'd do—both this morning and eve.
But my pen *can* but fail to describe, I believe,
What I then saw and felt if I make the attempt,
I think I must own that I did not repent,
Or do now, in the slightest degree, having sent
In my last the desired information, which must
Have been most gratifying to him ; and I trust
As much pleasure gave him as I thought that it might;
To hope gave reality, putting to flight
All doubt and suspicion.
                              He did not sit *quite*
At the front of the choir either morning or night,

But sitting just so he could look down at me,
With his face half in shadow, and half in light, he
Sat leaned slightly forward, his cheek in his hand,
His head resting sometimes 'gainst the pillar so grand
Which was close by his seat; his eye seeking my own
With a glance from which all of the bitter had flown,
And only the sweetness remained.   And, indeed !
His look volumes spoke ; in his face I could read
A depth and intenseness of passion I ne'er,
In my life, in another face saw.   And whene'er
I ventured to look in his fine speaking eye,
So dark, deep, and lustrous with tenderness, my
Foolish heart with its tremulous beatings almost
Seemed its bounds to be bursting, while through it a host
Of fancies both tender and sweet swiftly passed,
Till cheek flushed and eye drooped 'neath his glances at last,
To be again timidly raised, when I deemed
I had courage to meet the soft love-light which beamed
So plainly in his ; and shone over his face,
And, leaving on every feature its trace,
Rendered each of them, even the attitude, too,
Mutely eloquent of the strong passion which threw
Its charm over me as well, 'till in my own
An answering sweetness and tenderness shone ;
I trembled with rapture and every nerve thrilled
With emotion I could not controlled had I willed,
And which was too new, and too transient, too sweet—
A shadow of happiness much too complete,
To cause me a moment's desire to repress,
Or endeavor to check what gave me, I confess,
Such intense and exquisite delight.   So I quaffed
With eagerness, reckless, impatient, great draughts

Of the tenderness, passion, or love, I were blind
Not to read in the eye constantly seeking mine,
While he motionless sat nearly all of the time
Except when he sang.

     I have flirted before,
Quite desp'rately also, as well as with more
Than *one* gentleman, handsome and clever, refined,
Intelligent too; with large hearts, and fine minds,
And who liked pretty well insignificant me.
But yet, this I must say : that I never did see
In any man's face so much passion expressed,
As was written this morning, it must be confessed,
So plainly in his, my dear friend's; and I thought
His had been very eloquent *ere* this, but naught
To compare with its speaking to-day.

       Well! to-night
He also was there, as I said, the same light
In his eye that had shone there this noon, and as then,
Soft eyes *now* looked love to eyes speaking again.
The evening was but a complete repetition
Of to-day. In the same place he sat, same position,
And sent to me glances as tenderly sweet,
Which my eye just as vainly as then sought to meet
With aught like composure. No thought did he seem
To have but for me; and I, too, in a dream
Of pleasure delicious gave all mine to him,
Enshrining each smile my heart's chambers within.
And paid to the sermon, I fear, little heed,
Wicked girl that I am ! But how *could* I, indeed,
Beneath such a spell, such a rain of soft looks,
With before me a face like a wide-open book,
  5*

Written over with passionate ardor, each page—
How could there aught else my attention engage?
I suppose I *am* wicked—I know that I am!
Why am *I* not like others? How is it I can
With the usual routine be never content,
The same commonplace, every-day, tame events?
Why must I forever be looking beyond
For something beside, and which when at last found
Does not satisfy, but still urges me on
To new aspirations, and new flights of hope
Which in turn disappoint?

       By the way, in my note—
The last one I sent—I requested he'd write
Me a letter in church or to-day or to-night,
And give it to me after service. No one
But father and I went this eve, and alone
Was he, too, "*my own Antony*"—"*she*" did not come
This morning or evening.

      When service was o'er
He hastened downstairs, and just outside the door
He passed me—not stopping—but slipped in my hand—
Which touched his one instant—a note, and then ran
Down the street next the church, and I, too, hastened home.
Father went right downstairs, and I thus left alone
Did not pause to remove hat or cloak, but beneath
The dim light in the hall, I indeed scarcely breathed
As with eager impatience I hastily read
Its contents. 'Twas short, and it had at the head
"Sunday morn, in the 'corner'!" Began in this way:
"My own Bitter-Sweet!

     "What a bright lovely day!

You have lost all your powers prophetic, forsooth !
Well, well ! do my eyes now behold you, in truth ?
And have I been gazing indeed in the deeps
Of the eyes soft, cerulean of my Bitter-Sweet ? "
Then he told me that he had been reading my face,
And that a few lines strongly marked he could trace ;
But his feeble brain could not endure it this time
For a perfect analysis.   But would some time
Like to read it to me.   Then abruptly he said
" Behind Mrs. ——'s big hat why keep hiding your head ?
Did you find anything between some of the leaves
Of the psalm-book to-day ?

      " I suppose Christmas Eve
I shall be here at church.   Perhaps B. S. will, too.
I wish I could get a good chance to with you
Converse !   So you *did* intend, plainly, I see,
To have some amusement, and disappoint me !
You rogue !   I shall give you a tiny-sized piece
Of my mind when I see you.

      " The sermon has ceased.
' Let us pray ! '
    " Antony."

      Underneath he writes then,
" I intended to give you this note this A.M.
But did not have a chance."

      That is all, I believe ;
And this, too, must finish my record this eve,
For my fire has some time since entirely died out,
I'm quite chilled, and have caught a severe cold, no doubt.

December 24th, 1863.

   To-night's Christmas Eve! and to me it has been
Quite a pleasant one, also.
                But first, I wrote him
A letter on Monday, to ask if he thought
To see me this afternoon he could come up—
As I should be housekeeper. Ma at that time
Expecting to go up to T., changed her mind,
However, and so the next day I was forced
To write him that he must not come up, of course.
I asked and expected an answer to-day,
But did not receive it; but had yesterday
A' reply to my Monday's note, writing this way:
"I think, without doubt, I'll be likely to go
Up town the next Thursday P.M., and if so
Perhaps find B. S."
            So it seems he would come
If I had not written him not to. In one
Place he says:
            "Are you really *bitter*, or *sweet*,
Or both? Which predominates? Or are they each
Divided quite equally? *If* so, are they
Separately located, confined unto a
Particular place, or are they diffused through
The system, and so intermingled the two
Fine properties cannot be separately
Distinguished. Just possibly, now, I might be

Enabled to answer the question—who knows ?—
If women, like apples, were eaten.   Suppose
Me taking a bite out your cheek."
                              He went on
With much more in the same style, and then farther down
Writes—
            " Christmas is coming ; the Eve will find me
Stowed away in the corner.'
                        Abruptly, then, he
To a close brings his letter, by saying he's been
Several times interrupted, and now was again
Called off, so would close that he might get it in
To the office that night.
                        I have been this P.M.
Down town—sister Fannie and I—got my ring,
And really think it a quite pretty thing.
I meant my *dear friend* should have been the first one
To clasp in his own my hand with the ring on.
But was foolish enough to have placed it on my
Right hand, and a gentleman passing us by
On Broadway, paused to speak, and ere I was aware
I had been shaking hands with my brother.
                              As there
Was service in church to-night, all of us went ;
My Antony too, was of course there, and sent
Me many a glance, most impassioned and fond ;
To each one of them all my heart could but respond
In tremulous thrills of delight.   Oh ! what power
That man has o'er me !   Day by day, hour by hour,
It seems to increase, and I wonder where lies
The magic !   Is it in the glance of his eyes,

The smile on his mouth, or the exquisite tone
Of his fine voice, although heard in singing alone?
Or is there a charm still more potent than all
His soft smiles and fond looks?   The bewildering thrall
Which the tempter throws over us, when at our feet,
He lays the "forbidden fruit" lusciously sweet.
Alas! I am fearful that charm is more deep,
More entrancing, ecstatic, and powerful, too,
Than all others can be.   'Tis, I fear, but too true,
We're all nearly related to fair Mother Eve.
Young and frail, she was only too easy deceived,
Dragging down all her children in one fatal fall.
Ah!   "The trail of the serpent is over us all."
Eve, tempted, she yielded, and Adam when tried
Proved that *he'd* no more strength than his lovely, weak
        bride.
Then why should we hastily, rashly condemn
Their children for faults they inherit from them?

    Well! the voluntary which was given to-night
Was, "I know my Redeemer doth live."   It was quite
A nice thing in itself, and was rendered, I own,
Exquisitely—sung by soprano alone.
She stood somewhat back from the front of the choir,
And with self-possessed grace, which I could but admire,,
She sang the whole piece, then a moment paused, when
She had finished, as if about singing again,
Slowly turning at last, glided back to her seat,
While the tones of the organ, so low and so sweet,
Grew fainter and fainter, then slowly died out,
Until only the echo remained.   I've no doubt

There were few in the church could help feeling, to-night,
That " music hath charms " !
           And the sermon was quite
As fine a one also as ever I've heard
Mr. S. yet deliver; I think not a word
Was lost to my mind, notwithstanding, too, that
A little way from me my Antony sat.
All conspiring to render the evening to me
Quite as pleasant as I could desire it to be.
By the way, I did feel amused, somewhat, this eve,
At what little Harry remarked (I believe
I mentioned, some time since, my sister had come
On from Boston—of course bringing also her son),
And to-night Harry said, after we had come home,
" That man that was up in the choir looked at me
Nearly all of the time ! "
             Little innocent ! he
Took all to himself the sweet looks which were meant
For another—one who in return for them sent
Looks as warmly impassioned. He never once thought
There was greater attraction beside him than aught
He could offer, to cause that deep, soft sparkling eye
So often to turn toward us.
          By the by,
I wrote a short note to my friend, just before
I went out, to give him after service was o'er;
And succeeded in showing it to him, although
None but him I think saw it. But *I* needed no
Stronger proof that *he* did, than the soft, but faint glow
Which suffused his cheek instantly, also the quick
Intelligence beaming from eyes that a trick

Have, I fancy, of playing the traitor to what
Within his mind passes sometimes.   He is not
Aware, I presume, what a traitorous face
He carries with him, or how plain I can trace
In its changes, at times, his emotions and thoughts.

I was nearly or quite half-way home, ere he caught
Me and dext'rously slipped in my hand, as he passed,
A note—and which proved the reply to my last,
Which I looked for to-day—in return for the one
He found in my hand.   It was quietly done,
And none of those with me I'm sure saw the act.
He turned down the street we'd just passed, which in fact
Was his own.
            And his letter was pleasant and kind.
It commenced " *My own Bitter-Sweet!* "—this underlined-
" Christmas Eve.   In the ' corner,' " 'twas dated, and on
A small sheet of music was written.   He found
That he was mistaken in thinking, he said,
That he had there some paper, and so must instead
Use this " National Hymn."   He did not till this morn
Have my letter, as he out of town had been gone,
So in season for me to receive it to-day
He could not reply.   I've forgotten to say
His letter with kind Christmas wishes began.
He writes—
            " I imagine I noticed your hand
This eve to your face; and I thought it indeed
Quite pretty, although too far off to perceive
It very distinctly.   Do you recollect
What Romeo says to the fair Juliet,

When he at the casement has just perceived her,
In the scene in the garden ?   ' Oh, would that I were
A glove on that hand, that I might touch that cheek !' "
Then of various trifles he goes on to speak,
And writes just at closing,

            " The young ladies wish
To know what I'm writing.   I tell them it is
A *love letter*, and they are anxious to see.
In your rear, rolling up her eyes here, is Miss T.,
As if she thought she could read mischief in me,
And indeed I—
         " The sermon is now at an end.
           " Your
              " Antony."

         This little note from " *my friend*,"
And written in pencil on " National Hymn,"
Creased in folding, and soiled slightly, too, having been
Held some moments within his dear hand moist and warm,
Brings before me with such force the face and the form
Of my dear, *dearest* friend, that it now almost seems
As if he were here in reality.   Dreams
From which I awaken to find I'm alone,
That the charm of his dear—fancied—presence has flown,
To find there is now nothing left in my grasp
But a piece of the most senseless paper ; yet clasped
With fond warmth in the hand which in passing to-night
For a moment touched his.
         Am I dreaming tho', quite ?
If I am not I should be, and so I must say,
Christmas Eve, fare-thee-well, and good-night to to-day.

December 27th, 1863.

SUNDAY.

Stayed home all day Christmas, and most of the **day**
I sat in the parlor with book or crochet,
And in every stitch of the tidy I wrought,
I fastened of him a most kind, friendly thought.
With bright anticipations of when we should meet,
If that time *ever* comes—every hour was replete,
And the day swiftly speeded.   And yet I was blue
As any one could be, and all the eve too,
Although I went out.   Passed a quite pleasant eve;
But came home out of humor, somewhat, I believe,
And *my* Christmas closed with a hot storm of tears.

'Twas pleasant to-day, notwithstanding my fears
To the contrary ; but I can't say it has been
An exceedingly bright one to me.   I saw him
At service this morning, of course, and to-night;
But he—naughty boy—all the forenoon, sat quite
Far back in the corner.   I thought, though, that he
Was writing, but guess he was not.   This eve " *she* "
Was there ; and my father and I went alone.
I carried a note, which to him having shown,
He hastened downstairs soon as service was o'er—
Our seat is quite near to the vestibule door—
And so I was out in the entry, before
Scarcely any one else was. . And he was there, too,
As soon as myself, and he walked part way through

To the door, by my side, as he took from my hand
The note which was in it; but he—ugly man!—
Gave me none in return. I was vexed enough, too !
And I did pinch his hand just a little, 'tis true,
When I found it was empty. I wished I had not
Have given him mine, then; but never once thought
He would fail to give me one as well the same time,
And I think that he might!
                    I wrote him in mine,
To come out and see me next Tuesday P.M.—
My mother is going to Tarrytown then,
If she don't change her mind.
                    I believe I am quite
Too cross, or too blue, or despondent, to write
Any more, so my book I will close for to-night.

———

December 30*th*, 1863.

WEDNESDAY.

    Monday *was* to me one of the *most* wretched days
That I ever have passed, I think.   In the first place,
I felt as unhappy as could be, and then
To Brooklyn was forced to go in the A.M.
And ere I arrived there it started to snow,
Ard continued the rest of the day, and also
A part of the next.   I reached home about noon,
And Fannie was going to Tarrytown soon,
And wished me to accompany her.   I, 'tis true,
Did not like to at all; but then, what could I do?

I had no excuse, she insisted, and I,
As a matter of course, could do naught but comply.
And so one more brief note to my " own Antony,"
I wrote ere I started, and took out with me,
To mail on the way.   And I told him that he
Must not come out on Tuesday, as I had to go
Out of town for a few days, against my will, though,
But that I should be, without much doubt, at home
Next *Thursday* P.M., and if so, be alone,
And then should be happy to see him.   I know
Scarcely what, when he reads it, he'll think.   Somehow,
        though,
I felt that he cared not to come; yet each time
That we have arranged it, the fault has been mine
That 'twas not carried out—for he every time wrote
He should come at the time I had named in my note.
Yet the letter I sent him that day was somewhat
Independent, at least—he could come, or need not—
I made him perceive, just which pleased him to do.
And then wrote:
                " If you come, though, I shall not tempt you,
I think, from allegiance unto your wife.
I imagine, although, 'twould not be, in your life,
The *first time* it had swayed."
                          We called in at a store
On our way to the depot, and there right before
Me a gentleman stood I was introduced to
On last Christmas evening; who then, it is true,
Paid me some attention; but I've never thought
Of him since, and I certainly that day did not
Feel at all like conversing with strangers, that I
Cared nothing about.   So I'd not meet his eye,

Though he made, Fannie said, every effort he could
To attract my attention; but did him no good.
I knew he was there, so would give him no glance
Of recognition, warranting any advance
On his part.
        We had quite a time getting out
To T., for the snow gained so fast 'twas about
All the cars could then do to get through, and 'twas late
When at last we arrived at my brother Frank's gate.
The next day my depression of spirits was gone,
So I had a nice time, notwithstanding my strong
Aversion to going.
        Came home this P.M. ;
Found letters awaiting me, one from my *friend*—
'Twas short, but most kind, and he said he had been
Nearly " driven to death " for the whole day, and then
Was completely fagged out; but had just snatched a few
Brief moments to tell me, and hurriedly, too,
That he should go up town the next afternoon
If pleasant, about two o'clock, or as soon
Thereafter as might be, according to my
Instructions. I sent, since I came home to-night,
Him a letter, or rather a word—it was not
Hardly worthy the name of a letter, as what
I wrote in it merely was " *Come !* " and the date—
Though I signed it, of course. It was getting quite late
When I went out to mail it. A man spoke to me,
And frightened me so that I think I shall be
More careful in future about going out
In the evening alone ; I said nothing about
It, because no one knew that I went.

                                        Mother goes
Up to T. in the morning, if pleasant, and so
As my sister remained there, and Gertrude will be
To-morrow at school, of course, *I* cannot see
As there will be anything now to prevent
Our meeting at last.
                          Can it be my dear friend
I shall see in one more day? For once have him, too,
To my own self entirely? I cannot, can you,
My Journal, dear? yet realize it is true!
I have anticipated with so much of deep
And passionate longing his coming—in sleep
Have fancied him near me so often, to wake
And find it a dream, an illusive mistake,
That now that the time is so nearly at hand,
When my dreams shall become all reality, and
My hopes in fruition be merged, I cannot
Hardly give credence unto the sweet, happy thought,
Lest to-morrow I waken to find it but a
Delusion, which morning light scatters away.

————

December 31st, 1863.

THURSDAY.

How *can* I write down the events of this day?
Where shall I begin, and oh, what shall I say?
How can I describe what it's been unto me—
This *last day of the year*—one ever to be
Set apart? And " one brimful of sensations new,
And deep, sweet, and thrilling; of sensations, too,

Known but once in a lifetime." I think, too, that *he*
Will never forget it; and that it must be
To *him*, even, man of the world as he is,
A day of some import; and that I in his
Thoughts to-night can but have a conspicuous place.
As for me, I can now close my eyes, and his face
Seems right here before me.
                            He came this P.M.
About two o'clock—not much later—and when
He passed by the window I saw him, and so
To open the door I made all haste, although
He yet had not rung, and he stood before me,
Just as handsome and noble as ever; and we
Shook hands in a matter-of-fact, friendly way.
No confusion on either side; and I must say,
Notwithstanding that we to-day met under such
Circumstances peculiar, there was not a touch
Of embarrassment shown in his manner, and I
None experienced, certainly! even if my
Cheek was flushed with excitement, my heart beating fast,
With joy at his presence, long hoped for, at last
In its fulness possessed.
                        In the parlor we passed—
And sat down by the grate, in an easy-chair, I,
He seating himself in another near by,
Directly in front of, and facing, too, mine.
Of various matters we talked for some time,
And I found my dear friend to be quite as refined,
As intelligent, too, well informed, and as kind,
As pleasing in manner, in voice, and in speech—
As I had imagined him. Indeed! in each

He went far ahead of my fancy.   I find
He is thoroughly gentle, too, which, to my mind,
Is the most potent charm which a man can possess.
I always have thought he would be, I confess,
Sarcastic somewhat, but I never saw less
Of that than in him who was with me to-day.
And then he has, too, I can't less do than say,
The most fascinating, caressing, nice way,
Of any man which I have known heretofore,
And I'm certain that no one has e'er made me more
Intensely, unspeakably happy than he
Did to-day, when he sat here conversing with me.
I would I were able to write it all here,
Each motion and act, every word that his dear
Lips uttered; but that I can't do, it is clear.
It is all indistinct as a last evening's dream,
And I into form could not draw it, I ween.
I write a few words, and, ere I am aware,
I forget what I'm doing, almost forget where
I am, for the time, and my pen is laid down,
And I, in a reverie sweet and profound,
Live over again every moment of the
Two brief fleeting hours, so delicious to me,
So full of exquisite, entrancing delight,
A spell which yet rests on me.
                                        I *cannot* write !
I do not know how ; I cannot language find
To express what I wish—to convey from my mind,
To this paper insensate, the memory of what
Was so pleasant in passing.   I'm sure I cannot
Forget it, as long as I live, and so why
Should I care about having it written ?   Yet I

Suppose rather pleasant 'twould be, by and by,
These leaves of my life to turn backward, and read
Of a fancy—it is nothing deeper, indeed,
I am certain—and which may have long since burnt out,
And a memory, *that* half-forgotten, no doubt,
Be all that is left of the ashes. I'll try
And write what I can, though it should, by the by,
Be somewhat incoherent.
                    As saying before,
Of various things we conversed, and went o'er
Some points, too, of our correspondence.   Pretty much
The first thing he said was,
                    " How *dare* you make such
Grave charges against me ? "
                    And this with a smile
Arch and humorous ; I, though, could not for awhile
Understand his allusion, and so I told him,
And he only repeated the same thing ; but in
A moment or two it had flashed on my mind
To what he referred—what I wrote the last time—
That " I should not *tempt* him, etc.," and so
I answered,
                    " I recollect now, but you know
I *dare* to do anything, but to meet you ! "
He laughed then a little, replied,
                    " So you *do*
Think, then, it would not be the *first time*, do you ? "

   He hardly looks like the same man in the choir
That he does out of it ; not but what I admire
Him as much, or but what he looks quite as well, too,
Near by as he does farther off.   To the view
   C

Distance lends not enchantment, at least, in this **case ;**
He *is* very fine-looking, in form and in face.
I do not see how I could ever have thought
That Colonel Allair is more handsome !   He's *not,*
By any means ; though he in fact is somewhat
Of a different style, from "my own Antony ;"
Is darker complexioned, I think ; at least, he
Is less fair in face, and his beard darker, too ;
Is taller, not quite so broad shouldered.   I do
Not think that he either possesses such grace
Or polish of manner, allowing his face
To be nearly as handsome.

                      Remarking to him
That he did not look like the same person when in
The choir that he did out of it, he replied,
Laughingly, that perhaps he was not ; how did I
Know, indeed, but he *was* some one else ?

                               He to-day
To call on a lady a few blocks away
Was going—her name Mrs. Douglass, I think,
And a stranger to him—to engage her to sing
Next Sabbath at church.   I inquired whose place she
Was to take, the soprano's, or alto's.   And he
First replied laughingly, " Oh, the tenor's," and then,
Said that she was to sing in the place of Miss M.,
The present soprano.

                    Referred, by the by,
To the poem he sent me, " *You Kissed Me !* " and I
Asked if he knew the author.   He said he did not.
It purported to come from a lady, but thought
A woman naught half so exquisite could write,
And added that *in* the piece there was some quite

Strong language employed ; and then quoted, in his
Tones so matchless, the few lines commencing with this,
" And were I this instant an angel, possessed
Of the glory and peace that is given the blest,
I would throw my white robes unrepiningly down,
And tear from my forehead its glittering crown,
To nestle once more in that haven of rest "—
At the next line he paused, and with archness expressed
In his face, and I fancied some bashfulness, said,
With a little short laugh, tossing backward his head,
" I've forgotten the rest ! "

                He informed me that he
And my Sabbath-school teacher schoolmates used to be.
I exclaimed in surprise, " Why he's older than you ? "
He smiled, said, " I guess not, think he's fifty-two,
And I fifty-seven ! "

              " You are not so old ! "
I replied, and I knew by his face he'd not told
Me the truth when he answered me—" Why ! that is not
Very old, is it ? "

          " Oh, not so *very*, I thought,
Though that you was much younger ! " replied I, and he
Said, " No ! I am just seventeen ! "

                  Teasing me,
I of course knew he then was, or trying to do ;
So I said " No ! but tell me, just how old *are* you ! "
" Thirty-seven," he then said he was, and I knew
That this time, at least, he was telling me true.
Just to think of it ! He was last year *twice* as old
As I ! And how long he'd been married, he told
Me, as well. Fifteen years, I believe, and so I
Was scarcely four years old. He would, by the by,

Have had a long time to have waited for me.
He has two little boys, and the oldest thirteen,
The other one seven.   I never have seen
The youngest.

                   I spoke of a cousin of mine
Seeing him at a ball, one eve, some little time
Ago ; but he said he'd not been to but one
This season ; and that was masonic.   He'd on
A masonic ring, also.   I asked him if he
Was a mason, and could he not give unto me
The " grip," and he answered, " Oh, yes ! " as he took
My hand in his own, but of course merely shook
It, and naturally, I suppose, held it fast,
And pressing my fingers, retained in his clasp
The hand he had taken, although from his grasp
To release it I did once or twice vainly try.
But he then took the other, instead, by the by,
Both holding with firmness, yet gently, and I
Did not care very much.

                 I expected he would
Have made such advances.   I think that I should
Be affected and foolish if I should pretend
That I did not; or either that he did offend
By making such overtures.   I of course knew
When I sent my first letter, and also all through,
More especially, though, since becoming aware
That I knew he was married, and-so-forth, that there
Could not be much doubt but that he'd misjudge me
And not only weak, but unprincipled, he
Might possibly think me.   'Twould certainly be
Very natural, too ; and I could not blame him
If he did, yet I can but acknowledge he's been

Exceedingly generous, and, I have had
Occasion but once any fault to find—that
Was his sending the poem, to which some way back
I think I referred. Therefore, I was, in fact,
Prepared for injustice, yet still hoped he might
In the end change his mind, and I think that, to-night,
Of me his opinion is different quite
From what 'twas this morn. I repelled all I could,
Without being rude, the caresses he would
Have lavished on me; and I've no fault to find,
And he, I am certain, went home with his mind
In regard to my frailty quite disabused. And,
While making him fully, I think, understand
I was not what he thought me, I did not repel
What I knew was quite harmless, and also was—well,
There has been in my heart for so long an intense,
Half-unconscious desire for my friend's dear presence—
A longing just once to be clasped in his arms,
That now that my wishes could be without harm
Gratified, why should *I*, what he gave on his part
With so much of pleasure, refuse, while my heart
A rapid response beat to each fond caress
That he offered. And so I did not, I confess,
Repulse him, when he his head laid on my breast,
But suffered it there a few moments to rest,
While I to his forehead my cheek softly pressed,
As happy as he. Nor again, when he drew
Me within his embrace for a moment or two,
Just before he was leaving, and pressed on my lips
His first kiss, while to my very finger-tips
I felt the blood rush from my heart.

He, at last,
Having glanced at his watch, found that two hours had
     passed,
And 'twas then four o'clock; therefore, was about time
For Gertrude to come home from school; and to find
Him with me she must not; so I told him that he
Must go, which he already knew. So of me
Taking leave, very sweetly and kindly, he went,
And I was alone.
              One more hour was far spent
Before Gertie came home, so he need not have gone
So soon, had I known it would been quite so long
Ere she would have come.   Mother did not get home
Until about nine, and so we were alone—
I and Gertie—as father went down town this eve,
To hear—Wendell Phillips' address, I believe.
Gertrude soon went to sleep on the sofa, and I
Before the fire sat, in a rocker, with my
Elbows resting on each of the arms of my chair,
Both hands clasped o'er my eyes, and my thoughts—oh,
     well, where
Should they be but with him? And I wonder, too, whether
" *He* thought of to-day, of when we were together.
How? Where? Oh, what matter! Somewhere in a dream,
Drifting, slowly drifting down a wizard stream—
Where? *Together!* Then what matters it whither? "

   But midnight is rapidly hastening thither,
And I'll say good-by to to-day which has been
One of unalloyed pleasure; enshrining within
My heart's " white-washed chamber," its deepest recess,
The memory dear of to-day, and confess
" *Stolen waters* ARE *sweet!* "

And I also must blend
With adieus to the day a good-night to my *friend*,
To the future give hopes, to the past give a tear
Of regret, and farewells to the speeding " Old Year."

January 8th, 1864.

FRIDAY.

" The great laws of life readjust their infraction,
And to every emotion appoint a reaction."
That sentiment I indorse with all my heart,
And have realized fully, I think, for my part,
The truth of the sentence.   That pleasure must be
By misery followed inevitably.
No letter last Saturday did I receive,
As I hoped that I might; and the Sabbath, indeed,
Was a miserable day all around.   In the morn
I of course went to service.   My brother was down
And went to church with us.   My cousin came, too,
From Brooklyn, and as to myself, I was blue,
I thought, as I *could* be, before I went out ;
But my spirits, when I had returned, were about
Ten degrees lower still.
                    Well ! my friend was there too,
And he much as usual appeared, it is true ;
Yet I own I was rather dissatisfied, felt
Cross at him just a little, and more at myself.
I also was vexed that I had not received
Any letter from him Saturday, and believed

That he might to me written, if he had cared to,
As he promised, if I'm not mistaken, to do,
And was more disappointed than caring to own.
Then my brother and wife, after we returned home,
Had some words, which were called out by something I
　　　　said,
Though quite innocently; and then, too, my head
Ached almost as much as my heart, and I thought,
On the whole, 'twas a day as thoroughly fraught
With annoyances, trifling, perhaps, but yet none
The less irritating and vexing, as one
Very frequently passes.
　　　　　　　　There was, by the by,
In the chapel a prayer-meeting merely, that night,
And no service in church, and so I was quite
Content to stay home.
　　　　　　　　Well, I heard the bell ring
To-day, but supposed it was not anything
For me; consequently, was *much* pleased to find
I'd not only a letter from Antony mine,
But one also from Colonel Allair.　And I then
Felt better; for both were quite pleasing, and when
I had opened the Colonel's I found there enclosed
A photograph of him—a fine one !
　　　　　　　　Suppose
My Antony wished to make up for delay
In writing to me, for his letter to-day
Was much longer than usual, nor can I but say,
Was equally kindly and warmly expressed.
Commenced " My own Bitter-Sweet," and, for the rest,
I would much like to copy it here if I could,
But have neither the time nor the space.

　　　　　　　　　　　Thought he should
In the choir his position resign soon, although
He *did* " rather like the old ' corner,' " and so
Guess he'll not.   And his letter I answered to-night,
And mailed it.   I went past his house.   A bright light
Was in parlor and hall; but the shades were drawn down.
I saw naught of him—presume he was down town.
Sister Fannie to Boston returned yesterday.
I'm *so* tired, and think I have no more to say.

January 10*th*, 1864.

SUNDAY.

　Do not feel much like writing, have not much to write!
It's become second nature to write Sabbath night.
So, as is my wont, I have taken my pen,
And opened my book for that purpose.   But then,
As before I have said, I have not much to say.
The fact of the matter is, I am to-day
In much too low spirits for anything.   Too,
There's nothing of import occurred, since with you
I chatted, my Journal, a few nights ago.
Lorette was here yesterday afternoon, so
We went with some friends to the theatre.   Then
I'd an invitation to B. this P.M.
To dine, but 'twas so " bitter cold " did not go.
Went to church morn and evening as usual, and so
Of course saw my Antony.   *I* did not, though,
Pay but little attention to him, nor did he
To me either this morning; he seemed, though, to be
　　　6*

Very pleasant and smiling this evening, but I
Looked coldly away, and would not meet his eye.
I suppose that he thinks I am ugly—I, too,
Think *he* is a little, my Journal; don't you?

———

January 14th, 1864.

THURSDAY.

One more pleasant day in my changeable life!
Again I can write of some hours that were rife
With pleasure, instead of with pain.   A short note
I sent to my Antony Tuesday last.   Wrote
That mother was going to Brooklyn to-day,
And if he could come out this P.M., and stay
An hour or two with me, that I should be glad
To see him, of course.   I had hoped to have had
A letter in answer this morning, to know
Was he coming or not.   None arrived, though, and so
I hardly knew whether to expect him or not.
About noon, though, the bell loudly rang, and I thought
It sounded indeed like the carrier's ring;
But it was so late, thought it could not be him.
However, it was, and he brought me the note
I had been expecting; and yet, though he wrote
A long letter, for him, not a word did he say
As to whether he should, or not, come out to-day.
He asked near the end how I liked Sunday morn
The sermon; and said he dared hardly look down,
As it seemed just as though some one's eyes were on him
All the time.

Well, of course I was dressed and within
The parlor before two o'clock; but I had
Nearly given him up ere he came; but was glad,
Very glad, to see *his* well-known form, pass at length,
The window; and so to the hall-door I went,
And admitted my *friend.*

      Mrs. A., who has been
Staying here for some time, had gone out this P.M.,
Saying that she expected a call from a friend,
And asked me if I would not see him, and tell
Him why she was absent, and send him there. Well!
I promised to do so, and thought it was him,
When soon after my friend came I heard the bell ring.
So I went to the door; but a lady was there
Whom I did not know; proved to be a Miss Ware,
A teacher of music, and came here to see
If mother would not allow Gertrude to be
A pupil of hers. So I told her that I
Would speak to mamma about it, and would try
And at once let her know the result. She had then
Full particulars given to me; therefore, when
She asked me if she might come in, I was so
Much surprised that just what to reply did not know.
Nor did I think ahead far enough then to say
That I was engaged, and if some other day
She'd call, she would doubtless mamma find at home.
Hesitating one instant, the next I had shown
Her in the front-parlor. My Antony then
Had my albums, and sat calmly looking at them;
He was in the back room; both the doors, though, between
Were wide open, and so she of course must have seen

Him sitting there; but I did not at the time
Think anything of it, except, Journal mine,
That I wished she would go.   And she did not say one
Single thing except what she had previously done.
Remained a few moments, and then went away.
She gave me her card, and I found, by the way,
That she on the same street resided that he
Does.   He looked at her card, and he said she must be
But a few doors from him, and he guessed he would go
And take lessons in singing ; but *he* did not know
Her at all, in reply to my question, said.

Well !

We were having a cosey chat all to ourselves,
When some little time after the bell rang again.
You must know that I did not go *this* time, but when
In a moment Ann opened the door, I heard them
Enquire for my mother, and heard her reply
That she was away ; she believed, though, that I
Was at home.   So at once turned to show them into
The parlor, but—most fortunately, 'tis true—
The key I had turned when they rang, and she found
The door fastened.   And so after upstairs and down
She had looked for me vainly, informed them that I
Must also have gone out.   And when, by the by,
Their names they had given, I found them to be
Two of our own church ladies most prominent.   He
Wished to know who they were, and I told him.   How
    shocked
They'd have been, if the door had not chanced to be locked,
And they had been shown in the parlors, to find
Him and me there alone.   'Twould created a fine
Piece of scandal, no doubt.   But I wonder, in time,

That I thought to do so ; but 'twas well that I did,
Thus escaping unpleasant exposure.
                                            Amid
So much interruption, the afternoon passed
Away but too swiftly. Hours too bright to last
Glided rapidly onward. Why cannot we stay
The swift flight of Time ? Sometimes bid a to-day
So happy and joyous to tarry alway ?
We did have a nice, pleasant time this P.M.
It seems as if I had for years known my *friend.*
Was just as affectionate, gentle, and kind,
And charming, to-day, as he was the last time
He was here. And I *do* like him much, and I guess
That he does me a little. And yet, I confess
That my feelings have been vastly different this eve
Than they were the last time ; and think I may believe
I have conquered that fancy.
                                    The reason he wrote
Not a word about coming, within his last note,
Was that it was written on Tuesday ; the boy
Let the mail all lie over, and which did annoy
Him much ; but supposed that I'd receive mine
Yesterday afternoon. I coaxed him for some time
To give back my letters ; but he would not say
That he would or would not; only that he some day
Desired "reading them backwards." That's all the reply
I could get to my teasing. It seems he is quite
Immovable when he once makes up his mind,
And he's not to be coaxed, neither driven, I find,
Into what he decides not to do. But I thought
Him more pleasing in his conversation, and not

The less fascinating in manner, to-day,
Than when he was with me before.   Can but say
That in every respect he's a gentleman, too,
And I like him extremely!   My Journal, don't you?

I went out the evening to pass with some friends,
Which I'm sure I *could not* done the last time; but then,
As I've previously said, I am now feeling quite
Indiff'rent to him when compared to that night.
His presence to-day gave me *much* pleasure, though,
And the evening has been very happy also,
Filled with thoughts of his tenderness, manliness, grace,
His good sense, his kind words, and his loving embrace
As he kissed me at parting.   May he have to-night
Happy thoughts 'till he sleeps, and then dreams of delight!

January 24th, 1864.

SUNDAY.

One more dreary week has vanished and passed,
But I've naught to record, since when here I wrote last,
Except disappointment and pain, discontent,
Wounded pride, and displeasure.
                              Last Sabbath, I went
To church morn and eve.   Our new singer was there,
And he sat back with her in the morn.   Did I care?
Not so much as I should have a few weeks ago.
Remained in the " corner " that evening, although,
And sent to me glances both smiling and sweet,
Whenever my eyes I allowed his to meet,

Which was not very often. I'm sure he could read
Naught but coldness, indifference in mine, and, indeed,
I *felt* coldly to him. When they sang the last hymn
I saw the new singer and him whispering ;
They pretended that it was the music about—
Perhaps that it was! Mrs. ——, his wife—was out.
I wish *she* would stay home.

      Monday, went o'er to B.
It rained, I got wet, the result was to me
A cold most severe ; and the next day I could
Hardly hold up my head.

      Mother thought that she should
Go up to my brother's on Thursday ; at length
Decided she would not; so I did not send,
Of course, for my friend, until Frank that A.M.
Came up here and said that the baby was sick,
And wished her to go ; so she dressed just as quick
As she could, and went off; and then, writing to him,
I sent it down town by a friend who was in—
Making him understand 'twas an order for books.
I told him I knew he could come, and I looked
For him, too ; but he did not. I felt just as vexed
As I could do, of course ; and I thought I would next
A letter send him he would quite understand ;
Make a change for the better, or else be a grand
Winding-up of the whole.

      And I wrote, I could see,
I thought, how it was ; he was getting to be
Tired of our correspondence—disliked to say so ;
But he said voluntarily, some time ago,
That when weary of it he'd at once let me know.

So I meant that he should; and I said 'twas to me
Most certainly pleasant—but only while he
Wrote promptly; but since then had been much more **pain**
Than pleasure, indeed.   Then I wrote,

" It is plain

You care not for me, and I never once thought
That you did ; and I also can say I do not
Care much for you, either.   The crisis has passed !
Your recent neglect has been withering fast
All affection's sweet roses, too fragile to last,
Which had bloomed in my bosom for you, until naught
Remains but a few faded leaves which I caught
As they dropped from the stem ; and these, too, I shall now
Gather up, with your letters and words, and allow
The ' dead past to bury its dead.'   I shall see
You frequently, but you have lost over me
All your power.   I shall not forget you, indeed,
And neither shall you forget ' your Bitter Sweet ' (?)
While you sing in that choir, and I sit in the seat
I now do in church.   I am weary of wooing ;
New business it is to me, I've been pursuing ;
And I do not think I have had much success,
And shall not attempt it again, I confess ;
I will not coax *any* man, not even *you*,
And if there is any more wooing to do,
'Twill not be on *my* side."

And then, at the close,

I wrote that I left it with him to dispose,
According to his inclination.   That is
To say, at once candidly, if 'twas his wish,
To our correspondence close now ; and if so,
Or if not, I requested that he'd let me know

By a note Sunday eve without fail.   And I trust
It *may* bring a change, and indeed think it must.

Before I had sent this, the following day,
I an answer received to my other, to say,
He had just returned home from the country, and found
My note, but could not possibly get up town
That P.M., as he'd business he could not defer;
So we'd have to postpone it.   Wrote but a few words,
Scarce a page, but most kindly.   So then what to do,
About sending my letter, indeed hardly knew.
But at length thought I would, the result of it be
What it might.
            Lorette came up to-day, and with me
Went to church.   He sat back with the singers again.
She asked if I saw how he looked at me when
They were singing.   I *did* see, or rather I knew
His eyes were on me, though I would not, 'tis true,
Look fully at him.   After service, Lorette
And I went down town a short distance.   We met
My friend and his wife at the corner, and each
Walked down the same street 'till their door they had
            reached—
But we on the opposite side—and as he
Turned in closing the door he sent over to me
Smile and bow, too, of greeting most kind.   We came back
The same way, some time later.   Lorette said he sat
At the window; so doubtless he saw us, but I
Did not glance toward there while the house passing by.
This evening he sat in the "corner."   I thought
He was writing, but now I suppose he was not,

As he gave me no letter—most *provoking man !*—
Notwithstanding my urgent request. And how can
I avoid feeling coolly and cross to him, too,
If he does look so kindly at me ? And I *do!*

January 31*st*, 1864.

SUNDAY.

   The letter I so much desired last Sunday
Was on Wednesday received. Not a word did he say
About our correspondence now closing; but said
That he was last Sabbath so situated
'Twas impossible quite he should give me a note.
His letter was pleasant and kind, and he wrote
At some length beside, and he hoped that to me
It might be acceptable. Thought there would be
A change in the choir before long. There had been
The previous day a committee to him,
From some other church, and he could not tell what
Might be the result. But I hope he will not
Leave the choir. I am sure if I really thought
He would, I should be more unhappy than now.
Though 'twould hardly be possible, I will allow.
Said he saw me go up street on Sunday noon last.

   And as to to-day, it, as usual, has passed
Quite fleetly, if not very pleasantly. He
Sat back in the choir morn and eve; but on me
He kept his eyes fixed during singing, and the
Benediction as well, leaning over to see

Me as I passed out, though I would not give him
One full glance in return.   After all, though, I've been
And have *felt* toward him much less coolly to-day
Than I have for some time.   If he'd but keep away
From our new soprano, I think I'd not be
Quite so cross with him.   So, I am jealous, you see,
My Journal!   The fact is, I have not one bit
Of confidence in him; for if he sees fit
To flirt so with me, he with others will, too,
And I cannot respect a man who is untrue
In what *should* be the dearest relations of life.
Let me once get my letters from him, and then I've
Done with him.

        " *She* " was there, too, this evening—his wife ;—
She watches me closely, as if she might be
Just the least trifle jealous.   She need not—of me.
And I was of her once, but think I'm not now,
For *she's* much more cause than *I* have, I'll allow.

February 1st, 1864.

MONDAY.

I imagine the end can be not distant far !
That the time swift approaches when he and I are
To become merely strangers again.   And to-day
Has been an eventful one, I can but say !
In the first place, this morn I a letter received
From him, which was written on Saturday eve :
Was just going up to rehearsal, he wrote.

"'Twas a bore, should be glad when relieved!"   But I
        hope
That time will not come very soon.
                                        " I suppose
I shall see you to-morrow," he writes, near the close—
" But know not as then I shall hardly dare meet
Your eyes, lest I see that you look, Bitter Sweet,
So frowningly at me because I have not
Replied to your letter before, as I thought
To be able to do.   This is, though, the first chance
I have had."
                        But there was not much fear in his glance
Last Sabbath, nor did I frown much, I believe.
But he wrote before this—
                                " I a letter received
Anonymously but a few days ago,
In regard to my visiting up town; and so
It seems some one saw me, has taken the pains
To warn me of it, and attributes the same
To bad motives.   Perhaps 'tis as well, for although
My mind's free from wrong, others may not think so.
And a mere friendly visit construe thus into
Something worse.   Well! we all are quite likely, 'tis true,
To judge from appearance!) Unjustly, sometimes,
As in this case.   And we should perhaps bear in mind
The old proverb, ' Avoid all appearance of wrong.' "

   I knew in a moment just where it came from—
The caller I had the last time he was here;
From no one else *could* it have come.   It is clear
She saw him come in, and, they living so near

To each other, she certainly must have known him ;
So suppose that she made up her mind to come in
And ascertain why he was there. I thought, then,
Rather strange she should *ask* if she might, and, too, when
She'd already said all necessary to say.
She's contemptible ! Bad as I am, or she may
Think I am—for I fancy I'm not, by the way,
Any worse than *she* is—I would ne'er condescend
To do aught so mean. Force herself in, and then
Take advantage of what she discovered, to send
An anonymous letter to him. She is not,
Neither is her opinion, deserving a thought !
But it *is* rather galling to be so misjudged,
To a proud girl like me, it is true ! But then, fudge !
It is not worth minding, to come from that source,
Though for his sake, it could but annoy me, of course.
But if it don't get to his wife I don't care !

   Finished reading my letter, I went right downstairs,
And nearly the first thing, mamma asked me where
My letter was from. An evasive reply
Was I forced to make. This concealment, though, I
Can hardly endure. 'Tis quite foreign to my
Nature, habit, and wish. But it *shall* not be so !
I *will* sever all ties that now bind us, although
My heart it should break. Though there is not much fear
Of that, I imagine ! Instead, it is clear
'Twill be more a relief than aught else to me. Yet,
Can I give him up ? It will be hard, I expect,
Although it must be.
                         Mother said that a week
Ago yesterday, she had gone for a sheet

Of note-paper to my portfolio, and saw
It was locked.   But she thought that perhaps she might
    draw
Some forth from the leaves in between.   So she tried,
And she did; but she drew something else, too, beside.
One sheet of the letter—or copy—I sent
Him the previous week; and which also I meant
Upstairs to have taken, and placed in my desk,
And did the *next* day.   An envelope addressed
To him I have been very careful, all through,
Not to keep, lest some person should see it; and, too,
Whene'er there has been anything of the kind
Within my portfolio before, any time,
In the pockets I always have placed it, and not
The leaves in between; but this time my forethought
Seems quite to have left me.   She read it all through,
Told how it commenced, and some things I wrote, too,
And quoted verbatim—" I shan't forget you,
You shall not forget me, long as you continue
To sing in *that* choir, and I sit in the pew
That I now do in church."   So I saw that she knew
The whole story, and farther dissembling would be
Both useless, and also impossible.   She
Said she " *hoped* that it might be the bass-singer, and
Could not think I'd been writing to a married man."
And why *did* I do it?   Foolish girl that I am!
I told her I thought no more of him than she,
And, as soon as my letters I could obtain, we
Would be done with each other.

                So I must tell him
When I have a good chance.   I don't like to go in

To the store, so must wait until he comes out here.
And no knowing when that time will come, but I fear
'Twill be not very soon. And I do wonder what
Will come next? " It ne'er rains, but it pours!" and I
     thought
There was truth in the proverb to-day.

                      This P.M.

I wrote him a note ; have not sent it.

                      Well, when
We part, we'll part friends. One more meeting, and then—

February 7th, 1864.

SUNDAY.

  Nothing very important since here I last wrote.
Last Wednesday A.M., there arrived a brief note
From my friend ; and he spoke of the one he received,
And he writes—
           " Who it came from I cannot conceive,
Can you? You must see that will render it, though,
Impossible for me at present to go
Out to see you."
           I *do* wish that some people would
Their own affairs mind! It would do them more good,
And cause much less trouble. I had not sent mine
That I wrote him on Monday, so added a line,
And sent it that day. And I wrote him I thought,
After reading the rest of my letter, he'd not

Have much doubt where his came from, and asked him
　　　to send
It to me for perusal.   I told him I then
Expected that something would come of her call,
But thought not of that; neither cared I at all,
If it did not through her reach his wife.   And I hope
It will not, for her own sake and his too.   I wrote,
" I am *sure* 'twas from her, so you see that there would
Be no danger in your coming up, if I could
Opportunity give to you ; but I cannot
Just at present.   But *you* seem to have not a thought
That *I've* aught at stake."
　　　　　　　　　　　I wrote nothing about
My mother's discovery; 'till he comes out,
I thought I would wait ere I told him.   Have had
Not as yet any answer to that, though I half
Expected one yesterday morn.
　　　　　　　　　　This A.M.,
I of course went to church.   He was there, and again
Sat back with the rest of the singers, and I
Felt jealous as usual.   I do not see why
He does so, I'm sure! for he never used to
Until the new singer came ; now, it is true,
He does nearly always.
　　　　　　　　　　Was given to-night
In the chapel a Sabbath-school concert.   'Twas quite
A good one.   He was not of course there, but " *she*"—
His wife—was, and sat, too, one seat back of me.
After concert, her little boy came to her seat;
So I've seen him at last !   He's the image complete
Of his father.   He has the same eye, dark and deep,
The small mouth, pouting lips, and the same rounded cheek,

And, more like him than all, same expression of mild,
Sweet good-humor. And he *is* a beautiful child!
And I fancy that she thinks so, too, by the tone
Of fondness with which she addressed him. I own
That she well may be proud of her fine, lovely boy.
I wonder where *he* was to-night, how employed!

The Sabbath-school had a rehearsal last night.
I went. The choir, too, were rehearsing. I'd liked
To have looked in a moment on them, I confess;
But of course I could not, and was forced to repress
All longings to see my dear *friend*, 'till to-day,
And then was not quite satisfied, I must say.

February 12th, 1864.

FRIDAY.

Friday Eve! and once more all alone in my room,
With my journal before me, my pen I resume,
To inscribe on its pages the passing events
Of the week nearly gone, of a day of content,
Which also hastes fast to its close. And I, too,
Must with brevity say all I'm wishing to do,
And seek my repose.
                        Tuesday last, I believe,
From Colonel Allair I a letter received,
And one from my "*friend*" on the following day.
He writes—
            "I have felt much annoyed, I must say,
Since receiving the note which I spoke of to you,
In my last; and I cannot imagine yet, who

7

Its author could be. I can scarcely think, though,
It came from the party that called, as I know
I never saw *her* before; but it might be
Possible, I suppose, that she may have known me.
So vexed did I feel, then, that I destroyed it
At once! but have many times wished, I admit,
That I had not, as I would have liked you to see
The note, though 'twas not very likely to be—
The handwriting—familiar to you. I can't free
My mind from the thought that they're yet waiting for
The next visit."
                   But *I* don't at all think so! nor
Have I any doubt where it came from, as I
Said before, three or four days ago; or that my
Visitor and his new correspondent are one.

My sister has been wishing mother to come
And see her, for some time, and when she went home
Mamma promised to do so. She Wednesday received
A summons to come on immediately,
As my sister was ill. So she left us this morn,
And three or four weeks, I suppose, will be gone.
I sent him an answer to his yesterday,
And wrote him that mother was going away,
And asked him if he would come out this P.M.
I looked for his coming 'till half-past two, when
I quite gave him up, and had taken a book
And been reading some moments, when chancing to look
Out the window, I saw he was just passing by.
My book was thrown down in an instant, and I
At the door to admit him.
                   He said what I wrote
About coming up to-day, he did not note,

Until two o'clock. That my letter he then
Had just taken out to look over again,
And as soon as he saw that he came right away.
I wrote him in pencil, and that was in a
" P. S.," I believe, why he did not see it.

I told him about mamma, and I admit
He took it quite coolly, seemed vexed not one bit,
But laughingly asked why I did not permit
Her still to think it was the bass-singer !

            I
Enquired the first time he was here, by the by,
Where my letters he kept, and he told me within
A drawer in his desk; and to-day I asked him
If its contents he brought, and he said, no; that he
Could not get to them, as he had broken the key.
But so roguishly I could but know he was not
The truth telling me, and that he could have got
Them, had he desired to. I coaxed him to bring
Them out the next time that he came, but a thing
Satisfactory I could not get in reply,
Or nothing, at least, on which I could rely.
I told him I knew he would ne'er have the time
For " *reading them backwards !* "

           While teasing for mine,
He said not one word of my giving back his.
If he had, I should not. Had he told me, " That is
The condition alone on which I'll return yours,"
I should said not another word of it, I'm sure.
I *can't* give them up, come what may ! So I teased,
And coaxed, and persuaded, and he at his ease,
Leaning back in his chair, laughed in answer, or gave
Sometimes a caress for reply, or else made

Unto each argument some objection; at length,
He said—and his tone changed to ice—he would send
Them, certainly, if I insisted on it.
But that he had not all of them, he'd admit;
When they were about him sometimes, he had been
Obliged to destroy them, lest they should be seen.
He thought he would come out next Tuesday again.
From school Gertie came ere he left me, but went
Right downstairs; then he bade me good-by.

                      Well, we spent
An afternoon pleasant indeed; or at least
To me. He is *splendid*, I think, and was pleased
Much as ever, to-day, with him.

                   But I must not
Write more at this time. To my "*friend*" many thoughts
I am sending to-night, and with fond wishes fraught.

February 14th, 1864.

SUNDAY.

    Quite a nice, pleasant day this has been, and I come,
At its close, to write here of it; and I have some
News, my Journal, to tell you. Last night we received
A telegram, saying the previous eve
Mamma safely at her destination arrived—
Fannie's husband it came from—and that his dear wife
Had a very fine boy born that morn.

                      Gertie went
To Tarrytown yesterday; brother Frank sent

For father and I to dine with him to-day.
So we went after church.   Passed *his* house on the way.
When we first came in sight, he was standing between
The windows, but then he—I think, having seen
Us coming—sat down with a paper to read !
So I saw him distinctly.   And he is, indeed,
A darling, I think ; and was charming to-night !
But he sat with the singers.   The " corner " is quite
Deserted of late.   Well ! there is, I suppose,
More attraction elsewhere than that offers ; who knows ?

February 28*th*, 1864.

SUNDAY.

" I'm homesick, and heartsick, and weary of life ! "
Its pleasures, its follies, its turmoil, its strife !
I am weary of all that I've tasted below,
I am weary of friend, and I'm weary of foe.
And friends (?), what are they ?   When joy brightens our
 skies,
They flutter around us like gay butterflies,
Display their bright colors, their rainbow-hued wings.
Ah ! they're happy, and joyous, and beautiful things !
But touch their bright spots and their beauty is gone.
They spread their frail wings, and then soon flutter on.
Yes ! when sorrow's dark clouds have our heavens o'ercast,
We find, all too soon, their rich hues will not last.
On a frail " *broken reed* " we've been placing our trust,
Our friends are all false, and their vows naught but dust.

" Prosperity wins them, adversity tries,"
They're ours while the sun shines, when shade comes they
     fly.
" I'm homesick, and heartsick, and weary of life ! "
Its dearest enjoyment with poison is rife.
Enjoyment ? what is it, and where to be found ?
In fashion's gay haunts where mirth seems to abound ?
Ah, no ! Is not there beneath all this glitter
Some hearts that are aching—less sweet thoughts than
     bitter ?
Some one has said that "Home, Mother, and Heaven
Are the three sweetest words to our hearts ever given."
Home? Do we not find in each household band
Some chord that will vibrate, if swept by rude hand ?
A circle e'er find but *one* faithless one's there,
Ever a fireside, but has one vacant chair ?
Mother ? Though her love is as deep as 'tis pure,
Seek we not farther ? though find none that's truer.
Memory points us to counsels we've slighted,
To eyes dimmed by tears that sweet smiles should have
     lighted.
Heaven ? "Patience is bitter if the fruit is sweet ! "
The way's long and dreary, the thorns pierce our feet.
Though tempting the goal, beyond price the reward,
'Tis won but by toils, trials, faith in the Lord.
" I'm homesick, and heartsick, and weary of life ! "
Weary of love, friendship—yes ! weary of life.
Love ! oh, how fragile, how transient a flower !
And yet are not all of us swayed by its power ?
It brightens our pathway for one fleeting day,
We fondly imagine 'twill ne'er fade away.

But too soon we awake from the sweet, blissful dream,
To find hearts are faithless, love not what it seems.
Friendship ? 'Tis an empty, a meaningless word ;
'Tis fraught with heart-achings, with sighs breathed un-
    heard.
True 'tis to you when there is aught to be gained ;
When needed most, leaves your fond hearts to be pained
By its fickleness, untruth, and heartless disdain ;
To find your hopes blighted, your faith all in vain.
Life ! what is that ?   Ask the poet or painter,
Ask him whose weak voice with age daily grows fainter.
The poet in eloquent verse will portray
Its joys and its sorrows, smooth paths and rough ways.
The artist will paint you with light here, there shade,
A cradle—an altar—a grave newly made.
The old man will say 'tis a meteor bright,
One moment 'tis noonday, the next it is night.
" I'm homesick, and heartsick, and weary of life ! "
There's nothing but bitterness, nothing but strife !
Bickerings without, and temptations within,
Smiles battling with tears, and purity with sin.
Hopes are crushed at one blow, and true hearts are be-
    trayed,
Love's Eden is entered, home desolate made.
Dishonor is stamped upon many a brow,
Disgrace hangs o'er those that were happy but now ;
The death angel dark hovers o'er our bright land,
Touching here one, and there one, with his icy hand,
Gathering around him his mantle of gloom,
Only to drop it o'er some lonely tomb.
War o'er our country spreads its desolation,
Brother 'gainst brother, and nation 'gainst nation,

Pure streams dyed with hearts' blood, fields red and gory,
Lives yielding all up to country and glory.
Deep is the darkness, the night is dreary,
I'm homesick, heartsick, of life I am weary.

It has been a long time since I've written in here.
Two weeks! that in passing, have seemed long and drear.
Two weeks, which have brought in their flitting to me,
A few gleams of joy, but much more misery.
For writing no heart I have had, or for aught
Else beside where was requisite much composed thought;
And to-day I so restless have been all the time,
I thought that it possibly might ease my mind,
To talk for a short time, my Journal, with you,
And something tell you of the past week or two;
The record's too humiliating, though, quite
Too troubled and sad to be pleasant to write.

The week following *his* latest visit to me,
I received not a word from him, nor did I see
Him as I expected. You know he said then
He thought he would come the next Tuesday—but when
Tuesday came a most terrible storm raged. The next
Day was not much better, nor did I expect
Him of course! And the rest of the week was, although
Fair and clear, cold intensely, and *I* did not know
But possibly that might the reason be why
He did not come up. I wrote him, by the by,
Once or twice in the interim. Day after day
I watched for his coming—a letter—alway
To be disappointed. And no one can know
How restless, unhappy, I felt, and how slow

Dragged each wearisome hour.   In that way the week passed
With no tidings whatever ; and Sabbath at last
Arrived, and I went out to church.   He was there,
As usual ; but I, feeling too vexed to care
To see him, my eyes kept averted, nor met
His own scarcely once.   For I could not forget
How unkind he had been.   There may have, I concede,
Been something his coming to hinder, indeed ;
He *might*, though, have written, and not have kept me
In constant suspense the whole week.   Or if he
Did not *wish* to come up here why could not he say so ?
I'd like it much better than that he should play so
With my feelings and wishes.

                              My father went out
To my brother's to dine that day, but 'twas about
All that *I* could do home to remain ; and I knew
I could not be sociable if I tried to.
So I thought that the best place for me was at home,
And I spent the whole day between service alone.
Well ! the next day—on Monday—I sent him a note
Which was one piece of sarcasm all through ; and wrote
Him without fail to come up the next day and bring
My letters, and I'd nevermore say a thing
About his again coming up.   Tuesday, I
Was looking for him, and I saw passing by
A boy, with a book in his hand, and addressed
To some one : I saw one initial, the rest
His hand hid.   He went on to the end of the row,
Made inquiries, came back, rang our bell, then, and so
Of course I suspected that it was for me—
The book in his hand—and it thus proved to be.

          7*

No message he gave me, but when I removed
The wrapper, I found a sealed note, and which proved
To be written by him.   There were also with this
A dozen or so of my letters.   Well, his
I opened at once.   Commenced
  " My Bitter-Sweet : "
           " I was gone out of town nearly all of last week,
But your letters have all been received.   All I find
Is ' those letters I want ! '   I told you, the last time
That I saw you, I had not them all ; and you say
Not one word of returning me mine, by the way.
And now as the *letters* the uppermost thing
In your mind seems to be, I return half—will bring
Or send you the rest when *all mine* I receive.
This is no more than fair.   And you said, I believe,
That you still had them all ; and if you return them
You shall have all of yours, not destroyed, and you then
No more trouble about them will have on your mind.
So busy am I that I cannot find time
To go up town to-day, even if I dared to.
          " Yours in haste.
              " Antony."

         When I this had read through,
The first thing I did was to sit down and write
An answer to his, which I mailed the same night.
By the way, too, not one of the letters returned
Were of any account.   Notes, just fit to be burned.
I wrote him that I could not send him back his,
If I *never* have mine.   Suppose, therefore, that is
The end of the matter—as *he* said, in fact,
In his answer which I received Thursday.   And that

It was his intention to say many things,
But was feeling, that day, so unwell, could not bring
His mind to the subject; that also must be
The excuse for his brevity.
                                    I cannot see
What ails him, I'm sure!   There is something, but what,
I cannot conceive.   I am certain 'tis not
Anything *I* have done.   He is fretting about
The anonymous letter—mamma's finding out
About our correspondence—I think there's no doubt
It is one or the other, or something that I
Yet know nothing about.   In his answer to my
Reply to this letter, he writes—
                                    "I received
Yours this morning, and I can but say, I believe,
That nothing at all you have said angered me,
Though I *did* hardly fair, indeed, think it, to be
Compromised by your making acknowledgments that
I was your correspondent; as I could, in fact,
Not see the necessity."
                                    I, in reply,
Wrote, I thought that if one *certain lady*, whom I
Could mention, a similar question of him
Had asked, that mamma did of me, he would, in
His looks, if he did not in words, the whole thing
Have acknowledged as well.
                                    In the same he again
Writes—
                "I cannot your wish understand, that as friends
We should part.   Surely! *I* at least trust there'll be naught
But the most kindly feelings between us, or thoughts;

As I've, I assure you, no others to you.
His letter was most kind and pleasant all through,
And at some length was written. He says near the end,
" I cannot tell *when* I can come up, my friend,
As ' things is so mixed ;' some I cannot explain
At present, and had, perhaps, better remain
In ' statu quo.' "

    But as to what it can be,
Of course, I have not the remotest idea.
That was written on Friday, received yesterday.
He sat with the singers, as usual, to-day,
And looked very handsome. Well! I believe that
Is all, and I'm too tired to write more, in fact.

March 9th, 1864.

WEDNESDAY.

 The first part of the week which succeeded my last
Record here, my dear Journal, was quietly passed.
Father started for Boston on last Thursday eve
To bring mamma home ; but when ready to leave,
I could not go downstairs to bid him good-by,
So completely prostrate with a headache was I.
The night was a wretched one, and, the next day,
Though better, was not very well, I must say.
My brother's wife came about noon, and I went
Home with her, after I had first written and sent
A note to my friend as an answer to one
I that morning received ; and I wrote he could come,

Or not, as he pleased—he could write me again,
If he liked, or he need not—that 'twas to me, then,
A matter of perfect indifference; that
If he suited himself I was suited. In fact,
My letter was not cross but weary, as I
Was myself. I have often, of late, by the by,
In my mind had a poem I sometime ago
Was reading—the author of it I don't know—
Which commenced, "We are *so* tired, my poor heart and I!"

    On Sunday A.M. it was cloudy, and my
Sister made every effort she could to induce
Me not to go home; but 'twas not any use;
Go I would, and I did, and was very glad, too,
That I had, for he sat in the front nearly through
The sermon, and then in the corner; and I
Could not fail to perceive the soft light in his eye
Bent so constantly on me. And *I* could almost
Have fancied the last weeks a dream, as a host
Of sweet feelings then surged through my heart. I went home
For my letters, and then back to T.; and I own,
Though it rained, I got wet—as I'd taken that morn
The open carriage—I was glad I had gone,
And am still.
       Brother Frank and his wife went last night
In town to see Forrest; and so I was quite
Alone with the children and servants. I read
Moore and Shakspeare 'till weary, and then decided
To pencil a few farewell lines to my "*friend.*"
But wrote rather briefly, it being late then.
I came home to-day, and a letter received,
Saying mother and father would be home this eve.
They came about six.

And so this is the end!
The flirtation is over, and we are again
Merely strangers!   And yet, I can ne'er feel the same
Toward him that I did before it we began.
And I feel assured also, he, too, *never* can
Forget it or me.   Looking back now, it seems,
The three months just passed, much more like a long dream
Than it does reality.   It was to me,
Some parts of it, pleasant; yet *I* can but be
Most heartily glad it is over, and do
Not doubt but it is a relief to him, too.
The whole correspondence has been, in some things,
The most mortifying, humiliating,
Of any I ever have been engaged in.
But I think that from it I a lesson have learned,
And if a few leaves of the past could be turned,
And I could begin it again, it would be
On my part conducted quite differently.
The truth to confess, I am of it ashamed!
And presume many times I have thought him to blame,
When I have been mostly in fault.   We have not
Each other, somehow, understood.   I have thought
Him unkind, many times, very likely, when he
Was not conscious of it, nor intended to be.
But he's so *much influence* had over me,
And I *could* not indeed wear my chains gracefully,
But constantly struggling from bonds to be free,
Have wounded myself many times, I can see.
Of late, I have fancied, sometimes, that he meant
To punish me for keeping *him* in suspense
So long at the first.   If that *was* his intent,
He has had his revenge!

And so, this page ends
My journal, or this volume of it, at least.
For my book is quite filled, and this day must complete
The record of so many unhappy hours,
And a few most exquisitely happy ones! "Flowers
By the wayside!" And though springing up among thorns,
Blooming freshly and sweet, amid sunshine or storms.
Some time a new journal I trust to begin!
May it be much more peaceful than this one has been.
Farewell to this volume, to days bright and dreary!
"Rest is sweet after strife; I would sleep; I am weary!"

STOLEN WATERS.

PART SECOND.

"He tossed me bitterness, and called it sweet!"

J. G. HOLLAND.

"What was love, then? not calm, not secure, scarcely kind;
 But in one, all intensest emotion combined:
 Life and death: pain and rapture: the infinite sense
 Of something immortal, unknown, and immense!"

OWEN MEREDITH,

STOLEN WATERS.

NEW YORK.

April 24th, 1864.

SUNDAY.

To my new Journal, greeting!   Once more I resume
Book and pen with my own wayward heart to commune.
I seek, once again, a companionship I
Have most sadly missed in the weeks now gone by,
Since turning away from the record, which had
Been both *bitter* and *sweet,* and both joyous and sad,
Closed my book upon the irrevocable past,
And bent heart and will to the yet fruitless task
Of learning forgetfulness.   Lessons, I find,
Which no force of will, and no purpose of mind
Can make me achieve.
                               " The grief which doth not speak,
Whispers the o'er-fraught heart, and bids it break ! "

No fountain but must have some outlet! No heart
But must have some vent, or but longs to impart
Its sorrows and joys unto some faithful friend.
So to you, my dear Journal, I turn once again!
None more faithful than you, none more trusty and true;
So I'll give my confidence where it is due,
And gathering up all the now scattered threads
Of my life and my heart, will bring each tiny shred
To be again woven by *your* silent loom,
Into fabrics and colors of brightness or gloom.

The weeks which have vanished since bidding adieu
To my Journal's last volume, have not, it is true,
Been quite uneventful! And neither have they
Been tranquil or happy. Believing the way
To learn to forget what was painful and sad,
And once more to make my heart buoyant and glad,
Was within it to give to remembrance no place,
And cease in these pages its changes to trace,
I've kept tightly closed its escape-valves, and sealed
Every door to its innermost chambers—revealed
To none the emotion which almost, at times,
Seemed forcing an egress, all efforts of mine
To repress but indeed more rebellious made still,
Till my heart at length in its struggles with will
Has come off victorious, and given to grief
A vent—an escape—and in writing, relief.

Well! to-day for the first time since here I wrote last,
I have looked on the face of " my friend " of the past.
All these dreary weeks to a sick-room confined
He has been, and I, too, in a tumult of mind

Indescribable quite—first, of ignorance, doubt,
Then knowledge, anxiety, *have* been about
As restless, unhappy as I could well be.
And in the meantime, has *he* given to me,
I wonder, one thought?   Or already have I
Dropped out of his life with completeness, no sigh
Of regret for the past, for the future no hope!

The six weeks to me have passed by very slow.
For nearly a month he had been ill, before
I knew what detained him from service.   Two more
Sabbaths since then have gone.   When last week I went out
" *She* " was there, and I fancied knew something about
Our acquaintance, she then looked so queerly at me.
I presume 'twas all fancy, though!   By the way, he
This winter is wearing an overcoat light,
And during the service it hangs just in sight
In the " corner."   The first thing I noticed to-day,
When I went in, was Mrs. ——, his wife—and away
From her face to the " corner " I glanced ; and saw there
A light overcoat, yet even then did not dare
Hardly think it was his, fearing still I should be
Disappointed.   But when they began to sing, he
Stood before me as handsome as ever, although
Looking so pale and thin ; and a glad light, I know,
Filled my eyes, as I could not, indeed, fail to see
That when he came out his first glance was for me.
How happy it made me to see him again!
And so, my dear Journal, you see that his chain
Is still round my neck, and the clasp he yet holds,
But chains always chafe, although made of fine gold.

May 1st, 1864.

SUNDAY.

Again I'm in much tribulation!   This week
Father changes his business to Brooklyn.   He speaks
As if *we* should stay where we are until fall,
But expect when he gets there he'll soon want us all.
And how can I think of it?   How *can* I go
And leave *him*, " my own? "   I shall never, I know,
Never see him at all !
                        I to church went to-day;
He was there, and I *was* very glad, I must say,
To see he was looking much better—quite like
His dear self.   No service, but concert to-night.

May 8th, 1864.

SUNDAY.

Well ! this, I suppose, is my last Sunday here !
For the last time, my Journal, I come to this dear
Little sanctum of mine for a Sabbath night's chat,
Of which we so many before have had, that
I scarcely can force myself now to believe
That this is the last !   That this week I shall leave
This house in which so many hours I have passed,
So happy and joyous I knew they'd not last;
Hours of sadness, as well, which could not fly too fast.

That I must bid adieu to this dear little room,
With associations of both sunshine and gloom
So brimful; where so many castles I've built.
Some have melted in air, some have been all fulfilled !
My last Sabbath here has as usual been spent,
And is now nearly ended.   This morning I went
To church, and the first thing I saw was a dark
Overcoat, which was hung in the " corner." My heart
Sank sev'ral degrees.   Soon the bass-singer came
To the front with a gentleman ; both I saw plain,
And thought, " Well ! it seems we are having this morn
A new tenor, or organist !" And, although down
At my seat he kept constantly glancing, while he
Stood talking, I never once thought it could be
My Antony dearest ! and not until they
Were commencing to sing did I know him.   The way
Of it was, since the last Sabbath he's taken off
His beard, leaving only his mustache, so soft
And drooping.   It made in his looks such a change,
So distinct and decided, 'twas not very strange
That I did not know him, e'en though his dear face
Is so sweetly familiar, and in it I've traced
Each passing emotion so many a time.
He looks younger and handsomer ; yet, Journal mine,
I must own that I do scarcely like him so well ;
It makes him seem almost a stranger ; the spell
Of his presence has something of newness in it,
And seemed desecrating the past, I admit !
We intend to retain, for the present, our pew.
When I write here again, I suppose in my new
But less dearly loved home I shall be.   So adieu
To the memory of hopes, disappointed ones too,

Which cluster within this dear room; and a last
And lingering farewell to its dreams of the past!

-----cɔ-----

BROOKLYN.

May 22d, 1864.

SUNDAY.

Two weeks since my last writing! In my new home,
In my new " sanctum sanctorum," once more I come
To trace one more leaf of my life in this book.
I did not to church go last Sabbath; it looked
Like a storm, and I was not quite well. But to-day
We all of us went, and I thought I would stay
For the service this evening; so did not come home;
With a friend passed the interim. Father alone
Came over this evening. My friend did not go
To church to-night with me; my Antony, though,
Was there morn and eve; but he sat in his pew,
And we had a new tenor; so he has got through
With the choir, I conclude. On my going to-night
To service, I passed by his house; 'twas twilight;
The windows were open, and *he* stood near one,
Bending over a table with his oldest son,
Both consulting a large book then lying thereon.
I know not if he saw me; but had not been long
In church, when I saw them come in; and while she
Was taking her seat, my friend turned towards me

His dear face, with a smile most impassioned and sweet;
And my cheek slightly flushed, and my foolish heart beat
Just the least trifle faster, I own; it did seem
So strange, to see *him* sit downstairs! And I deem
It a pleasant coincidence our seats should be
So near to each other. Presume, though, that he
Will not be at church half the time, now he sings
No more in the choir. "There comes ever something
Between us and what we our happiness deem."
I shall now see my friend only rarely, I ween!

October 2d, 1864.

SUNDAY.

Four wearisome months have flown tardily past,
Since I opened this book, and made in it my last
Brief record. And though there has, in the mean time,
Been events of slight import to me and to mine,
I have not been desirous of writing them down;
Had no wish to commune with a heart I have found
More rebellious, and more uncontrollable too,
Then I care to acknowledge, now, even to you,
My Journal and confidante.
                          All summer long
We have had visitors, and the last are just gone.
My father went out West some three months ago,
Returning last week. As for me, you must know
I've been doing my best to attempt to forget
Scenes and friends of the past, but whose influence yet

8

Is felt in my heart.   And my efforts have been
Of but little avail; and now, down deep within
My heart, I am forced to acknowledge a fact
I was long in discovering; one, also, that
I would now fain ignore; and a truth, that to me
Is so full of bitterness, grief, misery,
And humiliation, it does seem, at times,
As if I could hardly endure it.   How blind
I have been! but my eyes are wide open at last;
And I now know, and *bitterly* know, why the past
Is yet so indelibly stamped on my heart;
Why I find it impossible, even a part
Of a certain three months to forget; and wherein
Lies the charm which has bound me so strongly to him;
Why I never could break the enchantment, and feel
That I once more was free.   No! I cannot conceal
From myself any longer, the fact that the thrall
That for months has enslaved me is this: That, with all
The intenseness and depth of my nature, I love
Him, my Antony dearest!   And that far above
All others he stands in my heart; and that no
Separation, or silence, or coolness, although
It might make me both grieved and indignant, could change,
Or serve in the slightest degree to estrange
My affection for him.   I may not ever see
Him again, unless 'tis at a distance, and he
May not even one tender thought give to me;
But yet he's my love, and my darling, my own!
And happiness, freedom, and peace, have all flown
From my heart, to make room for the unwelcome guest
Which I fain would exclude.   For, it must be confessed,

The knowledge is not very grateful and sweet,
Nor does it afford to me happiness deep.
Can it be, though, that *I*, independent and proud,
I, who, more than once, scornfully have avowed
I could think naught of one who did not care for me,
And imagined that I was " heart-whole, fancy-free "—
I am forced to confess, that not only unsought,
Unreturned, I have loved, but—the most bitter thought
Of all others, where none with much sweetness are fraught—
I have in my heart shrined the face of a man
Who is bound to another, and who never can
Anything be to me.   God forgive me, I pray,
And pity me, too !
     In the weeks passed away
Since herein I wrote last, I've a new method tried
To make me forget.   A flirtation, that vied
With the last one in nothing ; and was, on my side,
Carried on with such weary indifference, it
Could me not much pleasure afford, I admit.
I hoped to forget, in another's fond smile,
One whose sweetness had done, oh ! so much to beguile
My heart from its peace.   But the man was not one
I could ever care much for ! and now it is done—
The flirtation—and all there is left is a few
Fond letters, well-written and kind, it is true,
And a photograph.   With not a thought of regret,
I have laid them away.
     Many letters I yet
From Colonel Allair am receiving.   He writes
Notes most pleasing and fine ; and he says he is quite
Captivated by our correspondence ; and ne'er
Will forget me, he knows!   Well ! perhaps not ; if e'er

He is tried, we shall see!   But we always agree,
Never jar in the least.   Says he hopes to see me
Before very long, as his time has expired,
And he'll now soon be home.   I can't say I've desired
To see him this fall very much, and presume
He will alter his mind about coming so soon
When he my next letter receives.

                          I have been
To church frequently, but have rarely seen *him.*
One morn, I remember, when going up town,
I saw him on a car that passed by, coming down.
How *glad* just that one passing glimpse made me feel!
Though a slight tinge of sadness began soon to steal
O'er my heart, as the old potent charm was revived,
Bringing with it vain longings for what was denied.
I felt all the morn, I perhaps should see him,
But hoped that to church my dear friend would have been.
I went up to-day.   He was there ; neither gave
To the other much notice ; in fact nothing, save
An occasional most careless glance.   And he went
Out of church just ahead of me, talking intent
With a gentleman friend.   Afterwards, I passed by
Him so closely, my dress must have brushed him ; but I
Neither spoke, nor yet looked, just as if he was not
My Antony dearest! and in all my thoughts.

October 30*th,* 1864.

SUNDAY.

Was in town yesterday, and went into his store.
I have not for a long time been in there before.
I did not inquire for him, purchased a book,
And while I was doing so *he* came to look
For something near where I was standing, and asked
His partner some question about it, then passed
Back, returning a moment thereafter, and stood
By the counter, where when I should pass out I could
But see him. I sometimes have thought that he would
Ne'er again speak to me; I have so many times
Decidedly cut him; but he was as kind,
Yesterday, in his manner as ever; and I
Of course bowed and smiled too, as him I passed by.
But though I was outwardly calm and serene,
I trembled excessively; but did not mean
He should know I was moved; neither did he, I ween.

Were to-day both at church. He, my dearest, and I !
And his eye met my own more than once. By the by,
I think he still likes his quondam " Bitter-Sweet,"
Just a little, and no one with him can compete
In *my* heart, no person at least that I've met,
Though I *may* see some one that I like better, yet.

November 19*th*, 1864.

SATURDAY.

Been to church only once since the last time I wrote,
And naught has occurred that is worthy of note.
That day I remained all the noon time in church.
Went up in the choir for the first time, in search
Of traces of him; but found nothing; but sat
For a moment within the dear " corner;" in fact,
In the very same spot where my *friend* used to sit,
But one brief year ago; and from it to transmit
Many thoughts, looks, and smiles down to me.
                                        Do you know,
My dear Journal, that it was just one year ago
Yesterday that I sent my first letter to him?
How brimful of sweet recollections they've been—
The two days just passed. I wrote him, by the way,
A note to remind him of it, and to-day
Was in town, and went into his place, but did not
Have a chance to deliver, without doing what
I disliked very much—to inquire for him; so
I purchased a book, went where else I'd to go,
And returned, and accomplished my object that time.
How handsome he looked! and how pleasant and kind
Was his smile and his tone, as he took from my hand
The parcel I gave.   He *is* splendid, and grand!
My letter ran nearly like this:
    "*My dear ' John' !*

                    " Don't it look to you singular, some•
        what, that form

Of address at the head of a letter of mine?
For though I have written the same many times,
To you before, never! I write to you now,
Not thinking you'll care much to hear, I'll allow,
But because I just now know not what else to do,
And because I feel, too, just like writing to you.
I have not forgotten how wrong it is, though,
I wish that I could! But I ask you for no
Reply, and write only because to me 'tis
A gratification.
            " Do *you* know it is
Just one year to-day, since my first note to you
I wrote and despatched? It does seem, it is true,
Hardly possible, but so it is! Ah, my dear,
This cold, wintry weather, so frosty and clear,
Brings back very forcibly old times to me.
Does it to you also, my own ' Antony ? '
And do *you* ever think, I would much like to know,
Of *this* time, but one little, brief year ago?
A smile quite involuntary sometimes says
You have not entirely forgotten ' B. S !'
As to me, I like *you* just as well now as then ;
I liked you the first time I saw you, and when
Our brief correspondence was closed, you, my friend,
Were not the less dear ; and I like you, too, still,
Although inconsiderate, unkind, you will
Admit that you often have been—will you not?
I remember of your saying, once, that you thought
There was, 'tween the sexes, no such thing as love!
That 'twas mostly mere passion—or that was above
Pure affection predominant. *I* don't believe
You really thought so ; nor did you conceive,

My dear '*John*,' how conclusively that remark proved,
Though sixteen years married, you never have loved.
If this *is* your opinion, I differ with you !
For I—shall I say '*love*'? yes! for it is true,
That it, in this case, means no more than I like,
And I think it is, too, somewhat easier to write—
Yes, *love* you! but not with one passionate thought.
Am contented to see you, and, though I would not
Be sorry to have an occasional chat
With you, my dear friend, I am well aware that
I have to your love and caresses no right.
Nor do I care for them.   It is to me quite
Immaterial whether you like me or no ;
If you treat me unkindly or kindly; and so,
You see, nor your smiles nor your frowns can disturb
My calm equanimity ; neither can curb
Or enhance the full flow of my spirits.

                                " I thought

I saw you a few days ago, but was not
Quite certain of it—on Broadway, I believe.
Trusting you will with pleasure this letter receive,
And sending you love and a kiss, 'till we meet,
I am still and am only,

                    "Your own,

                        " Bitter-Sweet."

December 11*th,* 1864.

SUNDAY.

December! and almost the middle again!
Can it be that a whole year has flown by since when
I, with trembling delight, received letters from him
Who is still more to me than all others have been?
This fatal and singular passion! will it
Be *never* quite conquered? And must I admit
That my heart beats in fetters I'm powerless to break?

A heavy snow-storm, yesterday, could but make
It impossible I should go up town to-day.
I wonder if *he* was at church, by the way,
If my seat looked forsaken, and if my friend wished
That I had been there, or my presence once missed.

———

December 18*th,* 1864.

SUNDAY.

To-day was a beautiful one! and I went
To the old church this morning; and he, my dear friend,
Was there, and alone. In fact, "*she*" has not been
For some time at service. I could not see him
As he sat at the first, but then some one came in,
And he moved to the end of the pew. I would liked
To have been one seat back. Thought I noticed him write

8*

During prayer, but I might been mistaken. He came
Across after service, and passed down the same
Aisle with me, and directly behind me, in fact,
And with our soprano conversing; and that,
Of course, made me jealous. Her husband, although,
Was with her. And what he was writing, also,
For her might have been, or it might been for me,
And no chance to give it he had. Indeed, he
Might not written at all. I distinctly could hear,
As we came out, the tones of his voice, of that dear,
Perfect voice, which I've heard very little of late !
Those musical, fine, tenor tones ! which vibrate
On my ear ever sweetly. To-day I could see
He was some agitated ; perhaps it might be
From his then close proximity—was it?—to me ?
Or caused by the woman with whom he conversed ?
I dislike her ! Was jealous of her from the first.

We've a houseful of visitors ; have, in fact, had,
With but short intervals, since July. I'll be glad
When we're once more alone ; for I am all the time
So unhappy, or blue, or despondent, I find
It an unceasing strain on my heart and my mind,
And my nerves, and my temper, to be with my friends
Even decently sociable. What wonder, then,
That visitors bore me, and that I would fain
They were gone, that we might become quiet again !

December 25th, 1864.

SUNDAY.

Christmas greeting to you, my dear Journal, once more!
Went up town last evening, and called at the store
On my way, and saw *him*, too, my dearest! Did not
Have a chance, though, for speaking. Did *he* give a thought,
I wonder, to one year ago, or to me?
In the chapel last eve was a concert and " tree;"
I went, and remained with a friend for the night.
Went to service to-day, and I *was* surprised, quite
To see Mrs. ——, his wife, was there also, with him,
Looking fair, and as fresh, too, as ever. Had been
A long time since I'd seen her before. We'd to-day
A fine Christmas sermon, indeed, I must say.
This P.M. went to Sabbath-school, then returned home.
On my way to the car passed his house: and I own,
What I saw there both pleased and surprised me some, too!
Sitting back from the window, and yet in plain view,
Was my Antony dearest! and close in his arms
A bundle of cambric, and soft flannel warm.
Containing a baby, I could but suppose,
Sleeping sweetly, an infant's undreaming repose,
In arms that would fain shield from all earthly woes,
That tiny, frail blossom. I think *I* could sleep,
Held within such a clasp, a sleep dreamless and deep—
Sleep forever! and never again wake to weep.
" 'Twere delicious to die, if my heart might grow cold
While his arms wrapped me round in that passionate fold."

That is what I had never expected to see—
A baby in *his* arms, " my own Antony."

One thing somewhat vexes me : I've sometimes thought
Of late—though perhaps it is fancy—from what
I have noticed at church, that not only his friend
Mr. F., but his wife, from beginning to end,
Knows about our acquaintance. And yet, I can't think
He *could* make a jest of it ! Feel he would shrink
From aught so unworthy ; yet, think I will write
And give him a chance for defence, if he likes,
Not condemn him unheard, which would hardly be right.

December 31*st,* 1864.

SATURDAY.

Last Tuesday our visitors all went away,
And I wrote a letter, I think, the same day,
To my Antony, as in my last record here
I thought I should do.   Stated first, full and clear,
My suspicions, and grounds for the same ; the effect
Such thoughts could but have on my mind, hoping yet
I might be mistaken.   Would be but too glad
Could he prove to the contrary ; and if he had
Any wish to himself exculpate, or had aught
To say on the subject, I'd meet him, I thought,
Between one and three on the next afternoon,
If he chose to go up, at the L.'s reading-room.
The next day was stormy, but in the P.M.
Looked a little like clearing, so started ; but when

I had walked a few blocks it was raining again.
For a car I then waited a long time in vain,
So walked to the ferry. I caught one at last,
On the other side, tho' ; 'twas a few minutes past
Three o'clock when I reached the Library ; and he
Was not, of course, there at that hour. As for me,
Though I would have braved anything to have gone—
Did brave fearful travelling, a severe storm—
Yet regretted my folly when it was too late ;
Came home with the world out of humor, with fate
And myself in particular ; and in a state
Of discomfort in body, as well, being both
Cold and wet. Though I saw him not, still I am loth,
Even yet, to believe my own charges. I could
Not love him at all, I am sure, if I should.
Many things might prevented his keeping that day
The appointment I made. And indeed, though, he may
Have been there and gone ; or my letter might not
Have reached him in time ; or else he may have thought
That it was so stormy, I would not be there.
I'll give him one more chance.

                  I hope 'twill be fair
To-morrow, for I very much wish to go
Up to church in the morning ; but all day the snow
Has fallen unceasingly ; so I shall be
Obliged to stay home, very likely, I see.

   To-day is the last of this changeable year!
So filled with both sorrow and joy, hope and fear.
The last hours are speeding ! All day I have thought
Of one year ago—of those hours that were fraught
With so much of gladness to me ! Of that day,
The happiest ever I spent, I must say.

I shall never forget it! I wonder if he
Remembers it, too—if he but cared for me
Only just *half* as much as I do about him!
And, indeed, how do *I* know, but down deep within
The most sacred room in his heart, there is traced
My name, and in letters which naught can efface?
He is not demonstrative, and it may be
I am more to him, even, than he is to me.
Farewell to the year "sixty-four," so replete
With associations both bitter and sweet!

January 2d, 1865.

MONDAY.

It "made believe" storm all the day yesterday,
And there were no paths; consequently, away
From church I of course was obliged to remain;
So my "New Year's Day" this year, both opened and
       waned,
Without having been noted by any event
Of import; and so did the last, yet I've spent
Few days that were *more fully happy* than that.
And neither was this quite unhappy, in fact.
And to-day has been jubilant! For, this A.M.,
The carrier came here with letters; and when
He had given me two, he then said, "Let me see
If 1 have not another for you!" and then he
Passed me one, too, from—*him*, my own darling! and I
Could not tell you, my Journal, e'en tho' I should try,
How surprised and how pleased I was, too, to once more
Have a letter in *his* well-known hand, as of yore.

It was both short and cold ; but a very few lines;
Yet more precious to this wayward, fond heart of mine,
Than words of the most ardent love from another.
'Twas addressed my whole name ; and on each of the others
He has my initials used only, and I
Did not know that he knew what it was.

                     By the by,
I ought to have had it on Saturday.   States
Received mine on Thursday; adds, " *one day too late.*"
Said—

       " You do me, indeed, gross injustice !   I'm no
Such person.   Should written you some time ago,
But did not know where to address, and do not
Hardly think this will reach you."

                     I never had thought
Of his writing, and so, did not send my address.
That was all that he wrote.   There was not, I confess,
In that, aught to go into ecstasies o'er ;
Yet, coming from him, it has given me more
Of pleasure and gladness than aught else could do ;
And has rendered my New Year most happy, 'tis true.
I sat down at once and wrote him a reply,
Both loving and long; looked it o'er—laid it by,
And taking a fresh sheet, another one wrote,
As brief and as cold as his own icy note.
There was a great contrast the letters between !
One the heart had dictated, from th' wealth and the sheen
Of its jubilant love ; and the other was traced
By a hand which was guided alone by strait-laced
Decorum, and cold, worldly pride ; and the one
Which I sent was the *last.*

                   One more day is now done,
And auspiciously one more New Year has begun !

January 15th, 1865.

SUNDAY.

I made an appointment for Tuesday, P.M.,
But it rained hard all day; consequently again
It was missed.   Yesterday I'd a letter, although,
Saying any P.M. of next week he would go
To the L. to meet me.
                  To-day the wind blew
Exceedingly hard, and 'twas " bitter cold," too;
But I went up to church.   I'd forgotten to say
That a steward to me came, I think the last day
I was up there, and asked me if I would object
To sitting one seat farther back; he could let
Our pew to advantage, and thought as 'twas rare
For any of us, but myself, to be there,
That we did not care the whole seat to retain,
And that I'd very probably not mind the change.
And *did* I?   Well! not very much, I admit,
And certainly made no objection to it.
For, of course, if I sat just one pew farther back,
I should then be directly opposite that
Occupied by my Antony dearest.   If we
Both should at the inner end sit, there would be
But a thin, low partition between us.   This morn,
I did not know what was decided upon,
So took my old place.   The new occupants, though,
Were there.   This P.M. there was service, also,
To the mem'ry of one of our fallen heroes.
They were there, too, and thought it quite strange, I sup-
      pose,

To notice the change ; or, at least, she stared some
When I took my new seat. The number of one
Of the first hymns, she failing to catch, at once looked
At him, but his eyes were then bent on his book;
With a gesture just slightly impatient she then
Turned to me, so I passed her my hymn-book, and when
She returned it, of course bowed and smiled pleasantly;
We were both in the corner, and so could but be
Very near to each other. How little she knew
Of the ties indissoluble binding us two!
That *she* was the one only barrier between
Him and me, in more senses than one, too, I ween!
For as *she* sat between us at service to-day,
So in all things she parts us, both now and alway.

January 27th, 1865.

FRIDAY.

Last week an appointment for Thursday I made,
And again were frustrated my plans, so well laid.
One of the L.'s patrons is recently dead,
And I in the paper on Wednesday eve read
That the L. would be closed on the following day.
I was much disappointed and vexed, I must say.
But I not being able to help it, was forced
To make the best of it ; supposing, of course,
That he would have seen the same notice, also,
That morning at latest, and so would not go.
But lest he should not have, I wrote him again,

Saying why I that day should not come in, and then
Making one more appointment for Tuesday P.M.
There seems on our meeting to be a spell set!
But all obstacles only make stronger yet
My will and desire him to see.   It has been,
Oh, such a *long* time since I've spoken with him,
Since my hand with fond pressure has been clasped in his!
Almost a whole, long, weary year.   Yet he is
My love, and my dearest! and what wonder, then,
I desire with insatiable longing again
To stand face to face, hand to hand, with the man
Who to me is so much ; and that also I am
Quite ready to sacrifice any amount
Of pride to accomplish my wish ; and would count
It all nothing, compared to an hour's chat with him?
And thus far, in fact, our acquaintance has been
A sacrifice constant of pride on my part.
Pride is strong—strong enough! but yet *love* in my heart
Is more potent still! and I've found, it is true,
That in a contest 'tween the sentiments two,
Love always is conqueror ; that I'm a slave,
And each effort to sunder the fetters, which chafe
Me so sorely, but rivets my chains stronger yet,
While I 'neath their clankings still hopelessly fret.

   When Tuesday arrived I in town went once more,
And stopped on my way to the L. at the store.
He was in; I was certain he saw me, though I
Did not speak with him.   Oh! but I bought, by the by,
A paper, the first one I thought of, and found
When carelessly looking its columns a-down,
The first poem he sent me, " You Kissed Me!" was in i
I went to the L. and I waited, while minute

By minute flew on, and still *he* did not come.
I at last gave him up, and then started for home.
Vexed, provoked was I? No; those words cannot express
Half how *angry* I was. Far more so, I confess,
Than heretofore ever I *have* been with him.
Feeling certain he knew very well I was in,
And that, if he had not intended to go,
Or could not, he might at the least have said so
When I went in the store, why, how could I but feel
Very angry, indeed? Neither did I conceal
How incensed I then was, in the letter I sent.
I *was* very cross with him, and also meant
He should know it.

         To-day, I received a reply.
Though its contents were read with a quite tearless eye,
In my heart was such sorrow as never before
It has known; for I felt sure that now was all o'er,
And strangers we were to become evermore!
But I was not conscious how plainly was traced
The grief and despair I then felt, in my face,
Till a friend coming in had expressed much concern,
Being sure I was ill. I could but have discerned
From his note, that he was, indeed, only less vexed
Than I was when I wrote. Neither was I perplexed,
After reading his letter, the reason to know,
Nor could I then wonder at *his* feeling so.
He never has sent me one cross word before;
And I·—well! I've written to him many more
Cross letters than kind ones, I'm fearful; but then,
I got angry one minute, the next pleased again,
While a person not easily vexed frequently
Retains their displeasure some time. And so he,

Having once got provoked, or in anger at me,
Will now not forgive me, I fear, readily.
'My "note was insulting," he wrote, and I could
But acknowledge its truth.   He presumed that it would
Not be in accordance with etiquette, should
He a lady's word doubt ; and that therefore, as I
Said I *knew* that he saw me, he had in reply
Naught to say.   And again, both appointments he kept ;
The first time he found the L. closed, and the next
No one there that he knew ; and as *he* the last two
Had kept, so he *should not* the *next*.

                              What to do,
I at first hardly knew.   But then, conscious that I
Had wronged him, I could do no less, in reply,
Than acknowledge my error, and thus make amends
For my unjust, intemperate language, and send
An apology too, stipulating that he
His forgiveness should prove by his keeping with me
The appointment which I should make next ; so I wrote,
And he will to-morrow, I think, have my note.

———

February 7th, 1865.

TUESDAY.

   Nothing new or of import, since here I wrote last.
Have not been to service for two Sabbaths past ;
So him I have not seen, and neither have I
Received any letter from him, in reply

To the one which I sent more than one week ago.
If *he* could pass *that* by unanswered, I know
Not what he is made of.   I sent this P.M.
A very cool note, and appointing again
A meeting for Thursday.   And failure this time
Will crush out all hope from this poor heart of mine;
Forced to yield to despair, I will never again
Expect aught but misery, sorrow, and pain.
" He tosses me bitterness," truly!   Must I
With a stone be contented when bread is so nigh,
Or with husks, just because the fruit's hanging so high ?

February 9th, 1865.

THURSDAY.

Far more happy to-night than my words can portray,
I have seated myself, the events of to-day
To transcribe in my book ; but my heart is so light,
So jubilant, joyful, and so filled with bright,
Sweet thoughts, hopes, emotions, I scarce can compose
Myself to write calmly, this evening, of those
Events and sweet feelings.
     Well, *I* need not say,
I presume, my dear Journal, what rendered this day
Such a glad one to me !   What has rolled far away
The lowering clouds, shown the bright " silver lining,"
That " behind the dark cloud is the sun still shining."
And that ever 'tis " darkest just previous to dawn."
What else *could* have turned into roseate morn

My heart's midnight, except that to-day I've seen *him*,
And that he is still, that he ever has been,
My dearest dear friend!

          This P.M. I went in,
And at the Library I waited for him
Until three o'clock, when—he came! What a bound
Of delight my heart gave, as my darling came down
The long room, to where *I* was then sitting! How bright
Was the smile on his lips, and how sweet the soft light
In his eye, and how pleasant his musical tones,
As he murmured his greeting, and pressed in his own,
With warm fondness, the hand which I gave! Then he
    drew
A chair close to mine, and sat down. And I knew,
Without farther words, that my love was "still true."
What a nice chat we had! and all, too, was explained
To my satisfaction, 'till no thought remained
In my heart but of kindness for him; and it seems
All the trouble was caused by his " prudence " extreme.
He likes *me* just as well now as ever before.
And I—well! I own that I like him far more
Than words can express!

            Oh! the reason that I
To my penitent letter have had no reply,
Was that he was away, so it was not received
Until his return—I think yesterday eve—
When he found it awaiting him, also my last,
Appointing to-day's interview. So we passed
An hour or two there in the most pleasant chat;
And, as we were coming away, he said that
If *I'd* not get cross any more, he would be
A good boy in the future. He also asked me,

Once or twice, when I thought I'd be in town again;
And said, too, that if I would let him know when
He'd try and come up.   I of course was too glad
To promise.   We walked to my car, where he bade
Me good-by, and then left me.

      How sweet 'tis, once more
To feel we are friends! all unpleasantness o'er,
All difference reconciled!   What wonder, then,
In my heart smiles and sunshine are nestling again?

   •

February 12*th*, 1865.

SUNDAY.

 I have nothing to write of since Thursday, except
Our sweet reconcilement, and perfect, has kept
My heart constantly buoyant and glad.   Was to-day
Up at church, though it snowed when I started away,
And was bitterly cold.   He was not there this morn,
And I thought possibly on account of the storm
Might not be this afternoon either.   Of late
We've service had in the P.M., I must state,
Instead of the evening, as usual.   I'd not
Have gone up to church this cold day, but I thought
I would much like to know if my *friend* would appear
Any different now than before.   Well! my fears
In regard to his absence were all put to flight
When I saw him come in.   We were both of us quite

Alone in our pews, so had nothing to do
But look at each other; and we improved, too,
To advantage, the rare opportunity.   He
Sent *such* loving glances and smiles, too, to me;
Kept constantly turned toward me, in his face
The same look which I used to see there in the days
Long gone by.   And it *did* seem like " old times," indeed,
And I fancy that neither of us gave much heed
To the doubtless fine sermon; at least *I* did not,
And believe that he, also, had never a thought
But for me.   My own darling!   How *much* I love him.
How exquisitely happy this Sabbath has been!
And I felt fully paid, too, for going, although
The weather was very inclement.   I know
That I toward him can feel never again
As I have recently—until last Thursday—when
" Old things passed away, and all things became new."
By the way—and quite a coincidence, too,
I thought it—just one year ago, at the time
We to-day sat in church, at the same hour, in fine,
He and I were together in *my* dear old home
In New York, for the last time.   I did not, I own,
Remember it then.   And I wish I had, too!

    I wrote a few words, and dropped into his pew
The paper on which they were traced.   He did not
Perceive it, although and therefore, as I thought
That some one might find it whom *I* would not care
To have see or read it, I told him 'twas there
When we met at the door, and he went back for it.
I of course could not wait for him; that, I admit,
Would have been hardly " prudent;" but if he saw fit

He could join me. But Mr. S., when he came out,
Took his arm very coolly, walked with him about
Two blocks, and then left him. The rest of the way
I had him myself; and although, I dare say,
It was highly "imprudent"—our walking together—
'Twas none the less pleasant. It stormed, and the weath '
Was fearfully cold, yet I gave it no thought;
His presence with life, warmth, and sunshine was fraught.

February 23*d*, 1865.

THURSDAY.

Nearly two pleasant weeks have now glided away
Since my last record here. I had made for to-day
An appointment. 'Twas cloudy, and so, hardly knew
About going in, what 'twas best I should do.
At length I decided I would; and was glad
Afterward that I did so. A book, that I had
Been wishing to purchase, I ordered through him.
So I thought on my way to the L. I'd stop in
At his place, get my book, also thus ascertain
Was *he* going up; that I might not in vain
Have to wait if he could not. He sat near the door,
And he seldom remains in that part of the store.
He sprang up to speak to me, keeping me there
For more than an hour. It was quite private where
We were standing, and not many people were in.
But *I'd* not the slightest idea I'd been

9

There so long; and was quite surprised, too, I must say,
That he wished—as was evident—that I should stay.
And wonder he thought it quite "prudent."　Away
Time rapidly hastened, and forced me to leave.

To a masquerade ball, they were going this eve,
He and Mrs. ——, his wife.　I tried to induce
Him to tell me where now were my letters.　No use
I found it to coax or to tease; he refused
To inform me, or rather he told me, 'tis true,
So many improbable stories, I knew
Not which to believe.　I asked *him* if he'd come
Out to see me some time; but he thought he'd not run
Any risk; I inquired, if for no other one
He had risked any more.　Said, decidedly, "No!"
Very flattering, truly!　*Perhaps* it is so.
"With ease we believe what we ardently wish
To be true!"　He, however, did promise me this:
That if the next summer our people should be
Away, about three hundred miles, leaving me
All alone, he would try and come over.　He would
Go up to the L. the next time, if he could
Get away from the store.　Would have gone up to-day,
Very likely, if I had not called on the way.
Many thoughts and sweet ones of my dearest to-night!
God bless and preserve him 'till morning's fair light!

May 31*st*, 1865.

The last day of May!　And I find it has been
Three months, and more even, since I have within
These pages a single word traced.　Also find,
Glancing backward a little, this journal of mine
Has of late more a simple heart-record become,
Than aught else beside.　The truth is, to no one
Can I speak of the pain which at times I have found
Unbearable quite.　And the festering wound
Forced to ever conceal, it to me gives relief
Sometimes to give utterance here to my grief.
And therefore I write of it.　Common events
Have, of late, been to me of so little moment,
I have come to ignore them all here, though each week
And each day brings its own, either bitter or sweet.

　　And as to my love, we have met now and then,
Sometimes at the store, at the L., or again
A few times at church, once or twice in the street.
He has been just as charming whene'er we *did* meet,
But I've made some appointments that *he* did not keep,
And sent him some letters, to which a reply
I have failed to receive.　I wrote him, by the by,
About three weeks ago, a short note, to which I,
Requesting an answer, directed it sent
" To remain at the office 'till called for."　I went

In town to the L.—though it stormed—on the day
I looked for it; when coming down, on Broadway,
I saw on the opposite side of the street,
A face and a form too familiar to meet
Or pass without notice.   He did not, although,
Perceive *me*.   Ere I reached him he crossed to Park Row,
And taking a car moved away toward home,
Entirely unconscious his " Antony's own "
Had so nearly met him.   I *should* have been glad
With him just a few moments' chat to have had,
As a matter of course ; but I thought I would be
Quite contented if I should find waiting for me,
At the office, a letter from him, as I hoped.
And I did ; and a splendid one, too ; and I oped
And its contents with eager impatience perused.
And that for a time in my spirits infused
New life, strength, and joy.   By the way, we, I find,
Both gave up our pews in church at the same time,
And each quite unknown to the other.

                                This eve,
I again write myself disappointed !   Believe
No one *ever* was disappointed so much !
I *must* give him up.   I can *not* endure such
Aggravation and torture much longer.   I am
Of comfort and peace destitute.   And how can
Any one be so cruel as he is, at times !
He is *more* than provoking, is more than unkind.
And yet, I suppose he does *not* mean to be,
Does not know how fearfully he torments me.
Many times I've resolved I would never again
Either write him or make an appointment ; and then

Irresistible longings for tidings of him,
Or desires for one glimpse of his dear face, have been
Triumphant, my good resolutions dispelled,
And while pride remonstrated, and I have felt
To the utmost my folly, have written again.
Why my fate *must* it been to have loved thus in vain ?
But I will not complain ; right and best, I doubt not,
It is, and rebellion is quelled by the thought
That underneath all there's a long-broken vow.
Would I could forget him ! nor ever allow
Him a place in my heart any more.
                   I intend
At the sea-shore to pass a few weeks with some friends,
And expect to go soon. So, my Journal friend dear,
Until my return, I shall write no more here.

July 20*th*, 1865.

THURSDAY.

    At home once again ! And how pleasant it seems !
" There is no place like home ; " and although all my dreams
Of pleasure were fully, I think, realized,
And the time gayly passed by in sails, walks, and drives,
Yet sometimes my heart turned with longing, I own,
To the quiet and peace of my dearly-loved home.
While absent, some letters I had from a friend,
One with whom, I believe, I have previous to then
Had no correspondence. Permission to write
He requested, and *I* thought perhaps that it might
Be to me pleasant, also, so gave my consent ;
Stipulating, however, in its commencement,

No love-passage there should be in it.   He thought
Of the " heart disease " I'd a slight touch, but 'twould not
A lasting blight prove.   Would that *he* might be right !
He wrote me nice letters, and though I was quite
Glad to have them, yet I, caring nothing for him,
His letters in consequence, when they had been
Once perused and replied to, could not be to me
Of much farther value.

      From home frequently,
Of course, heard while absent; from Colonel Allair
Found, when I arrived, one awaiting me there.
I also had five or six others from him ;
Some from Annie, my friend, who a long time has been
My dear correspondent ; and from my love—*one !*
I wrote him before my departure from home,
To say I was going ; if *he* liked to write,
I'd be most glad to hear.   I'd been staying in quite
A different part of the town, a few days,
And so, when again I returned to the place
Where my letters were sent, I found several there.
And the first one I saw was addressed in his fair,
Well-known hand.   'Twas not long, and neither was it
Especially pleasing or kind, I admit,
And I sent him no answer.   Yet I was more glad
To receive it than any besides that I had.
Was not well—he wrote—and that letter to me
Was the first he had written in some weeks ; and he
Ought not even then to be writing.   Had been
Very busy indeed ; and expected, within
A few days, out of town to remove ; but did not,
Of course, tell me where, though he could but have thought
I'd be anxious to know.

                Mamma now soon intends
To go into the country a few weeks, and then
I think that for him I may possibly send,
And give him a chance to his promise redeem.
As he will, if he yet cares about me, I ween !

————

August 1st, 1865.

TUESDAY.

I am thoroughly wretched, and reckless as well!
What of late has come o'er me, I scarcely can tell;
But I've felt for awhile, as if at any cost
I *must* have my love!   And my heart, tempest-tossed
And despairing, is utterly desperate now,
And I *will* be something to him, I avow!
For him I have sacrificed my peace of mind,
Independence, my pride, happiness, and, in fine,
Everything but my honor—am tempted to say
That if I can have him in no other way,
Even that shall go also.   To him, all the deepest,
And freshest, and fondest, the purest, and sweetest
Emotions and thoughts of a heart only *he*
Has power to thrill—all the wealth of a free
And impassioned first love—and one, too, felt to be
The one love of my life—has been long consecrated,
And he cares for it nothing!   I *am* aggravated
Endurance beyond; past resistance am tempted;
Exhausted with being from pain ne'er exempted;

And weary, and heart-sick of struggles to gain
The mastery over this hopeless, and vain,
This humiliating, tormenting, and quite
Uncontrollable love. Indignation, grief, pride,
On my part—indifference, coldness, neglect,
On his own, do not have e'en the slightest effect,
Except more completely to make me the slave
Of this fierce, overpowering passion. Things grave,
And not pleasant, are these to acknowledge, I know ;
Nor anywhere else but here could I do so.
But all confidences are sacred with you,
My Journal, my friend ever silent and true !
Feeling thus, I have written a letter to him,
And written like this :

" My Dear ' John :'

" Opening

My casket of letters, the first thing that met
My eye was one written by you, and not yet
Acknowledged.   My time being quite occupied
While I was away, and I having, besides,
Many letters to write, I did not answer yours—
As it would not matter to you, I felt sure.
But since having seen it this morning, of you
I've been thinking much ; our relations unto
Each other reviewed, and have now come to write
To you the result.

" In the first place, I'm quite

Resolved upon this : that the state of things now
Existing between us I will not allow
To longer continue.   You very well know
It has been to me most aggravating, also
Unpleasant, at times—our acquaintance—although

I presume that it often has been my own fault,
More than yours; but some things have excessively galled
My sensitive feelings, when probably you
Were unconscious of giving offence. It is true,
I have written you letters, and more than a few,
Such as no gentleman to me ever would sent
More than once; and your very forbearance—well meant
As I doubt not it was—has sometimes made me more
Annoyed with you still. You have exercised o'er
Me a strange fascination; and, bent to your will
My high spirit has been, and pride also, until
I feel I can't longer endure it. I may
Have told you, perhaps, the same thing ere to-day;
But then it was written on impulse, and now
I am deeply in earnest; and you will allow
That if you have found me 'all things at all times,'
I at least have been always sincere !

       " Now, in fine,
I am ready to meet you upon your own terms,
Or to meet you no more! just as you shall discern
Will be best. You know very well *why* you came
To see me the first time; with *motives* the *same*
If you now desire calling upon me again,
I shall be glad to see you. You told me that when
Mamma was ' three hundred miles distant,' you then
Would come over; and now is the time to fulfil
The promise you made—and I'm sure that you will,
If you have the slightest regard for me still.
Should you come out here once, and you then do not choose
To do so again, I will ask you to lose
No more time for me. But I think you will not
Regret it, if you should decide to come out.

 9

And I think that indeed it is *much* more for *your*
Interest than it can be for *mine*, I am sure!
I expect to receive you on Wednesday P.M.,
Between one and five, unless I before then
Hear something contrary; and you will please write
Should you fail to come out.

      "Now in closing, good-night!
With kind wishes for you, and with hopes we may meet
Before many days, I am

    " Yours,

      " Bitter-Sweet."

I do not much think he will come, but he may;
And suppose, that it too would be best every way,
That he should not—for him, and me also—and still,
Notwithstanding all " prudence," I *do* hope he will!

———

August 4th, 1865.

FRIDAY.

My mother and Gertrude went off Wednesday morn,
And some five or six weeks they will doubtless be gone.
And when afternoon came I expected him some,
As no note I'd received, saying he should not come.
Watched and waited, but vainly.   I *did* think he might
Have written, at least; though 'twas possible, quite,
He intended to come, and could not get away,
And so would be out on the following day.

The next morning the carrier brought me a note
From him, and my heart seemed to leap to my throat
As I took off the wrapper, expecting to find
That he could not or would not come out.   But this time
I was, if disappointed, agreeably so.
I ought to have had it on Wednesday, although,
As 'twas written the first.   Said that he did not know
Until the receipt of my letter, that day,
That I had returned.   Then he went on to say,
Had business way down town that P.M., so he
Thought that he'd steal an hour, and slip over to B.
Told in detail his search for the house, and then writes :
" I rang at the door, which was then open wide,
At about three o'clock.   A young lady replied
To the summons, who was not B. S.; so I thought
I might justly conclude that your people *had not*
Gone ' three hundred miles ' out of town, or else they
Had come back in a hurry.   Am going away
To-morrow, and may return Friday ; if so,
Will see you if possible."
                              Well! you must know,
My Journal, this letter was, to the suspense
And doubt I then felt, a relief most intense.
I could not, at once, though, remember at all
At that day and hour there had any one called.
But at last recollected that some one did ring,
And of Gertrude, who went to the door, directing
A gentleman up the street farther ; and thought
At the time, what a soft voice he had ; but did not
Once dream of its being my friend ; and am glad
That *I* did not go to the door.   If I had

Some suspense, though, 'twould saved me, of course.   But
     Gertrude
Did not recognize him at all, I conclude.
I wondered if *he* heard me scolding; I know
I was fearfully nervous and cross; thought also,
He perhaps might have seen me ; I sat just inside
The back-parlor, with both folding-doors open wide.
But he said he did not.   That was Tuesday! the day
Before mother and Gertrude were going away.
And this afternoon he was here! and is still
My love! and my darling!   I feel that until
This day I've indeed never known him.   I find
I've often misjudged him; for he, good and kind,
Of the recklessness in my last letter expressed,
No advantage did take ; but, instead, I confess,
Treated me with the utmost respect.   Friendship true,
Regard deep and warm, and much tenderness, too,
Was betrayed in each action and word; and yet, he
Not even at parting so much as kissed me!
Conclusively proved how unjust I had been,
By an improper motive ascribing to him,
In his first visits to me.
             I never *can* read
Him at all; and his heart is a sealed book indeed !
To think evil of him, I am too much inclined.
So in this case, at least, I'm sure, love is not blind.
I am *so glad* to find that my darling's so true !
And feel I have in fearful peril been, too,
And thank God I am safe.   For had *he* proved to be
Less honorable—noble—had he tempted me—
I know not—I might have had strength to resist,
And natural virtue been roused to assist,

But I'm thankful, at least, that I then was not tried,
And that I have at length all his goodness descried.

I stood talking with Bella, my friend, at her gate,
And still hoping, although " my love he was late ! "
When I saw him approaching.   My heart gave a bound
And stood still, as I entered the house and sat down,
And endeavored my turbulent pulses to calm,
While I waited his coming, and knew that the man
Whom I love " with a love passing knowledge," would
    soon—
His dear self—be beside me in *this* very room.

He has moved up to Harlem ; next door, I believe,
To his father.   He went about six.   All the eve
My head has ached fearfully ; so, without lights,
I've sat in the window and dreamed.   And the night
Is perfectly lovely !
             One more happy day !
Yet a happiness, *doubtful*, somewhat, I must say.
He said he would come out again the next week.
God bless him to-night, and from all danger keep !

August 5th, 1865.

SATURDAY.

Can it be that but yesterday he was with me ?
That my hand was once more clasped in his, and that he
Then rested his dear head awhile on my knee ?

For he, world-weary man—he, my indolent boy,
Must needs have a lounge, and my lap must employ
As a pillow.   Am blue to-day! thoughts of " what might
Have been," crowd so close on my heart, that in spite
Of myself I am sad.   I expected, to-day,
A note from my late correspondent.   Must say,
Though none was received, I cared not; for, as long
As *he* is " my own," what beside can I want?
My dear one! yet *not* mine, and never can be.
But I must not dwell upon this; it makes me
Too entirely unhappy.   Ah, truly!   " The grief
Of affection betrayed is but tame and brief
Beside a forbidden love's utter despair!"
God pity and love me is my earnest prayer.

August 6th, 1865.

SUNDAY.

One more breaking out of the old wound!   To-day
I have been far more mis'rable than I can say.
Have not been out at all; and I hardly have left
My room since the morn, and for hours I have wept.
Wrote to mother, but only a note.   *Could* not write.
Why cannot I conquer this passion, whose might
And intensity chokes me, and fills my poor heart
With sadness so often?   Indeed! we *must* part!
I must give him up; he can never be mine!
I am very unhappy if he is unkind,

And if proofs of affection he gives me, then thoughts
Of—not what I have lost, but of what I cannot
Ever gain, and that he is not only not mine,
But another's instead, rushes on me at times,
With such force as completely to overwhelm me,
And my self-control, hardly-won, break down utterly !

September 12th, 1865.

TUESDAY.

Has more than a month been since I've written here,
And within that short time—oh, what ages of fear,
Hope, pain, and suspense I've endured and lived through.
I thought I'd before been most wretched, 'tis true !
But nothing that could in the least be compared
To this, have I ever experienced.   There
Has day after day been, when all I have felt
Was a longing desire for " escape from myself,
And oblivion of time."   When from this to that place,
With a quite tearless eye, but a white, anguished face,
Have I wandered ; now pausing awhile in my room,
Drawing down the blind close, and with darkness and gloom
Replacing the sunlight that mocked my despair—
On my bed for awhile, lying silently there,
Then crouched on the floor with my head in a chair,
Down stairs in the parlors, a book in my hand,
But the purport of which I could not understand ;
And then perhaps playing a half-dozen chords,
Which had much less of harmony than of discord,

Or leaning far back in a rocker, in vain
Endeavoring thus with the turbulent pain
In my heart to keep pace—Oh! my God alone knows
How brimful of agony to me were those
Few weeks, at length ended forever.   It seems,
Looking back on it now, like a long, fearful dream;
For a calm has succeeded the storm, or, at least,
The exhaustion that comes with severe pain's release.

Two weeks I looked for him almost every day,
And vainly.   A letter he wrote then, to say
He had met with an accident, somewhat severe,
On the cars, which some days had confined him, and feared
'Twould be several more before he should be out
Permanently; was going right home; when about,
He should try and come over.   My hopes this renewed,
And confidence too.   One more week ensued,
And then I began to expect him again.
One day I in town went, with Bella, my friend,
And so at the store called, in order that he
Might know I was not home in case he should be
Intending that day to go over to B.
But he was not in.   The clerk said had been out
For more than an hour, and 'twas doubtful about
His again coming in.   I supposed, of course, then,
He had gone to see me.   Was in torture again,
Until I reached home, and found out he had not.
The next day was in town again; therefore, I thought
To end my suspense I'd make one more attempt,
Or at least ascertain if he really meant
To come out or not; so I called; he was in,
But so busy I had but a few words with him.

He said he intended to come out that day,
But had so much to do he *could not* get away.
Had had some reverses in business, and then
Was not his own master.   I had that A.M.
A letter from mother received, saying she
Should be home the next Thursday.   I told him, and he
Said that he would come over that day, if he could ;
Could not say with positiveness that he should ;
But would unless business prevented.   But I
Then gave up his coming; and Thursday passed by
And I did not see him.

                The next morning brought
From mother a letter, and stating she thought
She should visit Boston before she came home ;
Consequently, should some two weeks longer be gone.
And one from him also, and saying that he
Intended that day to get over to B.,
But found it impossible; as he was quite
With visitors over-run, and had beside
His hands full of business, and knew not at times
Hardly what he was doing.   And then wrote, in fine,
" Don't feel cross with me, though, I have got a head wind
But hope for fair weather again, by and by ! "
This rather brought me to my senses ; and I
Felt ashamed that I *had* been so cross with him then—
Thus adding unto his annoyances, when
He already was quite over-burdened, although
I, of course, did not know he was troubled.   And so
I fully resolved that another cross word
I would nevermore send him, whatever occurred.
When I could not write pleasantly, I would not write.

My mother and Gertie arrived home to-night,
And the mis'rable past I am trying to seal
From sight, in my heart's darkest corner; but feel
Its effects will not be quite so easy concealed.

September 19th, 1865.

TUESDAY.

To-morrow our place of abode we shall change,
And I shall write " home " in a house new and strange.
To-night, for the last time, I sleep in this room,
And leave it with many regrets.   Just as soon
As 'round a place bright recollections of him
Have clustered most fondly and sweetly, we've been
Forced to leave it, and in a new place, to begin
Our home-life, and therein our home altars rear.
Better so, perhaps!   Thoughts of him are not, I fear,
Very good for me ; and, although I have to-day,
In outward appearance, been lively and gay,
'Twas only to cover the aching within ;
Only to drive away sad thoughts of him,
And my love that's so hopeless and vain.   Many times
Tears unbidden would spring to my eyes, and I find
Them hard to repress ; but I knew 'twould not do
To indulge them, so they were forced back, and none knew
Or dreamed of the pain I was hiding so well.
Many things occur daily, of him to impel
Remembrance; and when I begin to forget

Some light, trifling thing will bring all back, with yet
Greater force renewing each banished regret.

November 2d, 1865.

THURSDAY.

The morning my birth-day again ushers in !
And with it, of course, a new year I begin,
With most earnest hopes that its record may be
More tranquil than this one has been. Yes ! I see
That is what I desire—a calm, after the dark,
Stormy night ; and sweet peace for my sad troubled heart.
But when I shall have it, our God alone knows.
But not 'till I cease to do wrong, I suppose,
And learn to do right. It is so hard to feel,
At all times, that " all's for the best ! " hard to kneel
And kiss with submission the hand that would smite.
The last year passed swiftly away. If I might,
I would not recall it ; some parts have been quite
Too unhappy. I have not recovered, as yet,
From the anguish—or rather its blighting effect—
I endured in those drear August days. And must say,
I could fancy myself ten years older to-day
Than I was at that time. I look back, too, and feel
With surprise, what 'twere vain to attempt to conceal,
How much deeper, more tender my love is for him
Than 'twas three months ago. And yet, I within
These pages still hope, ere a year from to-night,
Of the end of this unhappy passion to write.

December 31st, 1865.

SUNDAY.

I've written " eighteen sixty-five," I suppose,
For the last time this year.   And I write at its close
One more anniversary to commemorate,
The dearest, and sweetest of all !   When, elate
With the joy of his presence, I had not a thought
But that he was with me.   And how fully fraught
Were the moments with gladness !   Yet *I* did not dream
That I loved him !   How strange that I could not have seen
What it meant—such infatuation !   That day
Was, without exception, I think I may say,
The happiest one of my life ; one which had
No bitter enwreathed with the sweet of its glad
Happy moments—just two years ago !

                                        It has been
More than four months since I have had one glimpse of him
I wrote him on his birth-day, some two months ago,
And once since—on the last anniversary, though,
Of our correspondence's commencement.   To these
No reply I received, or expected—though pleased
I of course should have been to have had one.   To-night,
In remembrance of *two years ago*, I shall write.

   For two or three weeks I have quite ceased to grieve,
And have not been so cheerful for months.   But last eve,
After I had retired, the old billows once more
Surged over my heart, breaking down, as of yore,
All the barriers my hardly-won self-control
Had attempted to rear, again flooding my soul

With the bitter and turbulent waters.   At times
It is *so* hard to feel he can never be mine,
But is always another's !   The Colonel, my dear,
Kind friend, does a great deal my sad heart to cheer ;
And his letters, so frequent and loving, to me
Of inestimable value have long come to be.

January 4th, 1866.

THURSDAY.

This day should be marked as a " red-letter day ! "
It has been, oh, so happy, and yet, in some ways,
So miserable also !   The bitter and sweet
In *my* cup invariably meet and compete.
The carrier brought me a letter this morn,
From my love ! And 'twas not short and cold, but more
    warm
And pleasing than any before I have had.
While its contents perusing, tears, happy and glad,
Welled up to my eyes, and, unheeded, brimmed o'er.
I glanced with haste through it, then turned, and once more
With loving delight read each word.   On my mind
Slowly dawning a consciousness for the first time,
The thought that it was barely possible he,
My love and my darling, might also love me.
I scarcely can credit it ; dare not believe
That it can be true.
           He wrote he had received
Mine the previous day, and intended to write
At once ; but was called off before he had quite

Got started, and so was obliged to forego
Until that time.   He blamed himself much—said also—
That he'd not before written in answer to mine;
Had honestly meant to, but from time to time
Had deferred it, till he was ashamed to, and then
Was fearful that it would not reach me.   Again
And again he most kindly assured me I'd not
Been forgotten, I was not to think it; had thought
Of me very often; and that he would like
Very much to see me; also said if I'd write,
And at the L. make an appointment, and soon,
But not 'till a late hour of some afternoon,
He'd keep it, if possible.   *I* must not be
Disappointed, although, if he should not; as he
Was upon circumstances dependent.

                                I've been
Expecting to go East this winter—within
A few weeks from now very likely shall go.
And in my last letter, of course told him so;
So when I am going he wishes to know,
And where.   And he says that he certainly must
See me ere I shall leave.   And his wishes, I trust,
And mine also, may gratified be!   And then he
In closing writes:
                        " Do not think hardly of me,
Or judge me unkindly.   I'm not what I seem
To be, in many ways, and would say many things
That I dare not, and possibly ought not."
                                    I am
So glad, now, I have not been cross!   But how can
I help thinking he loves me?   If I only knew
That he did—though 'twould be " stolen waters," 'tis true—

I could then separation or silence endure—
Anything, if I could of his love but be sure !
Thus the New Year again brings me happiness pure.

January 18*th*, 1866.

THURSDAY.

Is it possible that in my journal this eve
I write for the last time in Brooklyn ?   And leave
To-morrow the place endeared to me by so
Many sweet recollections ?   And although I know
That it is the truth, I cannot bring my mind
To realize it as a fact.
                                For some time
I've written so seldom and briefly, I find
I neglected to state that some ten months ago
My brother to Boston removed, and also
That father has been there some months, and intends
To have us all go in the spring.   Of course, then,
I shall not return.   And my last moments here
Are shadowed by a disappointment severe.
I made an appointment not quite two weeks since,
And which *he* failed to keep.   But yet, being convinced
That he was not in fault, I did not feel cross,
Although disappointed, as *he* doubtless was.
I am going away sooner than I have been
Intending to do ; consequently, wrote him
To that effect ; also appointing again
For Tuesday an interview ; but it rained then,

And *I* did not go. Yesterday I went in
And stopped at the store. On inquiring for him,
To my consternation as well as surprise,
That he was at home, sick in bed, was apprised.
Thus again were my dearest hopes blighted ; and I .
To Brooklyn and home forced to murmur good-by,
With no farewell word from my love, whom I've not
For five weary months once beheld. Oh ! the thought
Almost breaks my heart ! It is cruel, I'm sure,
And bitterly, *bitterly* hard to endure.
To my brother a letter I'd written that day,
Intending to mail it that evening, to say
I should be there to-morrow. I stood a long time
At the office, with it in my hand, half inclined
Not to send it at all, but to write them, instead,
That I should not come on. Looking forward with dread
To an absence from home while my darling was ill,
With no hopes of tidings of him, as, until
I should know he was well, I would not dare to write ;
And *he* knew not where to address. Well I might
Hesitate ! But the true reason I could not state,
And I had no other excuse. 'Twas too late,
I decided at length, to turn back ; so I sent
My letter, and then, with an aching heart, went
Up town, and the night with my friend Annie spent.
She had visitors, and the whole eve was to me
One long torture !
    And now, a sad farewell to B !

March 31*st*, 1866.

SATURDAY.

The first month of spring! and my record again
Is in Brooklyn, and home! I imagined that when
I once more was here I should quite happy be;
But there is so much of *him* to remind me,
That it keeps me sad constantly. Then I have not
Been well, either, since my return, and no doubt
That my spirits helped some to depress. Father thought
When I left, it was doubtful extremely about
Our moving to Boston this spring. Gertie, too,
Was quite ill, and they were " so lonely," I knew
That I ought to go home, and was glad so to do,
Although every effort to render my stay
In B. pleasant was made ; and indeed, I must say
Was unhappy much less than I feared I should be ;
And Fannie, my sister, returned home with me.

Of course, of or from my *friend* naught I had heard,
And was anxious, exceedingly, too, for some word.
So when I was home a few days, I went in,
And called at his place for some tidings of him.
Found he had been ill all the time I was gone ;
But was better then, and would be out before long.
About a week later was in town once more,
And having occasion to call at the store,
To purchase a book, casually inquired
If he was within, with no thought the desire
10

Of my heart would be granted fulfilment.   Was glad
To learn that he'd *been* down that day, though he had,
The clerk said, just gone out.   Some days after, we met
In New York, on Broadway ; but, to *my* great regret,
He had with him a gentleman—Fan was with me—
So content with mere greeting was I forced to be.
Nothing but aggravation was that, when not once
Had I seen my darling in seven long months.
Then I wrote ; but receiving no word in reply,
Went in to see *him*.   He was cordial ; but I
Was quite cool at first, 'till I found he had not
Been able for months to read, write, or do aught
Of the kind.   His physician forbade it, and feared
That another attack, if as long and severe
As the last, would entirely deprive him of sight.
My dearest !   May God, in His infinite might,
And love, such affliction avert.   I suppose
He suffers intensely when prostrate with those
Prolonged and repeated attacks ; and he says
He's often delirious, unconscious for days ;
And when sane, he can neither endure light nor sound,
And days of convalescence roll tardily 'round.
'Tis a nervous affection, and is the same thing
That confined him so long in the wearisome spring
Of two years ago ; but his health otherwise
Is robust ; and unmarred are his beautiful eyes,
Though his sight is impaired.
                              He said he wrote me
Last week, just as well as he could, although he
Was fearful that I could not read it, and thought
It was doubtful if he could himself.   He forgot

My address, and so it to the post-office sent ;
And I called there to get it as homeward I went.
'Twas written in pencil, and all sorts of ways,
And formed, to the usual neatness and grace,
With which he is wont his nice letters to trace,
Quite a contrast indeed.

     He told me that one
Of my letters was sent to the house; it had come
To the store, at the time he was absent—at home.
Mrs. —— thought that it " looked like a lady's fine hand."
'Twas quite likely a bill, he made her understand.
He does not come in town until late, he told me,
And leaves the store early. How nice it must be
To have him at home so much ! though perhaps she
Does not care about it as I should. But this
I must not dwell upon, a topic that is
Forbidden to me.

     I was quite calm that day
In my interview with him, and have been, I must say,
Ever since. Can it be I am loving him less ?
Oh, would it were so ! dare not think it, tho', lest
I'm again overwhelmed before I am aware
With its might and intenseness, its bitter despair.

<hr>

April 27th, 1866.

FRIDAY.

I saw my dear friend about two weeks ago,
When was made at the L. an appointment, although

He said if I came in he'd like me to call
At the store on my way. But I do not at all
Like to go there, and told him so also, but he
Insisting upon it, I could but agree.
The day previous to that we appointed, a note
From him I received, and in which he then wrote
He might be away the next day, but if not
He would at the store be, about three o'clock.
Hesitating awhile about going, at last
I decided I would; it was just quarter past
When I entered his place; on inquiring for him
Was informed he had stepped out, but soon would be in.
Supposing of course that such word he had left,
I waited and waited, until, quite bereft
Of patience, I paper inquired for, and wrote
With haste a few lines, of course leaving the note.
I *was* rather surprised at how *coolly*, though, I
Took the matter; did not, as in days now gone by,
Feel at all cross with him, neither was I so much
Disappointed as often I am under such
Circumstances. I feel quite encouraged! Before
I have thought I was not quite so much as of yore
In captivity to him, but one interview,
Or a letter from him, has dispelled, it is true,
All my fancied indifference; but it has stood
Now both tests. I was vexed with myself, that I should
Have waited. I never before have done so,
Nor should I then, had I not reason to know,
Or think, that he soon would be in. A few days
Thereafter, a note I received, when he says
He went in that day *purposely to see me.*
Waiting there at the store 'till twelve minutes past three,

And then returned home again, as he'd some men
At work on his place, and his presence with them
Was required.   He would see me this week.

In reply,

I wrote that I thought it was doubtful if I
Would be able to come in this week; if I could,
That I'd let him know, but, that I certainly should
Not call at the store.   Near the close I wrote, though,
If *he* made an appointment, I thought I might go,
And to do as he liked.   But it's now Friday eve,
And he has not; indeed, though, I hardly believed
That he would.   But I think the time *will* come when he
Will make an appointment, and anxious, too, be
That I should fulfil it.   And I'll wait and see.

———

April 28th, 1866.   .

SATURDAY.

I dreamed all the night of my friend, and to-day
The carrier brought me a letter, to say
He would be at the L. about five this P.M.
So he's made an appointment!   That's something that when
I wrote here last night that he *should* do sometime
I dreamed not would happen so soon.   To my mind
That was proof he was wishing to see me, as he
Must have seen by my note 'twas a matter to me
Of indifference.   So I proceeded to make
My toilet with haste, fearing I should be late.

But I reached the L. first. He came soon, and we spent
A happy hour there; then we parted, and went
Each our separate way—he desiring to see
Me again very soon, and I happy that he
Should have and express such a wish.

He told me

He sang at the "*old church*" last Sabbath, and should
To-morrow as well; I shall go up. It would
Seem indeed like old times to see *him* in the choir.
I go at his wish, and my own strong desire!
I asked if he sat in the "corner"; said, "yes,
And it *was* nice to be there!" Did thoughts of B. S.
And the sweet olden time make it nicer? I guess
That did not from the charm very largely detract.
We *did* have, as usual, a most pleasant chat!
I allowed him to hold my hand—gloved—in his own
For quite a long time.

Ah, my heart! where has flown

Thy boasted indifferent coolness? The last
Test was fatal, I fear. Since we parted, I've passed
Some moments most wretched; but, weary to-night,
I may feel quite different in morning's clear light.

May 1*st*, 1866.

TUESDAY.

Have been very unhappy for some few days past,
And not quite well either. On Sabbath morn last,

I went up to church. I was early, but he
Was there before I was, and given to me
Were his first glance and smile, when he came out to sing;
But there by his side was a woman I've seen
But too often already, and that I would fain
As long as I live behold never again—
Mrs. D., the soprano, I always disliked.
We had spoken of her on the previous night,
When we met at the L., and he said he had not
Even seen her since *she* left the choir. If I'd thought
That she would have been there, I'd not gone one step.
She was, though, and he must needs sit back, instead
Of his place in the "corner." It made me, indeed,
Most provoked and unhappy; though *he* paid no heed
To her, and did not stop to speak. But my eyes
With bitter tears filled many times; so surprised
And so disappointed was I! I had gone
Not far from the church when he passed me, his arm
In that of the bass-singer. Marked pains he took
To speak as he passed me. How handsome he looked!
Farther down, Mrs. D., sweeping by me, joined them
As they turned down Broadway, walking next him, though
     then
He was on the outside. That, indeed, was the last,
Bitter drop in my full cup of wormwood. They passed
From my sight, and I entered a car, homeward bound,
Sad and wretched indeed. But that day has torn down
Every barrier of coldness, indifference, that
I had fancied was raised. Alas! 'twas, in fact,
Only fancy, and I am as wholly his own
To-day as I ever was—his, his alone!

This morning, from Colonel Allair, I received
Just the nicest epistle he has, I believe,
Ever written to me; and had no slight effect
In raising my spirits, and helping to check
The sadness then weighing me down.   I know not
Hardly what I should now do without him; bright spots
Are his notes in my weary life.   In all respects
How unlike to *my other John* is he, and yet——

———

June 1st, 1866.

FRIDAY.

I went up to church a few Sabbaths ago.
My friend did not sing, nor did Mrs. D.   So
There was naught to disturb my devotions.   Relieved
I felt, I must own !   Some days since, I received
A letter from him, and a nice one.   He writes,
That he came on from Boston the previous night.
Had taken a cold most severe, and was then
Going home for a steaming.   He told me that when
He saw me up town at church was the last time
That he sang ; he went down for his car, and on mine
Saw me as we passed each the other ; but I
Was not looking that way.   And did he, by the by,
Surmise how I felt, and so told me to set
At rest all my doubts, and show *me* he was yet
My love and my darling?   While with Mrs. D.,
I imagined he was, he was thinking of me,

And watching to see me as I should pass by.
Oh ! *how* many times I've been conscious that I
Have done him indeed " gross injustice ! "

                  He wrote
He should soon find occasion to see me, he hoped,
That we might have a confab together.   I sent
Him a note, telling him that on Wednesday ma meant
To be absent, and asking if he would come out.
But she did not go, as it rained hard about
All the morning, and neither did he come.   That day,
However, he wrote me a letter to say
That he wanted to see me, and thought that he might
Appoint Friday, about four P.M. ; but that night
I had an engagement, and to that effect
I wrote him, of course ; but with after regret
That I had not kept his appointment.   To-day
I fulfilled my engagement ; the hours passed away
Very pleasantly, though I of course at the time
Could but think that I might been with " Antony mine,"
If I had not been there.

              He's done bravely, of late,
Not only one, but two appointments to make.
I wonder if there's a day passes but he
Sends many a tender thought over to me ;
And if musings of me are both pleasant and sweet,
And give to him happiness lasting and deep.
I never shall know more than now, I suppose ;
He is so reserved, he will never disclose
Them to me, or reveal me the depths of his heart ;
I only can judge by a passing remark,
An occasional word.   If unable to read,
He must of course think some, and can he, indeed,

    10*

Help thinking of one much and often, who so
Devotedly loves him? He *must* care, I know,
A little for me and my *letters*, or he
Would not cling to them so, and refuse utterly
To give them up ever. I said the last time
That *I* saw him, that *he'd* better give me back mine,
Lest something should happen to him. He refused
To do so, and said they were safe. And no use
To urge the thing farther, I saw it would be.
He don't like to own how *much* he cares for me.
" Oh could my fond ideas reality prove,
And one blissful moment give me all his love,
I would for that moment my life freely give,
And when he ceased to love, I no longer would live."

June 6th, 1866.

WEDNESDAY.

I hardly know when I so happy have been,
And so fully realized it, as within
The brief hours of this swift-flitting day.

                                You must know,
My dear Journal, that some five or six weeks ago,
My friend spoke of a series of " Gotham's wise men,"
Which is now being published ; and told me that when
His picture was out—which it would be then soon—
He would send it to me. And so, when this noon
The carrier brought me a paper, addressed
In the well-known handwriting of him I·love best,

I supposed it was that; neither was I, indeed,
Disappointed; but, opening it with all speed,
I found an engraving so perfect, it seemed
Almost as if he was before me.　Ma deemed
It not at all like him; but *she* has not seen
Him in two years or over, and doubtless forgot
How he looked.　And that *he* too has changed, it cannot
Be denied.　I have marked it in him, and it is
More evident still in his picture.　There is
On his face an expression entirely unlike
What it wore but three short years ago; then 'twas bright,
Smiling, happy, and careless; but now there are lines,
And he looks sad and anxious.　I cannot divine
The cause—perhaps business cares, illness, a mind
Or a heart that is troubled.　Whatever it be,
He's the dearest of all earthly objects to me.
" I ne'er wake at morn, but his name ever bounds
To my heart, the first hope of the day.　Ne'er kneel down
At evening, but it in my prayers, whether in
Thought or speech, mingles too.　If in this I have sinned,
God forgive me ! " for I have my punishment had,
In the " Consciousness of degradation, the sad
Despair which a woman o'erwhelms, when she dares
Unwooed, unrequited to love ! "　Yet how fair
And precious to me is my love !　All the day
I have trembled with my intense happiness.　Yea,
My thoughts constantly turned to the fact that at last
I have his dear picture; at each thought there passed
Through my pulses a thrill of exquisite delight.
Notwithstanding this, I'm feeling sad, though, to-night,
To think this poor semblance of him, of the dear,
Living, loving original's all that I e'er

Can hope for possession of! Naught but a bit
Of flimsy, insensible paper. Those lips
Can yield no response to my tender caress;
Those eyes cannot change from their sad earnestness,
Or give me e'en one glance of love. And with this
I *must* be content! Oh, my God! but it is
Bitter, *bitter*, this burden I ever must bear,
Of a hopeless and wasted affection. Oh, there
Are times when it seems it *must* kill me, this weight
At my heart which I'm forced constant effort to make
To keep back, and crush down, lest some cold, careless eye
Should sometime read the tale I so zealously try
To conceal. I'm yet young; must I go all through life
With the curse of unsatisfied longings at strife
In my heart, blighted hopes, and affection unsought,
Unreturned? O! God knows that against it I've fought
And struggled in vain! My love, gliding along
So smoothly, with naught to disturb the deep, strong
Serenity of his grand nature, I'm sure
Can't imagine what *I* daily have to endure.

His picture is lying before me! Each fine
Well-cut feature's indelibly stamped on my mind,
And impressed on my heart in most deep burning lines.
The smooth brow, and the eyes, so sweet, tender, and kind;
The full lips whose soft touch I can never forget;
E'en the poise of the head, the hair's careless and yet
Smooth adjustment; the cut of the beard and mustache
So familiar—and all that makes up the fine cast
Of form and of feature—are painted down deep
In my heart's fairest chamber, in colors soft, sweet,

And eternal.   Yet *'tis* good to have even this
Pictured semblance of him; and I own, to me 'tis
Indeed priceless.   While looking at it, I can ne'er
Forget that those eyes *have* looked love ; that those dear
Lips have, with a touch that no others can e'er
Resemble, met mine in love's pure, sweet caress ;
That my cheek has against that smooth forehead been pressed.
And my head pillowed on that broad, true, tender breast.

But midnight approaches ! My book I must close
On the record of this day, and seek my repose,
With thanks to the destiny which has, at length,
The fulfilment of one of my strong desires sent.

August 1st, 1866.

WEDNESDAY.

Two months, very nearly, since I've written here !
But though I've been silent, it's not, Journal dear,
Been because I've had nothing worth writing.   Instead,
The past weeks have been ones of strong and varied
Emotions.
            I've heard people say they could not
Keep a journal, because they would never, they thought,
Have aught worth the writing ; their lives were so tame
And quite uneventful.   I can't say the same !
If I should write all the events strongly marked
Which occur in my life, in fact even a part,
'Twould fill volumes.   I'm conscious *my* journal is quite
Incomplete ; is recording alone, of my life,

That part which is inner and hidden—that none
But myself ever sees; that it, too, has become
An escape-valve for long-pent emotion alone.
Were people to read it, to me quite unknown,
I fear they would think me a person of one
Idea—despondent and gloomy.　But though
I have lost the extravagant spirits, whose flow
At times was so brilliant, but three years ago,
Yet I often am cheerful, and lively, e'en now
Though not very gay ever, I will allow.
But I'm sure, did they know how completely I hide
The grief which sometimes bursts all barriers, they might
Their opinion of me somewhat change.

　　　　　　　　　Love, which is
To some but a sentiment, mere transient bliss,
Tamely felt, tamely lost, or at pleasure transferred,
To *me* is a life's one " grand passion "—oft heard
And read of, but seldom, I think, known or seen.
But though it pervades with its bitter-sweet sheen
Every fibre and pulse of my heart, yet it there
Abides, and is not in my face written, where
It by each passer-by may be read; and although
Within all my thoughts it may be, it has no
Part or place e'er in my conversation.

　　　　　　　　　　　Within
The interim since my last writing, I've been
So happy as from my love one or two notes
To receive, and in one of the latest he wrote
Mine had just come to hand; he expected to get
A " grand scolding " from me, for his recent neglect
In writing; he knew he was negligent in
All his correspondence; but that he had been

Quite unwell, and away a great deal.   At the end
He writes that he hopes we shall meet soon, and then
Have a long chat together.   And *I* hoped so, too!
Then adds—" Don't feel hard toward me, if I do
Not write you so often, or much as you like! "
He need fear no " scolding " from me, I replied.
I gave him my last more than one year ago.

 I *was* surprised, somewhat, a month since, or so,
At receiving a letter from one with whom I
Once flirted a little, and who, by the by,
At the time—about four years ago—sent to me
Some notes that were—well! very *warm*, certainly!
I then liked him much ; but had not seen or heard
From him, until then, since we parted, one word.
The acquaintance was closed amicably at the time,
By mutual consent.   I was quite pleased to find
I was not forgotten ; glad also to hear
From him once again after so many years.
The old correspondence he wished to renew ;
To this I objected, acceding unto
His desire the acquaintance might still continue.
Between us a few letters passed, and he came
To see me, of course.   And he seemed just the same
As in the old time.   Indeed! *I* could not see
As he'd changed in the least ; but he told me that he
Never saw such a change as there had been in me,
And my letters, as well—that, in fact, 'twas more marked
In those than it was in myself.   Not but what
They were fine, and as finished as ever, he thought,
But seemed so much colder, more formal, and not

So vivacious and gay. I asked did he think so,
And he said, "I *think* nothing about it. I *know*! "
How shocked I one evening felt at the receipt
Of one of his notes. " My own dear Bitter-Sweet!"
Was how it commenced; and I cannot describe
The feeling which passed o'er me, as I descried
Those words at the head of a letter from him.
The note from my hand dropped, as if it had been
A live coal of fire. When I saw him I asked
How he came to write that; and he said in times past
I signed one of mine thus (but that was before
The first to my love), and he thought to once more
Awake old emotions by using it now.
I replied somewhat bitterly, I must allow,
That it called up emotions entirely unlike
What he'd anticipated. And *he* did not write
Another addressed in that way. I had liked
Him always, as I said before; and awhile—
Shall I own it ?—attempted myself to beguile
With dreams of the possible chance of my heart
Being " caught in rebound," and transferring a part
Of my wasted affections to him. He came, too,
Just at the right time; when I was, it is true,
With the old love disgusted and weary, its place
Supplying, indeed, better, for a brief space,
Than I had deemed possible. But the dream soon
Was dispelled; for the old intimacy resumed
Showed *me*, also, that I had changed; how much he
To my love was inferior, proving to me
How impossible 'twas he should e'er satisfy
The cravings of heart, or of mind, or supply

The place by my darling left vacant, and brought
Me back to the old sweet allegiance. I thought
That mere strangers 'twas best we should be, as before,
And took measures accordingly. Yet, I was more
Disappointed than I can express, to again
Find my hopes for a new state of things blighted. Then
With that came despondency, even more deep
Than usual. Yesterday, wretched indeed
Was I ; and I felt like excluding myself
From society wholly, and breaking, as well,
All my correspondence—in future within
Myself live entirely ; to-day to begin
The new life. But I slept o'er it, and, as the morn
In roseate splendor from darkness is born,
So to yesterday's night so profound, gloom so deep,
Succeeds to-day's glorious sunshine.
                              To keep
This P.M. with my love, an appointment, went in.
I was late, altho' he was still later. I'd been
There some time, and was just about leaving, when he
At length came in. His partner was out, he told me,
And he waited for him 'till six nearly, and then
Left at once. We stayed there for awhile, and then went
For a walk. By the way, he to-day spoke again
About seeing me in the car that day when
I was coming from church, when he sang the last time ;
And said his surprise was not much less than mine
At Mrs. D. singing that morning. He bade
Me farewell somewhat hastily, as his car had
Already passed by ; bending low o'er my hand,
With a grace all his own, and a tenderness grand

And simple as well, he pressed it in both
Of his, with a lingering warmth, as if loath
To release it, then said he'd soon see me again,
And was gone.   But there was such a difference when
He was with me to-day, in his manner, from what
There was ever before—an air which I cannot
Describe, but that I perceived plainly.   A free
Familiar regard in his bearing to me,
Entirely unusual; and never did I,
His friendship appreciate more.   He's seen my
Worst qualities, surely, and yet is " still true,"
Notwithstanding, too, all I have done or can do.

August 17th, 1866.

FRIDAY.

I did not, I think, say, when writing here last,
There'd a much longer season than usual elapsed
Since from Colonel Allair I'd a letter received.
But though thinking it strange, his not writing, believe
There was a good reason, and that his delay
Was compulsory.   Two weeks ago yesterday,
The wished-for epistle arrived.   I was much
Pleased, indeed, upon opening it, to find such
A long letter, and thought that its kindly contents
Its late coming would amply compensate.   Intent
On this thought, I glanced first at the close, then again
To the head, and, all being as usual, I then

Prepared with much pleasure to read it; but down
The first page I had not far perused, ere I found
There was a great change. It was even more fond
Than his letters in general, yet he goes on
To say—while expressing unbounded regret
That it should be so, that he thinks 'twould be best
To close our correspondence—the reason expressed
Being his strong desire for a sweet retrospect,
And his fears, if continued, between us there might
Come something to render the mem'ry less bright
And pleasing than now. I might think this to be
Inconsistent, perhaps, with what hitherto he
Had written; he'd then thought to leave it to fate,
But now feared to do so; he knew it would take
From his life its sweet charm—would be parting, in truth,
With a piece of his heart. His pen almost refused
To transcribe the words—much like that in effect.
Hoped that some time it might be renewed upon yet
More agreeable terms; should he e'er visit me,
He trusted a most welcome guest he should be.
But if, before then, the time should be so long,
His desire to hear from me sufficiently strong
To his silence o'ercome, begged permission to write,
Granting me, too, the same; said he hoped that he might
Be allowed to retain still my letters, as they
Were dear unto him; I might do the same way
With his, or aught else that I liked.
                                 I read on
To the end of the fond, cruel letter, though long
Before I had finished tears blinded my eyes;
And I'd reached my room, scarcely, ere sobs hard and dry

In volumes broke forth ; neither could I control
Myself in the least. 'Twas so sudden, the whole
So quite unexpected! I ne'er was so grieved
In my life! So entirely I'd trusted, believed
In his truth, never doubting him once. I felt there
Was for me *nothing* but disappointment, despair!

Loving with supreme ardor all those whom I care
In the least for, I'm constantly wounded. Oh! would
That I *were* less extreme ; that, like others, I could
Sometimes keep a medium course. I expect
Never happiness lasting; in every respect
My organization's too sensitive, quite.
I feel everything too acutely—delight
And sorrow as well. I am one of those who
Desire, above all things, affection; and, too,
Manifested, not unexpressed love—to whom that
Is the only thing worth bearing life for, in fact,
And yet are too proud e'er to make manifest
Their desire for the love which they wish to possess;
Too reticent any endeavor to make
To win the affection they constantly crave,
By showing to others the same. But yet *I*
Cannot endure always in silence; and try
As I may to keep down all emotion, I must
Give way to grief sometimes. And having so much
Disappointment of late, which I'd swallowed and kept
Out of sight, this last hard, unexpected blow swept
Aside every atom of my self-control.
And in my despair, and abandon, the whole
I would have avowed—misplaced love, wounded pride,
Slighted friendship, and all, howe'er humbling it might

Be to me.   But with my self-command once regained,
Grief exhausted, accustomed reserve again came,
And I crushed it all down in my heart, buried deep
From all human sight, and of sympathy's sweet
Consolation deprived.   But this kept me prostrate
The whole day, and I did not go down until late ;
And with eyes then so swollen I scarcely could see,
Throbbing temples, and sad, aching heart.   Up to me
Ma and Fannie had both been, and anxious to know
The cause of my grief, but I begged them to go
And leave me alone.   And so, when I that eve
Went down, I took with me the letter to leave
With them if they wished.   With true delicacy,
Neither mentioned the subject.

       The colonel wished me
To write in reply, and I did so.   To-day
I an answer received, and it was, I must say,
A fine letter indeed ; and he said he had thought
Many times that our long correspondence could naught
But a bore be to me.   In its closing, the loss
Would be wholly on his side, and so that it was
On my account, merely, he wrote as he did.
At last owning, what I had half suspected,
The cause was my writing about the renewed
Intercourse with my old friend (I spoke of to you,
In my last record here, my dear Journal).   Of that
I wrote him, as I anything else do, in fact,
Which interests me, never dreaming that it
Would have such effect upon him, I admit.
He begged me to answer, and said he should write
Again in the interim.   So we, to-night,
Are just as good friends as before.

                          I'm perplexed
To discover what fate has in store for me next.

———

October 3d, 1866.

WEDNESDAY.

   I have from my love received two or three notes,
In the interval which has occurred since I wrote.
And one which he sent me I did not receive,
Much to my regret. He addressed, I believe,
To the office, and so it was lost. But how glad
I was, when to-day I another one had,
And such as he never has sent me before.
My love and forbearance the last year or more
Have not been in vain; and he loves me to-day,
And trusts, and respects me much more, I dare say,
Than if anger and sarcasm I'd not repressed.
Commenced as in general: " My dear B. S."
And said that upon the receipt of my last
He could not but blame himself that there had passed
Such an interval since he had written to me;
But had been away most of the time. And so he
Feels, it seems, his shortcomings, now I utter no
Reproaches; but when I found fault with him so,
He'd make no acknowledgments. I'm indeed glad,
For my sake, as well as his, too, that I had
Resolved to write no more cross letters, and my
Resolution have kept. Farther on he writes—
                                           " I

Can but say that it is real pleasure to read
Your letters : they're so entertaining, indeed,

So loving, and seem to come right from the heart."
How delighted I was at this earnest remark!
I have many times felt, that, instead of to him
Giving pleasure, they must very often have been
A source of annoyance; and though they could be—
Such feelings—but bitterly humbling to me,
I still sent them on, with faint hopes that I might
In answer a few lines receive, did he write,
Indeed, never so coldly and formal.   But now
I have my reward; for my darling avows
They *do* give him pleasure, and I've learned at length
That *he never* says what is not fully meant;
The confession, beside, half unwillingly seems
To have come, and which double force gives it.   I deem
That our correspondence, at last, has become
On a basis established more pleasant and firm
Than it has been of late.   In my last, I a kiss
Sent to him and to " Bertie " (the baby, that is),
Telling him to be sure and deliver it.   So
He writes me in answer :

             " The kiss, which you know
You sent in your letter a few days ago,
Was duly delivered to Bertie ; but, bless
His innocent soul, from whence came the caress
He indeed little knew."

             Since this note I received,
How many times I've fancied him, just at eve,
After his return home, clasping close in his arms
The beautiful child, pressing on his soft, warm,
Baby lips, a fond kiss from lips none the less sweet,
With thoughts of the love for him, boundless and deep,

Which had sent the caress to the unconscious boy—
The love for him, which would rejoice in his joy,
And grieve at his sorrow, and which renders dear
All the objects of his deep affection.　When here,
A few days ago, Lorette asked me if I
Had never desired that the woman would die,
Who stands between me and the man that I love.
But though loving him with a passion above
And beyond estimation, I thank God I've been
From that temptation spared ; that it has not within
My mind for a moment e'en once had a place.
I love him too well to desire to efface
From his heart or his home what she is, or had ought
Unto him and his children to be.　I do not
Like to see them together, or think, I must own,
Of them in the close intimacy of home—
The relation existing between them.　But those
Thoughts but make me unhappy, and never dispose
Me to feel hard or bitter to her or to him.
Of course, very different, though, it might been,
If he had not married until I had seen
And loved him—and harder to bear, too, I ween!
But I now can but feel that no censure is due
Anywhere ; but the cruel stroke was, it is true,
Unavoidable.　Closing, he says—

　　　　　　　　　　" Did you know
That I sang at the old church a few weeks ago,
For a single day merely ?　I'd sent you the word
Had it not been too late to do so, when I heard
I was wanted to sing.　It did seem like old times ! "
And so *his* thoughts sometimes turn to sweet " Auld lang
　　syne."

How *can* I help thinking he does care for me!
That I *am* dear to him, in some little degree!
His manner was always most tender and kind,
And perhaps it may be a fault wholly of mine,
That so brief, cold, reserved, his notes ever have been;
I've been cross and unreasonable often with him,
And, dear as he is, from him *I* could not bear
What he's taken from me.   But in utter despair,
So wretched, and chafing so under my bonds,
I sent letters sarcastic and bitter, when fond
And gentle ones would have been better.   But past
Are those days, forever, I trust.

               In the last
Of the colonel's nice letters, in one place he says—
" What a blessed thing 'tis a true friend to possess!
I do not know what without you I should do ;
I think sometimes my ' guardian angel ' are you,
If such things can be ; and I know that I owe
To your influence all that I am."

                  And if so,
If I some slight benefit may to him be,
I shall not have lived vainly.   My life seems to me
Such a failure, so wasted and weary, in it
So much disappointment and grief, I admit
I am thankful if there's even one that can say
They are better for my having lived.

                  Well! to-day
Our pastor called here and I gave my consent,
Though not willingly, very, to make an attempt
At teaching a Sabbath-school class.   I may like
When accustomed to it, but was fearful I might
   11

Find it irksome to feel that I always must go—
As I certainly should—if I wished to or no;
Nor do I feel competent either; and so
I fain would refused; but he *would* take from me
Nothing but a consent.   I *do* like to be free!
Don't like to feel ever the meaning of that
One little word "*must.*"   I suppose that, in fact,
Is why I have fretted so under the chains
I have worn for three years—years so brimful of change.
" From even *love's* rosy bonds I would be free! "
And yet it a glorious thing seems to me,
To feel one has such capabilities in
One's nature for loving; though it may have been
Undesired, unrewarded.   And is not that, still,
Love the noblest of all?   Nearly every heart will
Respond to another's deep passion, but few
Will dare to love where there is no hope, and, too,
Love on whate'er come.   Such affection is true !

October 24th, 1866.

WEDNESDAY.

Was in town some days since, and called twice at the
store.
But *he* was not in.   For the past week or more,
I have many times felt that I must, *must* see him,
And for one fond caress I have really been
Almost longing; have no hopes of having it, though,
As we ne'er meet alone.   I try not to feel so,

To think of it even; but out of my mind
I can't always drive it.   My heart is, at times,
So hungry for some of love's sweets ; and I get
Not much but its bitterness, pain, and regret.
I oft think of the time when I used to see him
Every Sabbath, receive in the brief interim
An occasional visit from him, which gave me
Such unalloyed pleasure.   I wonder if he
" Would care if his breast was my shelter as then,
And if he were here, would he kiss me again ! "

Well, my dear sister Fannie, who came home with me
From Boston last spring, will return soon, and she
Insists upon taking me with her.   But I
Am not wishing to go, as pa—who, by the by,
Returned some months since—seems determined to move
Out of town in the spring, so I fear this will prove
Our last winter in B. ; but much as I dislike
To go, I can't seem to avoid it.   Fan quite
Overrules each objection I offer, and so
I've at length with reluctance consented to go.
I suppose 'tis one more phase of destiny ; seems
To me nothing less.   I, of course, cannot dream
What might occur should I not go.   I have done
With struggling 'gainst fate ; and that 'tis but a turn
Of her wheel which to Boston this winter sends me,
I indeed can but think.   I've no wish there to be,
Had no hand in the matter, and bound so I am
By a tissue of circumstances, that I can
Do nothing but go.   Of it Colonel Allair
In his last writes, that I may be going to there

Meet my "destiny."　Truly !　I *may*, or my *death*,
There is but One knows.　So I've only to let
Events take their course and submit with what grace
I can, to whatever may come, and erase
From my heart every murmur, as far as I may.
But yet, when I feel as I have done to-day,
It seems as if *I could* not go.　I would like,
Above all things, one day's perfect quiet, and quite
Out the question in Fannie's home that is.

A note

To my *friend*, telling him I was going, I wrote
Some days since ; and I made an appointment, also,
For the eve of to-morrow ; have yet received no
Reply as I hoped.　In the morning may, though.

November 4th, 1866.

SUNDAY.

'Twould a volume require to write down here to-night
What I wish to.　My time, though, is limited quite,
And I must condense in a somewhat small space,
The record of what the past three or four days
Has occurred.　The day after I wrote last, from him
No letter receiving, I did not go in.
But Fannie deciding to go home somewhat
In advance of our former expectancy, thought
I would write him once more—which I did, saying that
Tuesday eve was the last I could meet him.　In fact,

I wrote rather coolly, and felt somewhat vexed
That he had not answered my last. On the next
Day but one I received his reply, which was quite
Satisfactory, and, just as much true delight
Afforded to me as the last one he sent.
My other he said was received, and he meant
To have written the following day; but he went
That eve to the theatre, and, coming home,
Took cold; had been sick ever since. I might known
There was cause for delay. I distrust him each time
That he disappoints me, and I yet always find
That he is not in fault. I shall learn, by and by,
To trust him, I hope—learn his truth to descry.
He wrote he regretted extremely that I
Should have been disappointed on Thursday, but still,
It could not be helped, and then adds that he will
Be there, if he's living and well, Tuesday eve.
Should expect me to write to him, after I leave,
He says near the close. His letter was long,
For his; truly kind, and in fact almost fond,
And gave me a feeling of *perfect content!*
An unusual delight, and not even yet spent.

On Tuesday it rained, so I did not go in.
I knew not but that the appointment by him
Would be kept. I that day was not well enough, though,
To have gone, had the weather been pleasant. And so
I wrote him I should not leave town 'till this week,
And Thursday, about six P.M., I would meet
My friend at the L. I intended, that day,
To leave home in season to stop on the way

At his place ; but being delayed, I did not
Reach the L. until two minutes past six o'clock ;
And five minutes later my love was with me.
I was going up town for the night, and so we
Did not stay there.   A carriage was waiting, which he
Then placed me within.   'Twas a beautiful night.
We drove part the distance, and then thought it might
Be pleasanter still to be walking—so then
At once put our thought into practice ; and when
From the carriage he lifted me, close in his arms
For a moment he held me, and then pressed a warm
But somewhat hasty kiss on my cheek—the first one
I have had from his lips for three years.   We walked on,
Going out of our way a short distance to pass
The " old church," so endeared to us both ; thinking, as
We in silence leaned o'er the low paling of iron
Enclosing the well-laid out grounds, of the time
When " Love's first dream " began.   And when turning
    away,
He said 'twas the nicest church, he could but say,
That he ever was in ; and 'twas so cosey, too,
In the choir.   I said, " Yes ; it was pleasant when you
Used to sit in the ' corner,' but was not so nice
When you next Mrs. D. took your seat ! "
                          He replies :
" Oh, but I in the ' corner ' almost always sat ! "
Up the avenue walking, I said to him, that
If he wished on my ring it should not be removed
While I remained absent.   " What ! over your glove ? "
He inquired.   But I had none on that hand—the one
He was holding—so said he would take off his own.

And while drawing it off, he between his dear lips
Placed my ring, and then slipping it on, with a kiss
Sealed his wishes for me; and the rest of the time
In his warm, ungloved hand with fond clasp he held mine.
To hear Madame Ristori was going that eve,
And said it was difficult for him to leave
That night, as some friends on from Boston were in
At the store when he left, and would not excuse him,
But he told them he *must* go, agreed to meet them
Between seven and eight at the theatre, then
Left in haste.   And he said he came up to the L.
When we made the appointment for Tuesday, as well.
And thought, though it did rain, that I would be in
As I left town so soon; and that I'd accused him
So often of breaking engagements, he meant
To keep that one, if through fire and water he went.
And he did go through *water* indeed, for it poured.
Said he sang the last Sabbath in church, but the word
Again did not get until too late to send
Out to me, but should sing the next Sunday again,
(That's to-day), and of course I consented to go.
'Twas not at *our* church that he sang, he said, though,
But at an Episcopal on the same street.
Many times he regretted that his "Bitter-Sweet"
Was not there when he sang at the old church.

                      When we
Reached Annie's—where I was to stop—he wished me
To walk on a short distance.   Of course I was glad
To comply, although then barely time he would had
To keep his engagement with promptness.   But that
Was nothing to me, if *he* felt satisfied.
We were on the same street where I used to reside,

And stood on a corner quite near my old home
For some little time; and it *was* sweet, I own,
To stand with my hand clasped in his, and the tones
Of his exquisite voice falling soft on my ear.
Sweet the stolen embrace when no person was near,
The petting so longed for, the perfect content
Which his mere presence gave me, the pure joy that sent
Every thought but of happiness out of my heart,
Though I knew time was flying, and soon we must part.
He was all the eve so affectionate, kind;
He called me " dear " once, and by name many times.
Though never addressing me by it before,
It could not have come from his lips now with more
Ease and natural readiness, if it had been
For long, a familiar " household word " with him.
Very pretty he speaks it, more as a caress
Than anything else, and it sounds, I confess,
Very sweet from his lips.

                He has never appeared
So tender and loving, and never so clear
And manifest was his attachment. Although
Always kind, he was then more than usually so.
More reason to think I *am* dear to him, he
Never gave me. Indeed! I am *sure* he loves me.
At least next to her, who in his heart claims
The first place. And am I contented to reign
As second within a divided heart? One
Who has often declared she would have all, or none,
Is with *this* satisfied? Yes! far better a part,
A moiety of his, than another's whole heart!

He spoke many times of my writing to him.
" You'll write me when Boston you shall arrive in,"

Was the last thing he said.   It was past eight o'clock
When again we before my friend's residence stopped.
Then taking my hands, both of them, in his own,
Left a kiss of farewell on my lips and was gone.
I fancy his friends tired of waiting, ere he
The theatre reached.

               Well! the evening, to me,
Was perfect!   My love every want satisfies ;
For the void in my heart sweet content he supplies,
Until it overflows with a love so entire, -
So sacred, and pure, passion can but expire,
So sweet I ignore all the pain gone before.
While I drank in the joy which his presence affords,
What wonder I should for a moment forget
That I " *stolen waters* " was quaffing!   And yet,
Is a love pure as mine such a deep, deadly sin,
And a crime each impassioned expression?   There's been
Very much to regret, and repent of—lose sight
Of the wrong, or excuse it, I do not—it might,
However, be *worse ;* and to One, who, if just,
Is loving and pitiful also, I'll trust
The sin and its punishment, knowing that He
Looks alone on the heart, each temptation can see,
Whether conquered or yielded to.   Once having worn
Our humanity, been by fierce temptations torn,
He knows how to succor, to pity, forgive ;
To His love and compassion the issue I leave.

   This morning was fair, so of course went up town
To church, as I promised.   Was early, and found
He had not yet arrived ; but the sexton gave me,
As requested, a seat near the choir ; and when he

    11*

Soon after came in, his face plainly betrayed
His pleasure at seeing me. *He* sang to-day,
Divinely, as ever! his voice seemed in truth
The impressive Episcopal service to suit,
And lost none of its richness and beauty, when in
The elaborate " Te Deum" heard. I had been
So proud of him, had we but met ere it came
To be sin he should love me—had *I* borne his name.
When service was over, I had not gone far
Ere he joined me. Together we waited for cars.
He said the last Sabbath " My Lady " was down,
But to-day it was too late to come, when she found
He intended to sing—I presume *no design*
There was in his failing to tell her in time (?).
I spoke of his being so late Thursday night,
Ere he kept his engagement; he said yes, 'twas quite
Ten o'clock ere he entered the theatre. When
He first left the car, about nine, he missed then,
For the first time, a valuable diamond ring.
He thought for a moment, then recollecting
That he drew off his glove where we stood a long time
Conversing, he took a car back ; failed to find
What he sought, so he borrowed a lantern near by—
Turned away unsuccessful again, when his eye
Was caught by the glitter. Indeed! he, I think,
Was most fortunate. It was a beautiful ring,
One his wife ordinarily wears.
                         So, I ween,
For the last time for many long months, I have seen
My love, and my dearest! I go, though, away,
Feeling sure of his truth and affection. All day

I have thought of a poem, expressing indeed
With perfectness my feelings to him.   Thus it reads:
   " What are my thoughts of thee ?
Ah, most serene and calm !   Amid the din,
The stir, and tumult of the busy crowd,
Like birds from far, they softly flutter in,
And breathe to me thy name, but not aloud.
I hear some voice with music like thy tone,
And start to know that I am not alone—
I look amid them all, if I may trace
Thy glance, thy smile, thy form's familiar grace—
And by the sudden flutter of my heart,
I know, my love, we are not far apart.
   " What are my thoughts of thee ?
All pure and fair, yet passionately sweet.
Moonlight and starlight whisper still of thee.
I breathe thy name, and o'er and o'er repeat
The words thou said'st beneath the whispering tree.
Again 'neath Winter's moonlight skies we stand,
I feel in mine the pressure of thy hand—
And words that touched my soul with sudden thrill
Are murmured o'er by lingering memories still.
And though our paths must part, 'tis sweet to know
Blest thoughts of thee are mine where'er I go—
Sweeter to know that with no vain regret,
We shall recall the hour when first we met."

It does seem so strange that we, after three years
Of misunderstandings, heart-burnings, and tears,
Should stand on the footing we now do ; and that
Our long correspondence, which has been in fact

Irregular, sparring, unpleasant—at length,
All jarrings at end—we, by mutual consent,
With mutual pleasure, propose to renew,
On a basis of confidence, knowledge, and true
Respect and affection, that neither could know
At its fatal beginning, just three years ago.
I *have* much injustice done him in the past,
But I'm glad I can truthfully say, that at last
My confidence in him is perfect, entire!

   I find, looking back for a year, I aspired
Ere to-night to be able the end to write here
Of this unhappy love.   But this record, I fear,
Looks not much like an overcome passion.
                            We leave
On the night train for Boston, on next Wednesday eve.
And so to my home I once more bid adieu,
To my darling, and also, my Journal, to you.

March 23*d*, 1867.

SATURDAY.

   Once more I'm in Brooklyn!   How happy I am
That, after a long, five months' absence, I can
Sit here in my own, cosey, dearly-loved room,
My old confidential chats here to resume
With my Journal; once more on its pages to trace
The sweet words "at home!"   There indeed is no place

So dear to my heart! I from Boston arrived
About two A.M. yesterday.
     Well! my life,
Since I left home last fall, has as usual not been
Uneventful; but on the contrary, within
A few months a great deal has been crowded. But it
Is so far in the past, I have now, I admit,
No time, nor, in fact, inclination to write ·
It in detail, and merely will give here to-night
A summary brief of a part.
     When I had
Been in B. a few days only, I was attacked
With severe fever symptoms, so suddenly that
'Twas with great difficulty that they were controlled,
And for a few days was quite ill. On the whole,
It was almost a wonder that I had escaped
A long run of fever.
     I wrote the same day
I arrived, to my *friend*; disappointed was I,
And greatly, that to it I had no reply.
I waited some two weeks, and then wrote again.
Still no answer! A letter to Annie I then
Dispatched, and enclosed one to him, the desire
Expressing that she'd take it in and inquire
For him—thus the state of his health ascertain,
And at once let me know the result. This was vain
(I had written to *her* two or three times before),
For from neither a word I received. And once more ·
I was in despair! and I cannot express
How unhappy it made me; and yet, none the less
Did I trust him, nor lose for one moment in him
My confidence; and I felt sure he'd not been

In fault in the matter.   When I could repress
No longer the grief which I can but confess
Each day but became more unbearable still,
The suspense and anxiety no force of will
Could suppress, which was killing me—Fannie would say,
"Why was I so sad, why not try to be gay?
She was sure I had nothing to trouble me!"   She
Would thought differently had she changed places with me.
Were her husband away from her, ill, perhaps blind,
Or sleeping in Death's icy clasp—and a line
Or a word of, or from him she could not receive,
She would weep, and imagine she'd reason to grieve.
I say this deliberately.   I believe
He's no less dear to me than her husband to her.
I was just as assured he was ill, as if word
To that effect I had received.

                     An event
Of some moment, six weeks or so after I went
To Boston, occurred, which I'll briefly state here:
When just finished shopping, one day, sharp and clear
A fire alarm struck from the "Old South" church bell,
And was echoed all over the city, as well.
A few moments later the engines rushed past,
A mad crowd in their wake.   They were all gone at last,
And crossing the sidewalk, I signalled a car,
Then leisurely walked out to meet it.   Not far
Had I gone, ere I heard shouts of "*haste!*" and was caught,
Dragged on to the platform, and thrust quick as thought
In the car, where a man on the left in his arms
Clasped me close—then a crash, a few screams of alarm,
Or of pain, and I, trembling and white, but unharmed,

Was released, and sat down.   And then, for the first time,
I knew what the danger had been, and divined
What a hairbreadth escape I had suffered.   It seems
That an engine, in all its mad fury—unseen
And unheard of by me—was directly behind
The car, which, obeying the signal of mine,
By stopping provoked the collision, which then
Could not be avoided.   They told me that when
They saw me approaching they thought I could not
Escape certain death.   I, unconscious of what
Was menacing me, must assuredly met
The fate which then threatened—I shudder e'en yet,
When I think of it—had it not been for the kind
And prompt action of those on the car at the time,
And the interposition direct of Divine
Omnipotent love and protection.   It seemed
A miracle, almost, that saved me.   I deemed
It indeed nothing less.   The pole of the engine
Was half-way through the car, and the door was crushed in,
The window-pane shattered, and weak women screamed,
And attempted to faint, and the crimson blood streamed
From both cheek and hand of one man near the door;
Another one had his coat torn; several more
Were injured in person or dress—yet was *I*,
More exposed than all others, by danger passed by,
And I stood there unharmed and untouched.   Not a word
Did I speak, but to answer, when if I was hurt
They kindly inquired.   I almost held my breath
At the Power which saved me from violent death.
And I thought that I never would murmur again
At whatever might come; or despair, feeling then

That there must be something in store for me yet,
Or I would not been spared; and, resolving to fret
No more at Fate's fickleness, wait for the end
With patience, with trust, and with hope.

                          To my friend,
My *dearest*, I wrote the last day of the year,
With hopes that would bring me some tidings. A mere
Note only, I sent, scarce a page, yet I knew
'Twas enough to assure him that I was " still true,"
And that if he was well he'd let *me* know the same.
In due time, to my joy, a reply to this came.
It was brief, but he stated he'd written me three
Directed according to orders. That he
Had been sick, as a matter of course, but was better.
That note I was not to consider a letter;
Was just leaving town, and had no time to write;
Would only be gone a few days, then I might
Expect to hear from him again. But although
I waited, and hoped, besides writing, also,
One or two more to him, yet not one other line
Did I receive from him, in all the long time
I was absent. And though I wrote Annie, again
And again, I heard nothing from her. This, too, when
From Colonel Allair I was hearing each week,
And from home twice as often as that, not to speak
Of others more transient; yet not one was lost,
And I thought it *was* hard those I wanted the most
Should have been just the ones to miscarry.

                               There was
In Malden a friend of my brother-in-law's,
Whose acquaintance I made while in B. There was not,
All during my stay, a week passed by, but what

He was there, and quite often more frequently still.
I liked him very much, and had reason to feel
The attachment was mutual.   Indeed, we at once
Became very good friends; and the long, weary months
Of my absence from home his society could
But render more pleasant, indeed, than they would
Have otherwise been.   And between us one bond
Of union there was, he knew naught of.   I found
That he'd "loved and lost;" and though *he* little thought
That I was aware of the fact, I could not
Avoid feeling for him, from the depths of my heart.
He, knowing the day that I meant to depart,
Met me at the depot, and bade me farewell
With regret that was evident.   *I* cannot tell
When again we shall meet—probably not for long—
But with pleasure I ever shall look back upon
Our pleasant acquaintance.

      We'd been a short time
In B. when my sister's health slowly declined,
And soon after the birth of the "Happy New Year,"
She seemed slipping from earth, while with anguish and
   tears, ,
We knew we could ne'er stay the fluttering soul,
Felt her feet would be soon threading streets of pure gold,
Her weary head pillowed on Jesus' true breast,
And her impatient spirit forever at rest.
My mother and father were summoned in haste,
And came on, expecting to see the dear face
Frozen, white, by the kiss of the conqueror, Death;
And indeed, we could fancy his icy cold breath
Had fanned her pale cheek, so near *his* portals grim
Did her faltering feet then approach.   I had been

Last to give up all hope, and I night and day passed
By her side, 'till upon the fair brow gathered fast
The cold dews of death, the pulse flickered and failed,
The soft loving eye became dim, 'neath the nails
The purple blood settled; then *my* hope was gone;
In my heart I then bade her a silent, and long,
Last farewell, thinking never to see her again,
'Till the jewel was lost from the casket.   But when
The night waned, the grim visitor slunk from our door,
And fair hope fluttered back to our sad hearts once more.
What a trying time 'twas to us all!   In despair
Was her husband—her children grief-stricken—all care
Devolved upon me, no less troubled, indeed!
Truly strength must be given to us as we need,
Or I could not endured what I did in those days.
When we gave up the loved one, I promised to stay
As long as they needed my presence ; although
The effort which it required, God alone knows !
But I counted the cost, and still felt it to be
A duty for me to remain.   I could see,
When, later she told me that I was indeed
Such a comfort to her when she felt that her feet
Were fast slipping over the brink, why impelled
I was to leave Brooklyn, last fall, and, as well,
One reason why God spared my life weeks before,
When 'twas in fearful peril.   When she, as of yore,
Was again in our midst, seemed as if we'd had one
Given back from the grave.   'Till her health had become
Sufficiently firm to permit a resume
Of her family's charge, I remained, and then soon
Turned my joyful steps homeward.

Awaiting me there,
I found a nice letter from Colonel Allair.
Have to-day been in town, and of course called to try
And some tidings obtain of my love.   Just as I
Had expected, I found he was ill.   'Twas about
Three weeks, they informed me, since he had been out;
Was no better when last they had heard—yesterday.
Though this knowledge made me very sad, I must say
Even that was much better than longer suspense.
Of late my anxiety's been most intense.
I knew not, of course, but in all this long time,
Death had entered *his* door.   Relieved was I to find
My dear one was living, though 'prisoned within
A silent and darkened apartment.   For him
It *is* very hard thus afflicted to be—
Hard for him—for all his—doubly painful for me,
Who must constant suspense and uncertainty feel,
And cannot be near him to nurse, soothe, or heal.

April 11th, 1867.

THURSDAY.

I had been home from Boston not more than a week
When somewhat surprised was I at the receipt
Of another nice letter from Colonel Allair—
Although none was due me ; and, wondering where
I could be all that time that from me he'd not heard.
He was anxious extremely, he said, for some word,
And feared there'd befallen me some accident
On my way home from B.   Not in any event

Expressing one doubt of myself.   My dear boy !
His letter was most kind, and gave me much joy.
A short time after my return, Annie one day
Came over to see me, and said, by the way,
That while I was absent she wrote me three times,
Yet not once did I hear.   'Tis indeed to my mind
Very incomprehensible.

                    How sad I was
All day Sabbath ! yet from no particular cause,
Or rather no *new* cause ; old griefs, and the old
And yet ever new wounds !   Not alone the untold
Despair of my wasted, unwise, hopeless love,
But my long-broken vows to my Father above,
Lost hope, and lost happiness.   *I* can't convey
To these pages, how heavy my heart was all day.
But 'tis gone, and I will not attempt its recall—
A passing cloud merely, yet, however small,
Dark and heavy with rain-drops ; but only such as
Have over my life-sky but too often passed,
And more and more frequently still, as the swift
Flitting years onward roll.   And to-day the cloud-drifts
Have been scarcely less dark.   All the night I had dreams
Of my *friend*—dreams not pleasant.   With morning's
        first beams,
I weeping awoke.   I'm *so* anxious !   It seems
As though I could not any longer endure
This racking suspense.   No one knows, I am sure,
Half how wearying 'tis.   Were it but allowed me
To see him, to soothe a few moments, 'twould be
A blest privilege ; but I have neither the rightt
Nor the power ; but 'tis very hard to be quite

Content always. Oh, why do I love him? And why
Can I not give him up?   When in B., by the by,
A friend casually said, " Two years is a long time
To be constant! "   But I, unto this love of mine,
So hopeless, perhaps unrequited, have been
Not two, but *four* years, nearly, constant.   And in
My heart, I must own, that the love is to-day
Warmer, purer, and sweeter, and in every way
More deep and enduring than ever before.
There *is* sweet with the pain, balm is oft sprinkled o'er
My heart's bitter anguish.   I love him with truth,
And with purity.   So there is nothing, forsooth,
In the love that should shame me; and only an act
Accomplished long years ere I knew him, in fact,
Almost in my babyhood, makes love like mine
A sin, and the simplest endearment a crime.
I did wrong, in the first place, I do not deny!
But most bitterly have I been punished, and I
Can but feel that the sin has been here expiated,
And by it the hereafter will not be shaded.
Over me for a long time the cloud has hung low;
Will its sable edge *never* roll backward, and show
The bright splendor beneath?   Or are the few sweet
Brief moments of happiness, exquisite, deep,
That his presence has always afforded, to be
The whole compensation intended for me,
For the anguish and pain I've endured, and must yet?
The one brilliant gem in a setting of jet?
The one gleam of light in the darkness so long
Enshrouding me?   " Sorrow and silence are strong,
And patient endurance is God-like! " one writes.
And if that end's accomplished, my heart made God-like,

If by patient endurance of this bitter grief
I am " purified, strengthened, perfected," in brief,
If through that I gain Heaven, I'll think it, indeed,
Lightly won, and give thanks for the glorious need.
A notice in this evening's paper just caught
My eye, and which proved to be, just as I thought,
Intended to summon to-morrow A.M.
Certain lodges of masons to meet, and attend
The funeral rites of a member. My heart
Stood still 'till I read it, and found that the hard,
Cruel dread at my heart-strings was not realized ;
That others were called to mourn, not me ; and eyes
And heart filled with gratitude. My mourning could
But be secret, and kill me it certainly would.
It seems as if that blow I never could bear ;
Me from that bitter trial, I pray God to spare.

May 4th, 1867.

SATURDAY.

About two weeks ago, I despatched a brief note
To my dearest, and after the date, merely wrote
" B. S. is at home ; when you're well enough, write
To the usual address."   And I hoped that I might
Hear at once ; but a week or more passed by before
I received a reply ; then he did not write more
Than a half-dozen lines. Had a few days been out,
He hoped permanently ; but he was about

Broken down.   For warm weather was praying, with trust
That his health would recruit.   My poor love! though it
    must,
Without doubt—summer's warmth—have the longed-for
    effect,
And bring his old buoyancy back again, yet
I fear winter's cold will prostrate him again,
And undo all the glad summer's work, and as then
Make him captive to pain.   If with him I could be,
I'd *such* care of him take!   Why did fate deny me
What would be such a boon!   Nothing more I'd desire
Than to watch o'er him, nurse him in sickness—aspire
To naught better than in all his joy to rejoice,
Support and give comfort in sorrow.   A choice
It is not mine to make.   Were he healthy and strong
It would not be so hard.   And if one of these long
And repeated attacks should my darling leave blind!
How could I endure it?   I've known for some time
That 'twas possible, probable even; yet I
Am not, and ne'er shall be, prepared for it.   Why,
When I think of that, should I forever be teased
With the memory of "Jane Eyre" and "Rochester"?   He
Was blind, also, and she was permitted to be
Light and eyes to him; yet, when he'd health and strength,
    then
Circumstances and stern destiny parted them.
But *my* "Rochester," he, my darling, my love,
Does not need me.   God grant me from Heaven above
Strength sufficient the weight of my sorrow to bear!
It grows very burdensome; and in despair
I almost sink beneath it.   Will *ever* there come
A better time for me?   The colonel, in one

Of his last letters, writes—" 'Tis indeed a long, long,
Weary night, that not *one* promise gives of the morn."
When will dawn for *me* break ?

                        I wrote him in reply
To his note, saying Saturday afternoon I
Would be in. For an answer I looked all the week,
But 'twas not 'till the day I appointed received.
I went to the door when the carrier called,
And he passed me three letters ; the last one of all
Was the one long desired. In the folds of my dress
I slipped it, and though I could scarcely repress
My expectant impatience the contents to read
Of the unopened letter, then lying, indeed,
So near to my heart, yet I forced myself to
Read both of my other long letters quite through—
One each from my brother and sister—and then
I hastened upstairs to devour the contents
Of the other. He merely wrote, though, he would be
At the L. about six o'clock Saturday eve.
I at once made my toilet, then up town to see
My friend Annie I went, and returned at the time
Appointed. But scarcely expected to find
My love at the L., as I wrote him in mine
I should not be in if it rained, and it did
Nearly all the P.M.; knew his health would forbid
Of his braving a storm ; and he came not.

                              I sent
Another, and made an appointment again
For yesterday. And I am able once more
To record pleasant things, and to write as of yore,
Of realized anticipations, and bright,
Sweet hopes all fulfilled. And if, while I shall write

Of yesterday's happiness, there should sometimes
A word of endearment slip out, from the mine
Of my love for him, why should I care?   Why repress
The impulse to utter the deep tenderness
That broods in my heart for him, when I well know
That these pages will be by no eyes but my own
Seen ever, at least while I live.   And when "life's
Fitful fever" is o'er, and I "sleep," why should I
Be concerned as to what may be then seen and thought?
Those who would for my weakness condemn me, do not
Know what they in the like circumstances would do;
And those, who in any degree have been through
The temptations and trials besetting me so,
Will pity me, rather than censure; will know
How utterly wretched I often have been.
And while to the dregs all the bitter drops in
The full cup of love I have drained, very few
Of its sweets I have tasted.   That life's to me, too,
But "a harvest of barren regrets," and a blight
All my sweet hopes of happiness, fleeting as bright.

My mother!   How *she* would feel did she know all!
She wonders why I am so sad, and why pall
All my pleasures so soon.   And she *may* some time know,
Some time solve the riddle that puzzles her so.
I would not have her now, as I know that it would
Cause her much pain, and could do no possible good.
I can't give him up! want the requisite strength:
I expect that I may be obliged to, at length,
By the strong force of circumstances; and 'till then
I cling to him; hoping as *my* love for him
Is involuntary, uncontrollable, in

12

All respects pure and true, that it may be forgiven
And not future punishment bring.   I *have* striven,
God knows, to o'ercome it, and think I have had
My chastisement all of the time, in the sad,
Bitter humiliation it caused, the frequent
Disappointments, the grief which seems ne'er to be spent,
The hopeless heart-achings for one who from me
Is eternally sundered.
                          I feared it would be
Stormy yesterday, also; as all the forenoon
Was cloudy, with strong, cold, east winds; but it soon
After noon cleared away very pleasant.   At four
I left home, and I then went direct to the store.
The first one I saw when I opened the door
Was my *friend*, and not far from the entrance.   He came
At once up to me; when we'd greetings exchanged,
I asked if to go up it was his intent.
He replied "Yes! at six?" and I gave an assent,
And hastened away.   I had waited for him
An hour nearly, and *he* a half hour too had been
There, before we discovered each other, through some
Slight misunderstanding.   I stood not far from
The entrance, and very much vexed I felt, too,
And thought if he did not come up, when he knew
That I was in town, and he'd promised to come,
I'd *never* forgive him, nor ever make one
More appointment, when just at that moment my hand
Was taken, a few words of greeting said, and
I turned, and my love was beside me.   Remained
There a moment, then went in.   Oh! how he had changed*!*
And how my heart ached as I saw in his face
The ravages which two months' illness had traced.

He had grown an old man since last autumn, and yet
To my heart he is dearer than ever.
                              He said
He wrote me thrice after the note I received,
None of which came to hand—and said last, he believed
He sent me a paper. It *is* strange, indeed !
At first we of mere commonplaces conversed ;
But after a time we dropped into the first
Serious conversation that ever has passed
Between us. I wrote him, I think in my last,
With my whole force of will I was trying to gain
The courage to give him up wholly ; obtain
The requisite strength to say, never again
I'd a meeting appoint, no more letters write him ;
When we met we would *talk* of a parting ; and in
The interim hoped he would think of it. Yet,
When first I referred to it, laughingly met
All I said with evasion, and when I reproved,
Retorted by saying, " But *you're* smiling, too ! "
But his playfulness he at length dropped, and became
As serious as I could desire. With his cane
Clasped in one hand, his other one holding his hat,
Which he from the table beside which we sat
Had taken a moment before, and his head
Bent slightly, he listened to all that I said,
Attentively, gravely, and answering, too,
As occasion demanded.
                      I briefly reviewed
Our long, desultory acquaintance, and when
I spoke of the grief he had caused me, he then
Asked what he had done. I referred, in reply,
To his frequent neglect of my letters, his slight

Of my wishes, his failure engagements to keep,
And the like.   But he answered, I yet did not speak
Of what he had *done*, only what he had *not*.
That he would prefer condemnation, he thought,
For omissive, rather than commissive sin.
I asked if he meant to imply that he'd in
Disregarding my wishes sinned less than he might
In fulfilling them; and, that if so, he was right,
I had not a doubt.   That was not, he replied,
What he meant; but for what he'd *omitted* to *do*,
He would rather be censured, when censure was due,
Than condemned for a wrong he had *done*.

As I knew
He had long been aware of my love, reckless, too,
As a woman is ever, when once she's betrayed
An affection she should have kept hidden away,
I told him quite plainly how dear he had been,
How much more than all others I still cared for him,
And added, I did not expect him to think
Any more of me, seeing how little I shrink
From telling him so—but he lifted his head,
And, " *No less, certainly !* " with much earnestness said.
Of course that was most gratifying to me,
And more so, as he the truth proved it to be.
I spoke of his letters, how cold and how brief
They had been, with exception of those I received
Just before I left home, adding *they* were, in fact,
Satisfactive entirely.   With quick, eager act,
Asked if that was the truth; said he *was glad of that*,
Very earnestly.   And, then I told him, however
We'd quarrelled in our correspondence, there never

Had been in our interviews aught to regret;
Those had been *very pleasant* in every respect.
With a smile most expressive, he looked up at that,
And my hand—he had taken in his 'neath his hat—
Warmly pressed, but said naught. Of how little to him,
And how much to me our acquaintance had been
I then spoke. And he answered in such an odd way,
As if all he wished to he did not dare say,
Or his strong feelings made it an effort to speak,
That to him it had been very pleasant indeed.
I spoke of how humbling the very fact was,
Of my caring for him, and the consequent loss
Of my own self-respect. But he " could not see why,"
He answered; and I in surprise made reply,
" Well, first, you are married ! " He raised his bowed head,
With a most meaning smile interrupting me, said,
" I know *that*, very well ! " I continued, that it
Was, of course, very wrong for me, *he* must admit,
To care more for him than for others, who were
Mere passing acquaintances; and, not a word
To speak or to write to him, had I a right,
Except what his wife with propriety might
Either hear or perceive ; and he surely must see
How deeply humiliating it must be
To one proud as I, to be forced to confess
I had lavishly wasted the deep tenderness
Of the first, only love of my heart upon one
Who cared nothing for me. While I spoke there had come
A slight flush to his cheek, though until I had done
Never lifted his eyes. Looking up then, he asked
How I *knew* that. " Knew what ? " I inquired, and there
      passed

A slight tinge of embarrassment into his tone,
As he answered—his hand pressing warmly my own—
" How know you that *I* do not care more for you
Than I do for all other fair women ? "   I knew
I'd no reason to *think* that he did, I replied.
He answered, of course he might say that he liked,
Or *loved* me, indeed! but, it never would do
To say all he might, and he had no *right* to.
Well! neither had I, I replied, but I did.
But he said there was naught to force *me* to restrict
My acts or my words.   I'd a right to say what
And all that I pleased; to another was not
Bound, as he was; I'd no one, of course, to object.
And I could but feel for him an added respect
For his truth to the ties that were round him, nor yet
Did I love him the less that his lips failed to speak
Words of love which to me would have been very sweet.

Then with much hesitation I told him, one more
Matter was there, I wished to refer to, before
We'd finished our confab.   That sometimes I'd thought,
Since we parted last fall, that I did not know what
He would think of me, as I at that time, I knew,
With scarce a remonstrance, submitted unto
The caresses he offered, and feared that he might
Not perhaps understand, that as almost a right,
From him I had taken what I should have felt
As an insult if offered by any one else;
And might think I would take from another the same.
He quickly replied, such a thought never came
In his mind for a moment; assuring me, then,
Most kindly, there never had been a time when

He had felt for me aught but the warmest esteem
And most thorough respect.
                              He, my love, did not dream
What relief and what gladness those words would afford,
Or how much of my lost self-respect they restored.
In return I said merely, I thought that he knew
That I'd ever reposed most implicit and true
Confidence in his honor.   We both had all through
Been feeling most deeply, and I had been forced
To make a slight pause more than once in the course
Of our conversation, my voice to control,
Though we spoke but in whispers.   And I, on the whole,
His character knowing so well, how extreme
Is his reticence, prudence, reserve—and supreme
His command of himself, think I ought not to be
Dissatisfied with the result.   For that he
Would say that he loved me, I did not expect.
Though his manner has often said so, in effect.

   After sitting a short time in silence, we rose
To leave, and together went out.   I proposed
To go from there up town, with Annie to spend
The night; so an errand it was his intent
That evening to do he postponed, that he might
Accompany me.   Took a car, and had quite
A nice chat on the way; and we left at the street
Where he used to reside; though he feared we should meet
Some one that he knew, and he said there were those,
And many, who'd be but too glad to disclose
To his wife aught like that.
                              He had *been* holding close
My hand, which he'd taken on leaving the car,

But between the two avenues, which was not far,
He released it, and folding his arm about me,
Held me thus while we walked a short distance; then he
Again drew my hand in his arm. We turned down
The avenue, paused at the Park, where we found
Ourselves shortly after, and leaned o'er the gate,
He proposing we leap in the fountain. I gave
A laughing assent, saying we would have thus
Death together, if life union *was* denied us!
"And I thought 'twere delicious to die then, if death ·
Would come while my mouth was yet moist with his
      breath!"
Again, taking me to my friend Annie's door,
Kissed, and bade me farewell, and we parted once more.

June 18*th*, 1867.

TUESDAY.

How one event crowds on another! To-night
I have, as in general, so much to write,
I hardly know where to begin. Much, I mean,
Which relates to my heart-life, by others unseen.

What an odd thing my friendship is with John Allair!
Our fates seem somehow strangely mingled, and where
It all is to end, I know not. There, indeed,
Is a warmth and affection between us, we read
Or hear of but seldom. He's called me, for long,
His "dear sister!" and that epithet covers strong

Expressions of ardent attachment.   In truth,
He makes love to me under that guise, and, forsooth,
Does it prettily, too!   He tells me that I am
His " pet sister," his " fondest attachment."   I can
Have not an idea how much benefit
My letters have been to him; and I permit
Him to say all the sweet things he chooses, while he
Thinks he gives naught but friendship, nor claims more
     from me.
And, indeed, he knows well that my heart is another's,
And that I can only " love him as a brother."
Well! since I wrote last, I in trouble have been—
Quite innocently on my part, though—with him.
It again is all settled, yet *I* hardly know,
What to think of him.   We, for two years past, or so,
Have written the other a letter each week;
Both written on Sabbath, both being received
About the same hour Thursday morn—though sometimes
Until the late mail he does not receive mine.
The week subsequent to my last record here,
His letter came promptly, as usual.   A dear,
Charming, flattering letter it was, too, all through!
In the course of it, he was referring unto
The receipt of my last, and as follows he writes:
" It seemed, as I read it, as if by your side,
In actual converse with you, I then sat.
I was in such a state of communion, ere that,
With you, and your letter then brought you, in fact,
So much nearer to me than you have been before,
That, when the spell vanished, it left me once more
The same feeling of sad and regretful *unrest*
Which I often have known, and yet cannot express

   12*

Or account for. But it was so *pleasant* and *grand*
To feel, yes! to really *feel* the full, bland,
Sweet influence of your lovely spirit! I'm sure
That my heart must have held conversation with yours,
And feel certain that you were then thinking of me.
Cannot you recollect where you were on that eve,
And what doing? Do try, dear! and in your reply
Fail not to inform me."

              Then thanks sent for my
Compliment with regard to the change I had seen
In his letters of late. He had hoped I would deem
They had changed for the better, and he was quite proud
To receive such assurance from me. He avowed
More indebted for it to the " dear little friend
Who had been to him more than a sister, and sent
Her blest influence him to assist in attempts
At self-culture," he was, than to any beside.
And 'twas *his* most sincere, earnest prayer that she might,
For the manner in which she that part had performed
Of her mission on earth, have a full, sweet reward.
Adding, " So do not think, little dear stricken heart,
That your life is a blank ! "

             Of this letter, a part
To Nettie, my dear friend, I read. Many times
She exclaimed at its elegance, praising its fine,
Pleasing sentiments, and, when at *her* strong desire
I had shown her his picture, which much she admired,
In her arch, pretty way she uplifted her head,
And, " how *can* you help loving him, darling," she said,
" When he is so handsome, and loves you so, too?
To say nothing of his charming letters to you ! "

She thought then, and 'till recently, we were engaged,
And believed naught I could to the contrary say.

I could not at first recollect how I passed
The evening to which he referred; but at last
It all in an instant across my mind flashed.
Sitting close to my love, in the L.'s reading-room,
In such deep conversation it might be presumed
I'd no thought but for him who then sat beside me,
And I wished it had been any other time he
Had desired information concerning: but knew
That part of his letter I must reply to
Or offend him: of course, I could tell him, too, naught
But the truth, which I did: but yet writing, I thought,
About it, in such a way he'd feel, indeed,
Rather flattered than otherwise.   Well, I received
His reply in due time.   'Twas brief, cold, and he wrote
Commonplaces alone.   And he said at the close—
" If this note, dear " (the only place where the first word
Of endearment—of which he is lavish—occurred),
" Proves uninteresting, does not satisfy,
You must excuse me, for a good letter I
Could not write you to-day, so unlike it I feel ;
And the reason I may, perhaps, some day reveal.
Be a good girl, and ever remember your friend ! "
I was both perplexed and indignant.   The end
Was much like the whole.   I could all overlook
Except one thing !—the coldness, constraint I could brook,
Thinking he might be troubled, in spirits depressed,
Were it not for the manner in which 'twas addressed—
" My dear friend ! "   At the head he in general writes,
" My sweet sister, " " My dear little pet, " and the like.

And I knew there was naught but displeasure with me
That could prompt him to write in that way; and could see
No cause for it, either, but what I wrote him
Of how I was occupied on the evening
Of which he inquired; and I could not see why
That should had such results. I regretted that I
Had written about it; though he, in effect
Forced me to. And yet, what is his right to object
To my passing the eve with whoever I choose?
Does he think all companionship I must refuse,
While I hold correspondence with him—a mere friend?
If he does, I imagine he'll find, in the end,
His mistake. And the more I thought of it, the more
I indignant became. Nettie, looking it o'er,
Declared that at length he had " found, with surprise,
That his *friendship* turns out to be *love in disguise.*"
And I thought even *he* could not censure me much
If *I* half suspected the same. There was such
An air, too, of misery all the way through;
And that no trifling thing it could be, I well knew,
To cause him to write in that manner to me.

I did not reply 'till the next Sabbath eve,
And then said—" Let us not repetition have, John,
Of last summer's experience. If I have done
Aught to vex you, why, tell me with frankness what, and
I'll apologize, or take it back, if I can.
Whatever it may be, you surely must know
It was done innocently, unwittingly; so
My conscience is clear, and I'd certainly no
Desire but to please you." The following week
Came his usual letter—although, of course, he'd

Not received mine as yet, as four days are required
For a letter to go, and so when we desire
To receive more than one in two weeks, it becomes
Necessary for *two* sets of letters, not *one ;*
So this was the answer to one sent before :—
It was long, and as loving as ever, and bore
To the other no reference ; but, there was quite
An undertone through it of sadness, unlike
Any I have had from him before.   Did not write
As early as usual, in fact, not 'till night.
Then said—" But while I've, dear, been silent all day,
I do not think you've from my thoughts been away
For more than five minutes at any one time,
And not often for such a duration.   In fine,
In my thoughts you've a fixture become ! "

This, I deemed,

Was a good deal to say !   Many other nice things,
And pleasant, he said, that I cannot write here.
It is too bad to tease him so, he's such a dear,
Good boy, such a kind, such a true, loving friend!
And to do so I certainly did not intend.
The next week brought an answer to mine, which
        contained
Of the cause a complete explanation, the same
Which I had surmised.   And then, lest that should not
Restore him in full to his place in my heart,
Wrote again in a few days.   Since then it has been
All right, and I think no more of it.

Within

The past month I have thought with more seriousness
Than I ever have previously done, I confess,

Of my love giving up.   And I ne'er realized
So fully before what a great sacrifice
It would be, what an effort 'twould cost.   Opening
A book, pencil-marks of his were the first thing
Which I saw there.   I entered the parlors, wherein
Were *so* many things to remind me of him—
The rocker he'd lounged in, the sofa where we
Together had sat, books and albums which he
Had handled.   Upstairs I came, opened my desk,
There were letters in his clear handwriting addressed,
His dear picture beside them.   Each time I exclaimed,
With a shudder, "How *can* I!"   And when evening came,
And I opened my journal to write, I discerned,
The first thing, a poem he sent me ; I turned
A few leaves, and a picture was there brought to view,
Which was eloquent of the bright hour when we two
Looked at it together—and *his* name I found
Upon every page.   Closed my book, and threw down—
Without writing—my pen.   My heart turned sick with
        dread,
And " I never can do it, I *cannot!* " I said.
I felt that there was a vast difference between
Giving him up entirely, and living on e'en
The terms we do now.   I dismissed from my mind
All thought of the sacrifice.

                        Some little time
Ago, I received a newspaper from him ;
Expecting it, answered the carrier's ring
Myself, and upstairs took it, ere I went back
To the room I had left, and where mother then sat.
She said naught of it, but it seems thought the more.
For, a few days thereafter, I slipped out the door

And ran to the box at the corner, a note
To him to deposit. Mamma did not know
That we, since we parted some three years ago,
Have had any intercourse. When back I came,
She asked if to him I was writing again.
I could not deny it, of course; on the whole,
Found "open confession was good for the soul."
I told her, with tears which I could not repress,
The whole bitter truth; nothing did I suppress,
And I'm *so glad* she knows it! It's taken, indeed,
From my mind a great burden. That I had deceived
My dear, kind, loving mother, has long been to me
A *most* bitter thought. And I knew, too, that she,
Felt almost contempt for my darling; but when
I told her how generous, noble, he'd been—
In all this long time how he never had made
One attempt, e'en, the slightest advantage to take
Of the love he had long known so well, and how true
His regard and esteem was for me, and how, too,
I thoroughly honor and trust him—how glad
I was I could say it!—she told me if that
Was the truth, he was one in a thousand; and said,
Though that I should love him she could but regret,
To our being good friends she would never object,
Nor, indeed, to our seeing each other, so long
As she now was assured there was nothing more wrong.
My dear mother! so kind to her sad, wayward child!
God bless her! and keep me from turning her smiles
To tear-drops of sorrow! It gave me such joy
She should change her opinion of *him*, my dear boy!
Such gladness to have her at length learn to know
All his true worth and honor.

A few days ago,
I was in at the store for a short time, and had
With him quite a nice, pleasant little confab.
All the good looks his illness last winter dispelled
He'd regained; and that day he was looking so well,
And so handsome, I fell in love over again!
He promised to write me on Friday, and when
The next morning passed by without bringing to me
The dear note, I was much disappointed; but he
Is as scrupulous, ever, a promise to keep,
As careful in making one; so I believed
He had a good reason. The note was received
Yesterday. 'Twas a nice, pleasant letter, indeed!
He said he was sorry that I should have been
Disappointed that morning in hearing from him;
But Friday he could not the time get to say
Even one word to me.

I've been feeling, to-day,
Very sad! For " forbidden fruit " pining in vain;
My heart aching with dull and incurable pain
For the soft " stolen waters " of *his* priceless love,
Which would be to me so passing sweet—sweet, above
All the passion and depth of another's! Once more
I revolved in my mind, as I have done before,
If 'twere possible for me my love to give up,
And from my heart's chambers his dear presence shut.
But from the dread prospect as usual I shrink,
And to him my weak heart still persistently clings.
How much I would like, on this beautiful night,
A ramble with him in the clear, soft moonlight;
Or a nice, cosey chat, in a nice, pleasant room,
Open casements, our only light that of the moon.

Others such bliss enjoy, why should *I* be denied!
How I envy her who has an undoubted right
To his presence, his love, his caresses! · And she
Does not know her good fortune, does not, I believe,
Her happiness prize as she should. And would I,
I wonder, if I could her place occupy?
I think *so*, yet " each heart knows its own bitterness,"
And how much there is of " connubial bliss "
In that household, I've no means of knowing. I've thought,
Sometimes, he loves *me!* but if so, or if not,
I never shall know. How unutterably sweet
Words of love from his dear lips would be—he who speaks
So little. Yet I could scarce love or respect
Him so much, were he not always so circumspect,
So faithful, so careful to ever be true
To her unto whom his allegiance is due.
My good, precious boy! lost forever to me,
Yet how dear to my heart must my love ever be!

July 14th, 1867.

SUNDAY.

Have been quite indisposed all the day, and to-night
Am so very unhappy! too much so to write,
Or to do aught but weep; for there's now going on
In my mind, such a conflict between right and wrong,
Religion and love! And oh! what can I do?
What *ought* I to do! How I wish that I knew
And had courage to do it. I feel there is naught
I can do in regard to the former, without

I make an entire sacrifice of the last.
Unless I can root from my heart all the vast
Wealth and power of this fatal passion.   How *can*
I give up my darling?   How part from the man
Who is dearer to me than the whole world beside?
Could the struggle I ever sustain?   Is there life,
Strength, endurance, enough in my heart to suffice
To support me, my broken heart heal?   God alone
Knows how bitter 'twould be.   *Could* I part from " **my**
     own "
Forever?   Put far from my sight everything
That in any degree should remind me of him?
Never *hope* him to see or to hear from again?
'Twould indeed be a trial most fearful!   And when
It was o'er, in my life what a drear blank 'twould leave.
Once resolved on, I would not turn back, I believe;
But I fear the required resolution will be
Not obtained very soon.   I'll think of it, and see.

July 15*th*, 1867.

MONDAY.   ·

Only twenty-four hours since herein I wrote last;
And more than twelve hours ago was the die cast,
The deed done, and the fatal words said that will part
Me forever from him who's the joy of my heart,
The dearest of all earthly objects to me,
And whose name is inscribed on this book's every leaf.
I write this with no tear; for my fountain of grief

Hours ago was exhausted. The tear-drops have all
Trickled down to my heart, and lie there like a pall,
A dead weight of sorrow.
                Last night I spent hours
In weeping, and deep, troubled thought; for the power
O! conscience, awakened, would make itself heard,
And pierced my poor heart with each soft-spoken word.
It told me that I had been sinful and weak;
Had yielded, where I should resisted. Like Eve,
I had suffered myself to be tempted, beguiled
Into tasting of fruit that's forbidden. And while
Unto the dominion of passion so wrong—
Notwithstanding its purity—I should succumb,
I never could hope to regain what I lost
Years ago, grace and favor of God. If I was
Not feeling to Him as I ought, I at least
Could my duty perform, and the whole issue leave
In His hands! And when at the untold sacrifice
My heart murmured, and in bitter agony cried
That its idol it *could not* give up, a reply
To my soul in a small, stilly voice softly came—
" Shall Jesus for you have died wholly in vain ?
Think what *He* for you suffered! and can you not do
This, even, for Him ? " Thus presented unto
My mind was the subject, and neither could I
Of it rid myself, nor its force could deny.
In a case such as that, how could I hesitate ?
To the tempter how list, when the *Voice Divine* spake.
And so " through many pangs of heart, through many tears
Was the firm resolve born that my idol for years
Should be shattered, torn out of my heart, given up
In a sacrifice whole and entire, ever shut

From all part in a life he had made bitter-sweet.
A resolve which ne'er faltered, amid all the deep
Pain and anguish, and bitter despair which it caused—
And my Father above knows alone what that was!
So religion and conscience have triumphed at length,
Done what coldness, and slights, all my will's force and
      strength,
The contempt of the world, or a mother's regret,
Or even the loss of my own self-respect,
Could never accomplished. A blank, oh, how dreary,
Is stretching before me! A life, oh, how weary
Must henceforth be mine! I can't think of it yet,
Cannot yet realize of my act the effect,   .
Or say to myself I shall never again
See or hear from my darling, from him who has been
My one thought, whether sleeping or waking, for years.
Oh, my burden is more, is far greater, I fear,
Then I ever can bear! God have mercy on me,
Or my heart it *will* break!   Such a pressure of grief
Is crushed down upon it, I scarcely can breathe.
Oh! my Father in heaven, give pity, relief!

    How full of sharp agony was the whole night!
And nothing but misery came with the light.
Yet I know but too well that the worst is to come,
When I from my heart must drive all thoughts of one
Still and ever so dear.   When I can but succumb
To the sorrow that must almost crush me; the dumb,
Speechless anguish I yet must endure.   I cannot
Anticipate it!   It is fearfully hard!
To him my decision this morning I sent,
Writing nearly as follows :

"My Dearest!

"Again,

And for the *last time*, I am writing to you,
To say, wholly and irrevocably, too,
I at last give you up!   Do not smile, as you read,
And wonder how many days there will, indeed,
Elapse, ere another from me is received.
I am not trifling now, but am, as you must know,
In most mis'rable earnest.   Nor do I say so
In a moment of pique at my sad, wasted love,
Nor of anger with you—you who always have proved
In the end, ever noble and kind, ever true—
But after a night's hopeless pain, such as you
May, I trust, never know.   Neither think, dear, that aught ·
You have done is the cause.   I am sure you will not,
When I tell you that never I one-half so well
Have loved you as this moment, when saying farewell—
Though the sad, fatal words that shall part us, my pen
Now refuses almost to transcribe.   'And what then?'
You will ask!   Simply this: that at length
My religion and principle's conquered, and naught
Beside such a great change could ever have wrought.
Between me and my God hitherto you have stood,
Though to you quite unconsciously.   I to Him could
Offer naught while I cherished a passion so wrong
As I knew was my love, notwithstanding its strong
And deep purity.   Nor dare 1 hesitate now,
Or longer ignore obligations and vows
I took on myself years ago.   You have been
The innocent cause of a blight rendering
All my happiness here, but I can't permit you
To make void all my hopes of felicity, too,

In the blissful hereafter.   I know that all this
You feel not yourself; but know, too, my love is
No sceptic, and in its existence I trust
You believe.   And some day, I am sure that you must
Experience what will unite us as friends
In that land far beyond the dark river, where ends
All sorrow and pain, where no partings are known,
Should we meet ne'er again 'till we meet at God's throne.
To this it has come!   Shall this thing I not do
For Jesus, who *died* both for me and for you?
I am no enthusiast; I do not feel
These things as I ought; but when duty's revealed
So plainly to me I can ne'er hesitate.
That at least I can do, though my heart it should break.
Do not think I am wavering, either, or that
My feelings will change.   I do nothing by half.
And as *I* have loved *you* with my whole heart, as your
Caresses, and letters, and words the most pure
And exquisite pleasure have given to me,
So now I, my darling, give them up, and " thee,"
At once and forever!   You never will know
What the effort has cost me; how fearful the blow;
Or what dark, dreary days I in future must see,
When the one bitter thought of my sad heart will be,
' My love I shall see never more, never more,
Until death's gates are passed, 'till life's fever is o'er!'
Some idea, perhaps, you may have, of how vast
Is the sacrifice, when, in recalling the past,
You think with what strong pertinacity I
Have clung to you nearly four years now gone by,
Notwithstanding the humiliation and pain

Which was caused by affection so hopeless and vain.
But you never will realize all the extent
Of the anguish with which this decision is sent.
Consider! You'd never give *me* up, I knew ;
Never say, ' I shall write no more letters to you,
Another appointment I never will keep ! '
Knew, if it was done, my hand *must* do the deed.
Indignation or anger I'd not, to assist,
Or urge 'gainst a heart, every fibre of which
Pleads so strongly for you.   And I knew I could see
Or hear from you often, and that you would be
Ever noble and true.   Think of this—how replete
With pleasure, how deeply, bewild'ringly sweet
Has our intercourse been, and you can but perceive
That 'tis after no *slight* struggle I these words write.
It *is* fearfully hard ! but yet rendered more light
From the fact that I suffer alone ; that you will
Not the cruel stroke feel as I must do.   And still,
I think *you* my decision perhaps may regret.
That 'twill cause you a few bitter pangs to reflect
That the fond little friend, true to you, at such cost,
And for such a long time, you forever have lost.
But you'll know that she'll *never* forget you—your name
Will e'er thrill her heart with a touch of the same
Old, beautiful music—that *she'll* never love
Another, as she has loved you—far above
And beyond all the world you must stand in her heart, ·
Though she writes, with her own hand, the words, ' we must
        part ! '
And that *you'll* forget *her*, she has never a fear.
You'll think of her on the last day of the year,

On the glad Christmas Eve.   Think of one, now and then,
Who loved you too well, if not wisely, and, when
She loved you most dearly, resigned you, because
She felt it was *right.*   And if I've ever lost,
In any degree, your respect—which, indeed,
I've no reason to think, and which you a few weeks
Ago kindly assured me had not been the case—
This I trust will restore it.   And I in this place
Wish to render you thanks for your kindness so true,
Forbearance, and rare generosity, too ;
Gentle patience, and noble, complete self-control,
Which enables us now to look back on the whole,
And think, notwithstanding we may have done wrong,
We have never been criminal.   Thanks to your strong,
Serene, and grand nature, your heart true and kind,
For your goodness to me ; and *God bless you !*

                                        " In fine,
I would see you once more ere the farewell is said.
Will you call on me here ?   Mother will not object ;
She knows all, and feels for you the same true respect
And honor that I do.   And while far apart
Our steps widely lead, the one prayer of my heart
Is that blessings may follow you all the world o'er,
And that God will my dear one preserve evermore,
'Till unto our rent souls comes a beautiful morn—
When succeeds to death's darkness eternity's dawn.
This is not my farewell !   That alone I can speak
When your arms are around me, your lips on my cheek,
And your true heart responding to mine at each beat—
Until then I remain

                    " All your own,
                              " Bitter Sweet."

A few days, and it all will be over ! The dream
So sweet will have ended.   My darling will seem
To drop out of my life as if dead—dead to me
Forever and ever, until we shall meet
Where all are united eternally, where
There can be no partings, no *marriage,* and there
I, too, shall be his, and he *all mine,* at last !
The feverish dream 's with the vanishing past ;
I to calmness must now school my heart, so bereft,
And in silence *endure* all the pain that is left.

July 30*th,* 1867.

TUESDAY.

Two weeks have elapsed since my farewell I sent
To my love ; yet I have not, until this P.M.,
Either heard from or seen him.   I did not know how
To account for it.   Feeling I could not allow
Him to slip from my life without even one more
Interview with my dear one, although, as of yore,
Pride rebelled, I resolved I would call at the store,
The cause of this long, cruel silence to find.
Felt I'd crushed down my pride before too many times
To yield to it now, and one more sacrifice
Could matter but little—let that thought suffice—
And went in to-day.   He did seem very glad
To see me, and I could but think that I had
Never seen him so handsome as *he* looked to-day.
Just my beau ideal in every way !

13

In looks, dress, appearance, a gentleman true,
My precious, lost darling! How plain to my view
Comes this moment his image before me, as he
Appeared when to-day he stood talking to me.
Leaning carelessly over the counter, thereon
Carving triangles, letters in various forms,
And list'ning attentively, smiling or grave,
To all that I said, glancing up as he gave
His opinion on matters of which we conversed,
Or his answers to me. Splendid, always! my first,
Only love! While on my part I both watched and marked
Every changing expression; anew on my heart
Stamped each feature, in deep, ineffaceable lines.

At once I referred to the letter of mine,
And his failure an answer to send. He replied,
That I asked no return; he thought none was required.
I requested that he would come out, and he thought
To do so as soon as he could, but had not
Found as yet opportunity. *I* said one thing
Was certain: he could not be gladder to bring
To a close our acquaintance, more glad it was o'er,
Than I was. He turned to me quickly, with more
Of pain in his eyes than I've seen there before,
And earnestly said, " Are *you* glad it is o'er ? "
That *I'm* inconsistent, I know very well!
But, forgetting love's sweets, at that moment I felt
Its bitterness only, and thought I could give
The former, if I of the last might be rid.
I told him I had not expected that he
Would care very much, but I thought that for me

And my feelings he'd have some regard.   With a touch
Of bitterness answered he, " *I* cared so much,
Had *so much* regard, I decided to go
Out to see you, but absent have been, and had no
Opportunity yet, as before I have said."
I told him I knew not but that he was vexed
At what I had written of mother, as when
She first knew about it he felt so.   But then
It was different, he said, and he rather was glad
Than otherwise, now, that she knew it, and had
No hesitancy about coming out.   Thought
He would quite like to see her—would rather than not.
He said that if possible he'd come this week.

In the first of my record this evening, I speak
Of my pride sacrificing by having gone in
To ascertain why I had not heard from him.
And I wish to say, now, that not one moment I
Have regretted it.   Neither have I, by the by,
Any similar sacrifice.   I never let
My love conquer pride, with an after regret.
And *he* never seemed to think 'twas any cause
Of triumph to him, or involved any loss
Of my dignity or self-respect.   When I've felt
Mortified at my own want of firmness, myself,
And weakness in yielding so much to my strong,
Overpowering love for him, potent so long,
Never word, look, or act of his added unto
My humiliation, or showed that he knew
Or had e'er thought of it.   And how late I have learned
To prize all his goodness to me—to discern
His grand generosity, charity, truth.

Only after a four years' acquaintance, forsooth,
And when I am losing him, too.   But I am
So thankful that I have known him 'till I can
Be assured that I have not unworthily loved.
But one who on every occasion has proved
How superior he to myself is, as well
As the most of his sex.   He's so good! I'm impelled
More and more to esteem him each time that we met.
And I left him to-day, loving him with more deep
And perfect a love than I ever have done,
Were that possible.   Yet I must give up the one
Who is *so* dear to me!   And I thought this P.M.,
After my return home, 'twas indeed hard, that, when
A brief interview with my love gave to me
Such pure and entire happiness, I must be
Deprived of that, even; that I from my heart
Must bid his dear image forever depart,
And learn to be reconciled to the sad thought
That I never shall see him again.   Oh! how fraught
With anguish those words are!   Of that when I think,
" All my sunshine grows suddenly dark," and I shrink
From the fearful ordeal I yet have to bear;
And my calmness is but the falsehood of despair.

August 6th, 1867.

TUESDAY.

With a heart almost broken beneath its dread load
Of grief and bereavement, with eyes overflowed

With hot tears, trembling hand, and a faltering pen,
In this book, which has been for so long my dear friend,
Companion, and confidante, come I to make
My last record. For I can but feel that this day
Should close the account of the baneful, and yet
Most beautiful past, all its love and regret,
All its sweetness and pain, all its sorrow and trust;
And that when I shall open another, it must
On its pages no traces contain of the sad,
Troubled waters that these have long flooded.

                                              I had
No visit last week from my love, but received
On Saturday morning a note, saying he
Had thought he should see me ere that, but was quite
Unwell, and unless he should get out that night
Would be forced to defer it 'till Tuesday—to-day.
I expected him this afternoon, and must say
I was much disappointed when failing to come.
But I had, just at night, such a headache come on,
I half wished that he still might defer it, although
'Twas with heart-throbs of pleasure I saw him approach,
And with warm, happy welcome met him at the door.

    What an evening we spent! All the sweet shadowed o'er
By the pain of the parting that yet was in store.
Sitting close on the sofa, my hand in his clasp,
Conversing of future, and present, and past,
Living ages of happiness in the few brief,
Fleeting moments of this all too-swift-passing eve ;
And yet, with a thread of despair through the whole,
Realizing with pain which we could not control
That this was the last! Oh ! but *it was*, indeed,

To us each, in one moment, both bitter and sweet,
Both happy and sad.
                    We referring again
To mamma's knowing of the relation which then
Existed between us, he said that he felt
Much pleased at that part of my letter, as well
As greatly relieved.   Was *most* glad that she knew
All about it, and that I'd told *him* of it, too.
Surely! that alone proves how sincere, pure, and true
His regard for me is.   I reproached him, that he
Had ever so very reserved been with me,
And he said all his friends of the same thing complained.
But so strong were his feelings that he was constrained
To use much reserve, or he could not keep them
At all under control ; and also to prevent
His saying a great many things he ought not.
How true that " deep waters flow stilly," I thought,
And that natures which *are* most reserved are the ones
Most exquisitely sensitive, most finely strung,
And susceptible unto emotion most strong.
He has great self-command—I have known it for long.

    What a pleasure I felt it to be, to tell him
How greatly endeared to my heart he had been
By acquaintance more close ; how much more I'd esteemed
And honored him as the swift years, like a dream,
Flitted onward ; and added—as *my* cheek I pressed
To his, which was then on my shoulder at rest—
" And I think that you *are* a much better man, too,
Than you were when we met four years since ; do not you ? "
In a voice with emotion all broken, he said,
" I *hope* I am, dear ! "   And I *know* that, instead

Of being to *me* a defilement, this sweet,
Entire, perfect love, has been to me of deep,
Lasting benefit, and a strong safeguard, as well.
Loving him, I from others attentions repelled,
Which, received, might my happiness ruined for life.
Who knows not through suffering we're purified?
And as I've suffered deeply—*how* deeply, there's One
Alone knows—so I trust that my soul has become
Purified by the discipline which it has known.
And, to-day, feel that not in religion alone,
But in character, principles, morals, I am
Better now than I was four years since. No one can
But acknowledge a high, pure, and perfect love has
A refining influence upon the heart, that
Reads the discipline of disappointment aright.
I believe the effect upon him has been like.
And though I in all cases the tempter have been,
Yet I feel that the influence *I've* had o'er him,
On the whole, has been only for good. And I'm *glad!*
How rejoiced, too, I am that I now can look back
And say *he's* never offered to me one temptation;
But has, in all things, been the impersonation
Of truly magnanimous honor. My own
Peerless love! I am glad, very glad to have known
Him, although it has brought me such pain as to-night
I've been forced to endure.
                When I asked him not quite
To forget me, he said, no; it was not with ease
We old, sweet recollections ignore, and that he
Should think very often of me; he supposed
He should not ever see me again! Very close
Was the clasp which he held me within, as we felt

All the force of those words.   We could *not* trust ourselves
To speak much of that time, and each moment it seemed
More and more that I never could give up the dream
That had been, oh, so sweet ! or the farewell words say
That should part us forever.   Oh ! how my heart ached,
As the time swift approached when I knew he must go—
Go to come nevermore.   Oh, why *must* it be so ?
God help me to bear this unutt'rable woe !
We sat for a long time in silence complete,
His arm holding me tight, his face pressed to my cheek,
Our hearts almost bursting with anguish so vast,
With full realization that this was the *last.*
Oh, how bitter-sweet these moments were as they passed !
How we clung to each other with pain at the dread
Ordeal through which we both had to pass yet.
When our last we must look in each other's dear eyes,
Where despair could but enter as hope slowly died,
When our hands must be clasped for the last time on earth,
And our quivering lips speak the last farewell words.

I begged him to tell me *once* ere we should part,
That he loved me ; but only more close to his heart
Did he press me, and murmured, " Oh, *don't* ask me, dear ;
Do not ask me ; you ought not ! " His voice, soft and clear
In general, now sounded husky and strange.
I urged him no longer—was answered—'twas plain
That he loved me ; I needed no words to assure
Me of what I were foolish to doubt.   And though pure
And perfect the joy would have been from his lips
The sweet words once to hear, I did not, I admit,
Love him less that those words were withheld.   Very few

Would temptation so strong have resisted, I knew.
And I felt very thankful my love was so true.

It was time he should go! He arose, crossed the room.
Returned, and beside me his seat he resumed;
With his arm around me, his cheek on my bowed head,
He so earnestly, sweetly, caressingly said:
"I will tell you, dear, how it shall be! We'll forget
Everything that is bad, all the good recollect.
The remembrance of all that is sweet, that reflects
Any pleasure to us when the past we recall,
We will cherish forever; and we will let all
That's bitter or painful from memory fade,
And never again in our thoughts have a place.
Say! shall it be thus?" And I, too much moved
To reply, by my silence alone could approve.
For a moment he strained me again very close
To his warm, throbbing heart, where he held me, as though
He could *not* let me go; then he once more arose,
But paused 'neath the chandelier, taking a book
From the table, at which he indeed scarcely looked;
Then, laying it down, toward me turned again;
I had also arisen, stood leaning against
The table behind him—eyes drooping, downcast,
And a sad, bleeding heart; both my hands he then clasped,
Leaned his brow against mine and looked into my eyes;
They were brimful of tears, and as *he* turned to hide
His emotion, I said to him, "This is the *last*,
And *you* do not care!" What reproach and pain passed
Into both eye and tone, as he said in reply
Merely, "*Do* not talk so!"
                              But time fleetly flew by,

13*

And we knew he must go ; that the moment had come
When my darling must leave me to never return.
What a lifetime of anguish was crowded in those
Few moments of parting !   Again clasping close
The hands he still held, stooped and—for the first time
This evening—with warmth pressed his dear lips to mine,
In a passionate, lingering kiss of farewell.
What love and despair it expressed, who can tell ?
I stood where he left me, despondent, cast down,
With no hope in my heart, and with eyes on the ground,
'Till he turned, with his hand on the door ; then I raised
My eyes, and how *radiant* was his dear face,
With the strong love for me which would not be denied,
In a moment like this, *all* expression !   Shall I
Forget *ever* that look ?   Not while reason and life
Shall endure.   And half-sobbing, "You *do* love me, then,"
I sprang toward him and was folded again
Within an embrace so impassioned and strong,
As my fluttering breath to impede—and how long
I scarcely can tell.   But he murmured at last,
"Farewell, and God bless you ! " released me, and passed
From my sight ; and the closed door shut out all the light,
Joy, and hope of a life that is henceforth a blight,
A dreary and wearisome blank.   Oh, my God !
Have pity, I pray ; give relief to this load,
Which is more than I ever can bear !

         Of the time
Just after he left me this evening, my mind
Retains no recollection.   But know that I found
Myself on the sofa, reclining face down,
My head on my clasped hands, with no sob, and no tear,
But my heart almost breaking with bitter and drear

Hopeless agony, such as I pray I may ne'er
Experience more.   While it cried in its pain,
"Oh my darling, my love, come back to me again!
Come back, oh, come back, I can *not* let you go!"
But the echoes with mocking despair answered, "No,
Nevermore, nevermore!"

                          It is midnight! and sleep
Refusing her watch by my pillow to keep,
Though my temples are throbbing with pain, and my hand
With exhaustion is trembling, and with no command
Of my fluttering pulses, I've risen to write
In my journal these faltering lines, and unite
With my last sad farewell to my sorrowful love,
My adieus to this also; erecting above
This grave of my heart the one blank, brittle stone
Of forgetfulness; praying for what one alone
Can bestow, peace and calm to the storm in my breast,
A rebuke to the troubled waves never at rest.

"Stolen waters are sweet!"   But the most abject woe
Lies hidden their glittering wavelets below,
No more shall the baneful and beautiful draught
Touch the lips, which before have so eagerly quaffed
Of the bright, sparkling waters.   No more shall I know
The bliss or the pain it so long has bestowed,
Love's goblet is shattered! the contents, I found
Both bitter and sweet, are all spilled on the ground.
God forgive all the wrong of the past, and again
Unite us, where all are eternally friends.

STOLEN WATERS.

PART THIRD.

"What matters a little sorrow if the end is bliss?"

MRS. GREY.

"The bitter past, more welcome is the sweet!"

SHAKSPEARE.

STOLEN WATERS.

Part Third.

BROOKLYN.

August 13th, 1867.

TUESDAY.

ONCE more I commence a new journal! and close
The last, leaving it, with its story of most
Intense pain, pleasure, passion, and letting the dear
Inspirer of all drop from out my life here,
As one that has never existed. *Shall* it
Be thus? Shall I not any mention permit
In these leaves of my heart, of the one whose dear **name**
Has filled the last volumes with beauty and pain,
As it has for so long filled my heart with its deep
Thrilling music, so passionate, soft, low, and sweet?
I *can't* cease to think of him often, and much!
I know not that I *wish* to forget, or to thrust

The record aside of what has to me been
So delightful in anticipation, and in
The realization and sweet retrospect.
For as *he* asked that I would alone recollect
All the *good* in the past, how can I a request
So exquisitely tendered refuse! No! I'll cease
To think of the sorrow, suspense, grief, that he's
Oft unconsciously caused, and remember alone
The supreme happiness and delight I have known
In his presence; the joy of expectancy, too,
And fond recollection. For 'tis indeed true,
Though to anticipation I've given full rein
When thinking to see him, my hopes ne'er were vain.
But the realization was far in advance
Of all I had fancied. Though followed by blank
Disappointment, extravagant hopes e'er have been
In all other matters, but *never* with him.
On our interviews, brief and infrequent, in fact,
With not one regret, e'en, I now can look back.
All has been perfect harmony, truth, tenderness,
And how much *I* have lived, I can never express,
In the few fleeting hours we together have passed.
Years, I might say, for their recollection will last,
Will cling to and bless me for long months and years,
And give to my sad heart much brightness and cheer,
Replacing with pleasure the darkness and gloom.

So the pictures that hang on the walls of the room
Dedicated exclusively unto my love
In the castle of memory, cheery above
All the others, the most sacred chamber, indeed,
Of my heart, shall all brightness and loveliness be;

With the richest and softest hues all shall be tinged,
With lustre most sweet and pure all glittering,
With the cord of eternal remembrance all hung,
By the hand of undying love, fond affection.
They shall be scenes of hope all fulfilled, friendship true;
Of scrupulous honor, sincerity too,
Temptations resisted, and faith tried and proved,
Confidence ne'er betrayed, and love, constant and quite
Involuntary and enduring.   The light
Shed by stars of esteem, true respect, and regard
Shining over the whole, added charm to impart
To the pictures so fascinating in themselves,
Which must ever be dearer to me than aught else.
"'*Tis* sweet to remember! I would not forego
The charm which the past o'er the present can throw."
And so I will *not* put him out of my heart,
And my heart and life's journal.   I'll try—although hard
Is the lesson to learn—him to never regret;
But my life's sweetest dream I must fail to forget
Long as being endures—the bright dream, that to one
Of *my* temperament only once ever comes,
"The *sole* love that life gave to me."   It is true
"There are loves in some lives for which time can renew
All that time may destroy.   Lives there are in love, too,
Which cling to one faith, and die with it, nor move
Though earthquakes may shatter the shrine!" and such
        love
I have given to him! If I would, I cannot
Forget him.   My journal would be, too, without
Interest to me, should his dear name cease to find
A place in its pages.   If I through all time

Shut him out of my life, shall I also deny
Him a place in my heart, and heart-record?　Shall **I,**
When he said he would never forget *me,* do less
Than remember him, too?

　　　　　　　　　　　Much surprised, I confess
I was, some days since, when in town on Broadway
To meet Mrs. ——, his wife.　I had not, till that **day,**
For years seen her ; and then I should not, I dare **say,**
Have noticed her, had she not given a glance
Of recognition unmistakable, as
We passed.　She was looking indeed very nice !
Of course that little incident did not suffice
To make *me* any happier.　Only brought back
Old times with more force, and made me very sad.

　　Last Sabbath, in church, when I found the first **hymn.**
"June 12th, '64," was traced on the margin.
How strongly that also the past did recall !
And the day when 'twas written, more plainly than all:
Sitting there, in that beautiful church, on that bright
Lovely morning in June, Mr. S. in his quiet
Deep voice the words reading—above me the face
Ever dear, dearly loved even then—all the place
Hushed to silence, unbroken except by the low
Thrilling tones of the reader; then softly and slow
His voice sang the beautiful words, and made them
Sweeter far than before.　It all came back again,
As the words so familiar now fell on my ear,
While my eyes slowly filled with such sad, bitter tears.
I have not, until then, been at church since that time
When that hymn has been sung.　And now, when I **am**
　　　trying

To forget, in a measure, all this, comes to taunt me
With " bliss that's remembered." How he and his haunt
    me !
Fate seems to forbid my forgetting. Far more
Do I love him than ever I have done before,
Now I know that to me he forever is lost.
The preacher that day said, when any one was
Peculiarly tried, or had any great grief,
They might be assured there was some glad relief,
Some great blessing in store for them; as tried and proved
Was an article ere it was ready for use.
It comforted me very much. And as I
Have, God knows ! been of late indeed fearfully tried,
It may be that something's still waiting for me,
To make up for the pain I've endured recently.
I hope so, and that it may come speedily.

    To-night, at the time he came one week ago,
I of course thought of him, as I have done also
Through to-day, and in fact every day ; but this eve
My dear Nettie was in, and it passed, I believe,
For a very few moments, quite out of my mind,
'Till I looked at my watch, found 'twas just half-past nine,
The hour of our parting! At that very time,
Only one week ago, on my lips he'd just pressed
His kiss of farewell—his last lingering caress,
The sweetest that man to a woman e'er gave !
And my heart and my pulses stopped beating, as wave
After wave of remembrance rolled over my soul,
Recalling of that bitter evening, the whole.
Stood still with grief, pain, and unbounded regret.
" *'Twas* sad that our parting should be ! " sad but yet

Inevitable. And perhaps better then
Than later. It must have come some time, and when
Less than now should I love him? for each added year,
Could but have made him to my heart still more dear,
And the parting yet harder to bear. The last week
Has, God knows, been to me a most sad one, indeed!
I have *lived* through it, though, as I *must* do all those
Yet to come. Oh, how *many* before life shall close!
I am yet, oh, so young! Life to me looks so long!
Twenty-two, and its brightness and beauty all gone!

August 2d, 1868.

Almost a year, since I have opened this book!
And how has it passed? One would think but to look
At my external life, that 'twas calm and serene,
Would not deem I was mourning a bright, broken dream.
Very quiet indeed, has my outward life seemed,
And as to my *true* life, that hidden within
The depths of my heart, that's diversified been.
Some days have been very unhappy. Days when
The winds and the waves my frail barque have o'erwhelmed,
When I found it impossible quite, to suppress
The sad, intense longing for one dear caress
From the lips loved so well; for his presence, a sight
Of the one dear, dear face, which would bring joy and light
To my poor, aching heart; for a touch of his warm,
Loving hand, and the clasp of his strong, tender arm.
When some slight trifling thing would bring all back again
With such force to my mind, it would seem to me then

That I never could bear it. And yet, I believe
That the days which are saddest are those that succeed
To a night when my dreams have all been of him. Nights
That came but too oft—dreams which but tantalized.
I *could* thoughts of him in some measure control;
But over my dreams I had none; and my soul
They have made very sad, many times. Not a day
In this long, weary year, now, thank God! passed away,
But I've thought of him much. Not a night, but my last
Thought and prayer was for him. How has *he* the year
    passed?
Oh, would that I knew! Yet the burden I've borne
Philosophically on the whole, and have known
Some pleasant if no *happy* hours, e'en in this
Most desolate year, dreary as my life is.

   To the "old church" last Sabbath a visit I paid;
But I did not see there the one dear, handsome face
Whose eyes used to meet mine so kindly. The place
And service, without him, were quite incomplete;
And I'd only the pleasure of retrospect sweet,
To compensate me for the lost charm.
                  August seems
A fatal month to me; and what will *this* bring?
From Colonel Allair I'm expecting this week
A visit. It long has been talked of, indeed,
And now the time seems to have come. I am much
Anticipating from his stay, and I trust
We may with each other some pleasant hours spend.
Oh, would 'twas my *darling* instead of my *friend!*
My "other John"! Were that the case, though, I fear
I should not so tranquilly write of it here.

But that never, oh, never can be!   One more year
Of my life is now gone.   One year nearer are we
To the meeting eternal.   How joyful 'twill be!
I've been reading a book about heaven, of late,
A beautiful thing, too!   And as it portrayed
The reunion of friends, it occurred to me then,
Though I oft think of meeting my love there, to spend
A happy eternity with him, the thought
That we may be in separate places has not
Ever entered my soul.   And when that suggests it,
Does my mind for one moment a place there permit
The thought to retain?   No; with all of my heart
I believe, that as here we are kept far apart,
There we shall be united in all the sweet bonds
Of friendship and love—love *perfected* and fond.
I trust it to Jesus who died for us both!
And it *is* very sweet unto *Him* all to owe,
And feel He's not only the power, but wish,
This loved one of mine to bring safe into His
Precious fold.   And I pray God, through Him, that if none
Of my morning and evening petitions shall come
To His ear, and find gracious acceptance, save one,
That my prayer for my love, from a full, penitent,
And sometimes aching heart, may like fragrant incense
Ascend even unto the foot of the Throne,
And an answer in blessings on him shower down.
God sees not as man sees!   And Christ, who has borne
Our weak human nature, our weakness has known;
He uses mysterious means to work out
His designs, and bring his wise purpose about.
And may I not hope that what all the world might
Think a serious error, at least, if not quite

A crime, may the means be of bringing to Christ
One wandering lamb? Oh! how happy and glad
'Twould make me, to think that my influence had,
Under God, been the means of directing the feet
Of one so beloved into paths that shall lead
To the gates of the city eternal. God keep
My darling through all of life's wild, stormy blasts,
And bring us together with Him, safe at last!

———

August 16th, 1868.

SUNDAY.

Since I last wrote the Colonel has been here, and gone,
And I on my lips wear his troth-kiss, and on
My finger his ring! Am I happy in this
New relation? I scarcely can tell, I confess!
I like *him* very much, very much indeed! More,
I think, than I have any one heretofore,
Excepting my love of the sweet olden time;
And *I* do not know as that passion of mine
Interferes in the least with the strong, warm regard
Which I now have for John. The place held in my heart
By my old love's peculiar and sacred to him;
No other can ever approach it. Within
That chamber no footsteps may enter. The door
Is fast, and my love holds the key. Nevermore
Shall it open, 'till life's joys and sorrows are o'er.
And yet, my attachment to John is, I think,
Strong enough to make me unto him everything

That he may desire; and *he* feels it is so.
Our engagement is only conditional, though,
And if either should think, in the future, 'twould be
Best it should not be consummated, why we
Are to make it known instantly.

       He was with me
Scarcely more than a week. The first few days passed on
Quite fleetly to us, in reviewing our long
Correspondence so pleasant. But *one* day, he'd been
In town since the morning, and, waiting for him,
Just at twilight, was down in the parlors, and leaning
My head on the mantel-piece, stood idly dreaming
Of what—I indeed scarcely know; but I must
In my reverie *have* been absorbed very much,
For I heard not his ring, nor his step in the hall,
Nor the opening door—in fact, was not at all
Aware of his presence, until some one's arms
Were around me with passionate pressure and warm,
And my head to a manly breast gently was drawn.
Too surprised to be very indignant, I raised
My eyes, and o'er me there was bending a face,
With a look in it only one passion can trace.
I said nothing, but would have withdrawn from his clasp.
But he held me the closer, his heart throbbing fast
'Neath my cheek, which was resting against it, and said,
"This, dear, is the best place for *your* weary head!"
Then rapidly, eloquently, he went on
To tell me how dear to him I had been long;
How sad would his life be without me; how strong
His desire was to shield me from all of the storms
Of life, which had hitherto visited me
With such roughness; how kind, and how tender he'd be.

And looking up into his true, honest eyes,
I felt that in *his* hands my happiness I
Could give, and the trust would be never betrayed;
And the answer he wished for I readily gave.
In a year he will come for me, if before then
Neither think it were better he should not. And when
He bade me farewell, 'twas with tears of regret
And sorrow I saw his departure. And yet,
I thought of a parting but one year ago,
And felt, for the first time, it could not be so—
The conditional promise could never be kept.
But that feeling soon passed, and I'm now quite content,
And think that my life with him will be, indeed,
A tranquil and happy existence, and lead
My heart into safe, pleasant paths. And to-night,
I thank God for His goodness, and pray that aright
I may use my strong influence over the man
Whose happiness now has been placed in my hands.

October 10*th*, 1868.

SATURDAY.

Scarcely two months have sped, and already do I
Beneath my bonds chafe. My heart already cries,
That it never can be! and beside me there lies
A letter, signed, sealed, whose contents shall dissolve
The engagement on which we so lately resolved;
And I wonder, now, how I could ever have felt
That *I* could the marriage vows take on myself,

14

And promise to love any other but *him*
Who must still be my dearest, as ever he's been.
For John I've indeed the most sincere and true
Attachment, and know well that *he* loves me, too.
And yet, my heart shrinks from the intimacy
Of married life, even with him. And think he
Will feel, as I do, 'tis but justice and kindness,
Thus early to sever the ties which now bind us.
I suppose my decision will give him much pain,
And so it does me; for I, too, hoped, in vain,
Together, a bright, happy future to spend.
And it hurts me, indeed, to cause grief to my friend;
Yet, I feel that it will be as nothing compared
To a life-time of sorrow, the grief and despair
Of within his arms holding a cold, loveless wife;
That the promise, if kept, could but make us for life
Both wretched, indeed! For one face ever must
Between us have come, and thus, marring for us
All happiness, rendered our fancied bliss naught
But a mockery. Feeling thus, I, of course, thought
It but right to tell *him* without further delay;
And therefore I wrote him a letter to-day.

'Tis best so! Not sufficiently large is my heart
To contain more than one love; for every part
Is filled to o'erflowing with that. I feel, too,
That 'tis sweeter, far sweeter to love *him*, my true,
Only love, with no hope of again seeing him
While life lasts, with no thought of there ever being
Between us one sweet, tender tie, than to be
Worshipped by any other. The *mem'ry* to me,

Of his love, is far more than the most warm, heartfelt,
Passionate adoration of any one else.
With such feelings, I can't wrong a friend that's so dear,
By a ruined heart giving to him, or a mere
Pretence of affection.   So sorry am I,
So sorry, that he should have ever a tie
Between us more close than warm friendship besought
Or desired; and so sorry, too, that I should not
Seen at first that his hopes could be ne'er realized.
Still, I trust that his love not so deeply does lie,
That it is not so lasting and strong as he thinks;
That, before many years their swift flight shall have winged,
He will find one more worthy of such a dear, kind
Companion as he would be; who, through all time,
Every craving shall satisfy of his true, warm,
Loving heart.   And who shall not alone fill his arms,
But his mind and his soul.
                    Thus once more I become
All my love's, with no thought but for him—my dear one!

———

December 18*th*, 1868.

FRIDAY.

'Tis with saddest of sad hearts I sit down to write
A few words in my journal's still pages to-night.
Such sorrowful news as to-day I've received!
This morning a paper was handed to me,
Addressed in my love's well-known hand.   Oh, how *long*
It had been since I'd seen it before!   What a strong

Thrill fluttered my pulse as I recognized it!
Was so happy and glad about it, I admit
That I never once thought it was strange he should break
In that manner our long, cruel silence. With haste
I tore off the wrapper, and looked, but in vain,
For a written word which should the sending explain.
But when carelessly glancing its columns adown,
I observed a marked paragraph, which I soon found
A notice to be of the death of his wife.
I scarcely more shocked have been, in my whole life!
How my heart aches for him! How it *has* ached all day!
How grief stricken he must be! Oh, would in some way
I could give to him comfort. His dear children, too—
His sweet little Bertie! Oh, what will he do
Without his own loving mamma. 'Tis, indeed,
Very hard for them all. And it makes my heart bleed,
When I think of how lonely they *must* be to-night.
God, I pray, cheer their sad hearts!

       Of fever she died,
After scarce a week's illness. I can't realize
It were possible that her fair face should lie now,
White and still, 'neath the snows of December. Oh, how
Can he bear it?—my darling! 'Tis sad, oh, so sad—
This most bitter trial he ever has had.

 I wrote him this evening a few lines of deep,
Heartfelt sympathy; feeling I never could sleep
Until I had told him how truly I grieved
At his sorrow. And wrote, with the earnest belief
It was right that I should. Jesus pity and bless,
And to his troubled spirit send cheer and sweet rest!

December 31st, 1868.

THURSDAY.

The last day of the year! I have been looking o'er
The journal I've kept for six long years, or more;
And I could not help thinking that, were I to read
The same in a book, I should think it, indeed,
Over-drawn, and extravagant, too. Yet, God knows
That I felt every word from beginning to close.
Felt bitterly, sweetly, the fullest extent
Of what was expressed. And a nature intense
As mine is, could scarcely feel less, influenced
By the same circumstances, I'm sure! As I knew
'Twould be no criticism subjected unto
More severe than my own, I have freely expressed
All my heart's bliss and pain, happiness and unrest.

The old year is dying! The moments speed fast!
As they vanish away among things of the past,
My thoughts backward roll to one bright afternoon,
Just five years ago—five long years! yet how soon
Have they slipped from beneath our oft-faltering feet—
When my heart the first time wildly throbbed 'neath the
        cheek
Of one who's become since so dear; when my lips
Felt the pressure of his in his first tender kiss,
And I eagerly tasted the first drops of bliss,
In the goblet of love which his ready hand raised
To my parched, thirsty lips. Oh, how sweet was the taste!

Happy then in the present, so happy to see
That I filled all his thoughts for the moment, **that he**
Was all I had deemed him—a gentleman true.
Not thinking, or *caring* indeed, then, this **new**,
Sweet feeling to analyze, reckless of what
The future might bring forth—in fact, with **no thought**
That moment beyond, and delirious, too,
With the joy of his presence, the glad moments **flew**
But too swiftly, and brought our first parting.　**And then**
Succeeded the eve's dreamy retrospect, when
I sat with my hand o'er my eyes tightly pressed,
Recalling with pleasure each offered caress,
With rapturous thrill every word of the man
Who, in truth, even then, held my heart in his hand.
And nobly has *he* used the power possessed.
True, indeed, has he been to his trust.　Kindest, **best**,
Most generous ever.　What wonder, above
All others, I honor, admire him, and love!
What wonder that I joyous mention should make
Of each of these glad anniversary days,
As the untiring wheels of time roll them along?
What wonder that sweet recollection, with strong,
Fond emotion, should linger around them, each year
But rendering them indeed all the more dear?
Oh, blessed be memory!　"There is no time
Like the old time, no love like the old love."　I find,
In the whole of my world, not a man who is like
Unto *my* love!　God bless and preserve him to-night!

December 31*st,* 1869.

FRIDAY.

" The day of all days " to me, *my wedding day !*
It is now six P.M. ; in two hours I shall say,
God willing, the words that forever will bind
Me to *him,* my heart's idol, for such a long time,
My own love and darling!   And sitting here, clad
In my pure bridal robes, I am making the glad,
Last record in my little journal, which has
Been a brief one, indeed ; for since it was commenced
I've no heart had for writing.   But *this* blissful end
Compensates for all of the pain gone before.

'Tis a night of deep beauty !   I look WITHOUT, o'er
My shoulder, and see the full moon, large and bright,
Shining calm and serene from the far East ; while light,
Fleecy clouds hover near it and o'er it ; but do
Not its brilliance obscure.   But a dark one's there, too ;
Sailing near, and yet nearer ; and if that should flit
Over, will it not hide with completeness all its
Matchless beauty and brilliance ?   With interest deep
I watch it move slowly along ; now it sweeps
Over every part ; but the radiance still
Escapes, and the ether surrounding it gilds.
In the cloud there are rifts, too, through which I its calm,
Silvery beauty still see.   Now it rises, with grand,
Imperial triumph, above the dark and
Most envious clouds shining forth once again,
With its lustre undimmed, and its beauty unchanged.

I turn from that picture, and look WITHIN !　There
I find perfect happiness !　And, though aware
That it by passing clouds may, and *must* be, indeed,
Temporarily dimmed, yet I trust there may be
Rifts, through which I may still its bright radiance see.
That *they* will soon pass, and its brilliancy leave
Untarnished, unchanged !

　　　　　　　　This is my " PROLOGUE " brief,
To what I've to write.

　　　　　　　　Just one week since, to-night,
In the parlor I sat in the gathering twilight,
Idly rocking and dreaming, with cheek in my hand,
Of present and past, when the bell loudly rang.
My position I still did not change, till the door
Was thrown wide, and a gentleman, crossing the floor,
Paused by me.　I looked up, and with rapturous joy
Recognized at one glance my own love ! my dear boy,
Who for more than two years I have never once seen.
Oh, how glad was my heart !　How entire and supreme
The delight with which once more I felt his dear arm
Around me, his kiss on my lips, long and warm !
And how happy was *he* to again hold me thus !
Oh, that moment alone quite compensated us
For the anguish of parting, the longing, and grief
Of the past two sad years.　Neither of us could speak
For a while ; then he drew me with him to a seat,
And as we sat down side by side, he to me
Said tenderly, softly, and how wistfully—
" I have come for you, dear, and I want you at once,
Entirely, forever !　And nothing more must
Ever separate us.　And no longer can I
Live apart from you ; every day want you in my

Now desolate home, every hour in my heart.
You are all mine! my darling, my wife, are you not?"
I against the dear hand which I held laid my cheek,
And looked up the dear eyes true and loving to meet,
And the answer he wished in my face let him read.
No words were required; for too long had he known
That my heart's every fibre for *him* throbbed alone.
And as *his* lips met mine in the lingering kiss
Of betrothal, I thought that no other caress
Was ever so sweet.
    Then he went on to tell,
As the darkening shades swiftly gathered and fell,
All that I'd for so long from his lips wished to hear.
How much and how dearly he'd loved me for years;
How it had sometimes almost overcome him;
How hard to repress words of love it had been,
When they trembled on *his* very lips; how with pain
He'd allowed many letters of mine to remain
Unanswered, from feeling he never could trust
Himself to reply; and how bowed to the dust
He was at our last bitter parting.
    How great,
And exceeding the joy which all this to me gave!
And to Him who bestows upon us all good gifts,
How thankful I felt that such full, perfect bliss,
Was at length me accorded—my most ardent wish
For long years, and the very desire of my heart.
And not what I wished for alone, He imparts—
The boon of his love—but He grants me, beside,
What I never dared think of, the privilege, right,
The remainder of life with my dear one to spend.

14*

That was one week ago! Every evening since then
He's been with me; and we're to be married to-night !
He thought we had been kept apart too long, quite,
To delay any more, and would give me but one
More brief week of freedom.   Nor did I, I own,
Desire it.   *These* chains are of silk, do not fret,
And bondage to *him* is, I think, sweeter yet
Than the most entire liberty.

                   What a soft light
Filled his eyes all the eve !   And my thoughts then took
    flight
To those beautiful Sabbaths six years ago, when
We both sat in church, and he down to me sent
Such sweet, thrilling glances—like, but not the same.
And *he loves me !*   My heart the sweet music again
And again doth repeat.   I am his, he is mine.
His heart warmly beats for me, mine through all time
Throbs for him truly, tenderly.   Friends *here* we are,
Friends we shall be in heaven ; loving here, loving far
Through the endless eternity.   He will soon come
To leave me not 'till the words making us one—
As we've long been in heart—shall be spoken.   That voice
So exquisite I once more shall hear ; meet the eyes
Whose glance is so loving and true ; feel the warm,
Thrilling clasp of his hand, the embrace of his arm,
The touch so caressing of *his* bearded cheek,
And the pressure of his mustached lips, as they meet
My own in the sweetest of kisses.   And this
Is *not* "*stolen* waters," but God-given bliss !
And how *can* any person, who ever a kiss
Of love has received, think of yielding their lips

To passion's profane touch, formality's cold,
Or friendship's indifferent pressure.   I own
I cannot.   And from *any* one's kisses I shrink
When he's left a caress on my lips.   For I think
A kiss sacred and very expressive, and it
Should be neither profaned nor abused.   I admit
I *like* kisses, but not a profusion, or those
That are cold and indifferent.   Though I suppose
My ideas are somewhat peculiar—in fact,
Have been *told* so—I'd not have them changed.   And am
    glad
He the luxury uses so rarely, indeed,
That 'tis not rendered common.   Am glad, too, that he
Is reserved; that he's not prodigal in professing
Attachment to me; is not free in expressing
His strong, full affection.
                I love him, he me !
I with my whole heart, my might, mind, strength; and he
As I wish to be loved.   And how thankful I am,
Every day, every hour of my life, that the man
On whom I have lavished the first, only love
Of which I am capable, who has above
All others for long been enshrined in my heart's
Sweet " holy of holies," who, " be the days dark
Or bright," must abide there forever, is one
That is worthy of all; a rare man, who's become
More honored and trusted each time we have met.
With whom a familiar acquaintance, instead
Of breaking the charm, or of weakening the depth
Of my passion 's enhanced it a thousand fold, swept
Aside every barrier, rendered it yet

More strong, deep, enduring, and shown him to me
The one love of my life—a man, manly—to be
My own, here and hereafter.

                  The name that I chose,
When I sent my first note to him *so* long ago,
How pertinent 'twas! " *Bitter-sweet !* " Seems almost
Prophetic. Impulsively chosen, no thought
Except for the present, no glance into what
Was then dim futurity, *no care*, indeed,
For what fruit might grow from the rashly sown seed.
A very child was I, dependent on each
Passing moment for happiness; joyous or grieved,
Glad or sorry, as by influences around
I was swayed. Not reflecting once, as to the wrong
Or right of the step I was taking, and not
One thought of with what results it might be fraught.
By the sweet, witching glances of his soft, dark eye
Fascinated, bewildered by the sweet, dreamy smile,
Which not alone wreathed his lips, dimpled his cheek,
But gave added beauty and softness to each
Fine feature of his speaking face ; and to him,
Looking up, as unto a superior being ;
List'ning week after week to the magic of his
Lovely voice, he a spell far too strong to resist,
Too gradual, subtle, bewilderingly sweet,
Wove around me, which deeper grew each passing week,
'Till, reckless of consequences, secure in
My disguise, longing passionately for something
Tangible, in connection with him—a line traced
By his hand, or the paper where it had been placed,
Something, *anything*, which was or had been his own—
I sent my first letter, and, as has been shown,

Prophetically chose as my disguise
The name " *Bitter-Sweet.*"   Six long years have passed by,
And a few days ago I another one sent,
In the same manner signed.   But I wrote to him then
As unto a stranger, unknown to him quite,
But now as my darling, my love, my delight !
What was then a dream only has long since become
A blessed reality ; and, more than once
I've experienced what I then longed for, the press
Of his arm around me, of my head to his breast.

Bitter-Sweet ! bitter has been indeed that note's fruit ;
Sweet, intensely sweet, also !   The plant's language, too,
Which I carelessly then as an emblem chose—*truth*—
Has run through the whole of our lives' warp and woof,
Since we ceased to be strangers.   I *have* been, I feel,
To him faithful, and he is, I know, *true as steel.*
The sweet's been predominant ; and, though 'tis plain
The bitter has also been present, it came
At the first, as the name indicates ; and the sweet
Followed swiftly, is thorough, and lasting, and deep.

Just six years to-day, since we met the first time !
And to-night God will make me all his, him all mine.
It is now half-past seven !   A few moments more,
And he will be here.   And though I've lingered o'er
This hour's pleasant task, I must leave it and haste
To my " EPILOGUE."
         Love is the " Alpha " I trace,
The " Omega " is joy.   I've for once known the taste
Of the rare, ruby wine of *entire happiness !*
Something seldom attained, scarcely known when possessed.

Every burden is lightened, each cloud is dispelled;
Every sorrow is banished, all gloom is expelled,
By the bright influence of the rosy contents
Of that magic goblet.   Whatever is meant
For me in the future, I then can look back
To these moments so joyous and glad, thinking that
Once, at least, have my heart-strings been swept by the
   hand
Of true happiness; and strains of music, both grand
And sweet, his magnetic touch followed.   Soft strains
Which vibrated and echoed, until they became
All lost in my joy's deep immensity.
       Then,
" What matters some sorrow, if blissful's the end? "

 The voice of my love ! and I think, as with fleet,
Eager footsteps, I hasten my dear one to meet,
That " the bitter all past, far more welcome's the sweet ! "

FINIS.

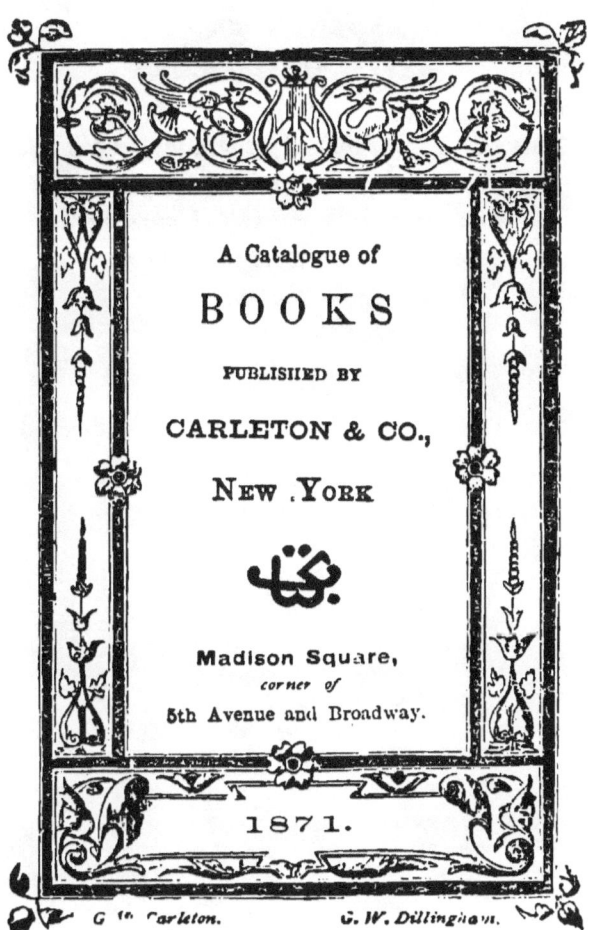

A Catalogue of

BOOKS

PUBLISHED BY

CARLETON & CO.,

NEW . YORK

Madison Square,
corner of
5th Avenue and Broadway.

1871.

G. W. Carleton. G. W. Dillingham.

"*There* is a kind of physiognomy in the titles
of books no less than in the faces of
men, by which a skilful observer
will know as well what to expect from the one as the
other."—BUTLER.

NEW BOOKS

Recently Published by

G. W. CARLETON & CO., New York,

Madison Square, Fifth Avenue and Broadway.

N.B.—THE PUBLISHERS, upon receipt of the price in advance, will send
any of the following Books by mail, POSTAGE FREE, to any part of the United
States. This convenient and very safe mode may be adopted when the neighbor-
ing Booksellers are not supplied with the desired work.

Marion Harland.

ALONE.—	A novel.	12mo. cloth,	$1.50
HIDDEN PATH.—	do.	do.	$1.50
MOSS SIDE.—	do.	do.	$1.5e
NEMESIS.—	do.	do.	$1.5c
MIRIAM.—	do.	do.	$1.50
AT LAST.—	do. *Just Published.*	do.	$1.50
HELEN GARDNER.—	do.	do.	$1.50
SUNNYBANK.—	do.	do.	$1.50
HUSBANDS AND HOMES.—	do.	do.	$1.50
RUBY'S HUSBAND.—	do.	do.	$1.50
PHEMIE'S TEMPTATION.—	do.	do.	$1.50
THE EMPTY HEART.—	do.	do.	$1.50

Miss Muloch.

JOHN HALIFAX.—A novel. With illustration. 12mo. cloth, $1.75
A LIFE FOR A LIFE.— . do. do. $1.75

Charlotte Bronte (Currer Bell).

JANE EYRE.—A novel. With illustration. 12mo. cloth, $1.75
THE PROFESSOR.—do. . do. . do. $1.75
SHIRLEY.— . do. . do. . do. $1.75
VILLETTE.— . do. . do. . do. $1.75

Hand-Books of Society.

THE HABITS OF GOOD SOCIETY; nice points of taste, good man-
ners, and the art of making oneself agreeable. 12mo. $1.75
THE ART OF CONVERSATION.—A sensible work, for every one
who wishes to be an agreeable talker or listener. 12mo. $1.50
ARTS OF WRITING, READING, AND SPEAKING.—An excellent book
for self-instruction and improvement. 12mo. clo., $1.50
HAND-BOOKS OF SOCIETY.—The above three choice volumes
bound extra, and put in a handsome box. . $5.00

Mrs. A. P. Hill.

MRS. HILL'S NEW COOKERY BOOK, and receipts. 12mo. cloth, $2.00

Mary J. Holmes.

'LENA RIVERS.—	. . . A novel. 12mo. cloth,	$1 50
DARKNESS AND DAYLIGHT.—	. do. . do. .	$1.50
TEMPEST AND SUNSHINE.—	. do. . do. .	$1.50
MARIAN GREY.—	. . . do. . do. .	$1 50
MEADOW BROOK.—	. . . do. . do. .	$1 50
ENGLISH ORPHANS.—	. do. . do. .	$1 50
DORA DEANE.—	. . . do. . do. .	$1 50
COUSIN MAUDE.—	. . . do. . do. .	$1.50
HOMESTEAD ON THE HILLSIDE.—	. do. . do. .	$1 50
HUGH WORTHINGTON.—	. do. . do. .	$1.50
THE CAMERON PRIDE.—	. do. . do. .	$1.50
ROSE MATHER.—	. . do. . do.	$1 50
ETHELYN'S MISTAKE.-—	. do. . do. .	$1.50
MILLBANK.—	. . . *Just published.* do. .	$1.50

Augusta J. Evans.

BEULAH.—	. . . . A novel. 12mo. cloth,	$1.75
MACARIA.—	. . . . do. . do. .	$1.75
ST. ELMO.—	. . . . do. . do. .	$2.00
VASHTI.—	. . . . do. . do. .	$2.00
INEZ.—	. . . . do. . do. .	$1.75

Victor Hugo.

LES MISERABLES.—	The celebrated novel, 8vo, cloth,	$2.50
DO.	Two vol. edition. fine paper, do.	$5.00
DO.	In the Spanish language do.	$5.00

Algernon Charles Swinburne.

LAUS VENERIS, AND OTHER POEMS.—Elegant new edition $1.50

Captain Mayne Reid.—Illustrated.

THE SCALP HUNTERS.—		12mo. clo.,	$1.50
THE WAR TRAIL.— .	} Far West Series	do.	$1.50
THE HUNTER'S FEAST.— .		do.	$1.50
THE TIGER HUNTER.— .		do.	$1.50
OSCEOLA, THE SEMINOLE.—		do.	$1.50
THE QUADROON.— .	} Prairie Series	do.	$1.50
RANGERS AND REGULATORS.—		do.	$1.50
THE WHITE GAUNTLET.—		do.	$1.50
WILD LIFE.—		do.	$1 50
THE HEADLESS HORSEMAN.—	} Pioneer Series	do.	$1.50
LOST LENORE.— . .		do.	$1.50
THE WOOD RANGERS.— .		do.	$1.50
THE WHITE CHIEF.—		do.	$1.50
THE WILD HUNTRESS.— .	} Wild Forest Series	do.	$1.50
THE MAROON.— . .		do.	$1.50
THE RIFLE RANGERS.— .		do.	$1.50

Comic Books—Illustrated.

ARTEMUS WARD,	His Book.—Letters, etc.	12mo. cl.,	$1.50
DO.	His Travels—Mormons, etc.	do.	$1.50
DO.	In London.—Punch Letters.	do.	$1.50
DO.	His Panorama and Lecture.	do.	$1.50
DO.	Sandwiches for Railroad. . .		.25
JOSH BILLINGS	ON ICE, and other things.—	do.	$1.50
DO.	His Book of Proverbs, etc.	·do.	$1.50
DO.	Farmer's Allmanax. . .		.25
FANNY FERN.—Folly as it Flies. . .		do.	$1.50
DO.	Gingersnaps	do.	$1.50
VERDANT GREEN.—A racy English college story.		do.	$1 50
MILES O'REILLY.—His Book of Adventures.		do.	$1.50
ORPHEUS C. KERR.—Kerr Papers, 4 vols. in one.		do.	$2.00
DO.	Avery Glibun. A novel. .	.	$2.00
DO.	The Cloven Foot. do.	do.	$1.50
BALLAD OF LORD BATEMAN.—Illustrated by Cruikshank.			.25

A. S. Roe's Works.

A LONG LOOK AHEAD.—	A novel. .	12mo. cloth,	$1.50
TO LOVE AND TO BE LOVED.—	do. . .	do.	$1.50
TIME AND TIDE.—	do. . .	do.	$1.50
I'VE BEEN THINKING.—	do. . .	do.	$1.50
THE STAR AND THE CLOUD.—	do. . .	do.	$1.50
TRUE TO THE LAST.—	do. . .	do.	$1.50
HOW COULD HE HELP IT ?—	do. . .	do.	$1.50
LIKE AND UNLIKE.—	do. . .	do.	$1.50
LOOKING AROUND.—	do. . .	do.	$1.50
WOMAN OUR ANGEL.—	do. . .	do.	$1.50
THE CLOUD ON THE HEART.—	do. . .	do.	$1.50
RESOLUTION.—	do. . .	do.	$1.50

Joseph Rodman Drake.

THE CULPRIT FAY.—A faery poem, with 100 illustrations.		$2.00
DO.	Superbly bound in turkey morocco.	$5.00

"Brick" Pomeroy.

SENSE.—An illustrated vol. of fireside musings.	12mo. cl.,	$1.50
NONSENSE.— do. do. comic sketches.	do.	$1.50
OUR SATURDAY NIGHTS. do. pathos and sentiment.		$1.50
BRICK DUST.—Comic sketches.		$1.50
GOLD DUST.—Fireside musings.		$1.50

John Esten Cooke.

FAIRFAX.—	A brilliant new novel. .	12mo. cloth,	$1.50
HILT TO HILT.—	do. . . .	do.	$1.50
HAMMER AND RAPIER.—	do. . . .	do.	$1.50
OUT OF THE FOAM.—	do. *Just published.*	do.	$1.50

Books of Amusement.

THE ART OF AMUSING.—With 150 illustrations.   12mo. $1.50
ROBINSON CRUSOE.—A Complete edition, illustrated,   do. $1.5c

By the Author of "Rutledge."

RUTLEDGE.—A deeply interesting novel.   12mo. cloth, $1.75
THE SUTHERLANDS.—   do.   .   .   do.   . $1.75
FRANK WARRINGTON.—   do.   .   .   do.   . $1.75
ST. PHILIP'S.—   do.   .   do.   . $1.75
LOUIE'S LAST TERM AT ST. MARY'S.—   do.   . $1.75
ROUNDHEARTS AND OTHER STORIES.—For children. do.   . $1.75
A ROSARY FOR LENT.—Devotional Readings.   do.   . $1.75

Richard B. Kimball.

WAS HE SUCCESSFUL?— A novel.   .   .   12mo. cloth, $1.75
UNDERCURRENTS.—   do.   .   .   do. $1.75
SAINT LEGER.—   do.   .   .   do. $1.75
ROMANCE OF STUDENT LIFE.—do.   .   .   do. $1.75
IN THE TROPICS.—   do.   .   .   do. $1.75
HENRY POWERS, Banker. do.   .   .   do. $1.75
TO-DAY.—   do.   .   .   do. $1.75

M. Michelet's Remarkable Works.

LOVE (L'AMOUR).—Translated from the French. 12mo. cl., $1.50
WOMAN (LA FEMME).—   .   do.   .   .   do. $1.50

Ernest Renan.

THE LIFE OF JESUS.—Translated from the French. 12mo. cl..$1.75
LIVES OF THE APOSTLES.—   do.   .   .   do. $1.75
THE LIFE OF SAINT PAUL.—   do.   .   .   do. $1.75

Popular Italian Novels.

DOCTOR ANTONIO.—A love story. By Ruffini. 12mo. cl., $1.75
BEATRICE CENCI.—By Guerrazzi, with portrait.   do. $1.75

Geo. W. Carleton.

OUR ARTIST IN CUBA.--With 50 comic illustrations.   . $1.50
OUR ARTIST IN PERU.—   do.   do.   .   . $1.50
OUR ARTIST IN AFRICA.—(*In press*)   do.   . $1.50

Julie P. Smith.

WIDOW GOLDSMITH'S DAUGHTER.—A novel. 12mo. cloth, $1.75
CHRIS AND OTHO.—   do.   do. $1.75
THE WIDOWER.—   do.   do. $1.75

Mansfield T. Walworth.

WARWICK.—A new novel.   .   .   12mo. cloth, $1.75
LULU.—   do.   .   .   .   do. $1.75
HOTSPUR.—   do.   .   .   .   do. $1.75
STORMCLIFF.—   do.   .   .   .   do. $1.75
A NEW BOOK.—   do.   .   .   .   do. $1.75

Miscellaneous Works.

FRENCH LOVE SONGS.—By the best French authors.	$1.50
BEAUTY IS POWER.—An admirable book for ladies.	$1.50
ITALIAN LIFE AND LEGENDS.—By Anna Cora Ritchie.	$1.50
LIFE AND DEATH.—A new American novel..	$1.50
HOW TO MAKE MONEY ; AND HOW TO KEEP IT.—Davies.	$1.50
THE CLOISTER AND THE HEARTH.—By Charles Reade.	$1.50
TALES FROM THE OPERAS.—The Plots of all the Operas.	$1.50
LOVE IN LETTERS.—An interesting and piquant book.	$2.00
OUT IN THE WORLD.—A novel. By T. S. Arthur.	$1.50
WHAT CAME AFTERWARDS.— do. do.	$1.50
OUR NEIGHBORS.— do. do.	$1.50
LIGHT ON SHADOWED PATHS.—do. do.	$1.50
ADVENTURES OF A HONEYMOON.—A love story.	$1.50
THE BIBLE IN INDIA.—From the French of Jacolliot.	$2.00
AMONG THE PINES.—Down South. By Edmund Kirke.	$1.50
MY SOUTHERN FRIENDS.— do. do.	$1.50
DOWN IN TENNESSEE.— do. do.	$1.50
ADRIFT IN DIXIE.— do. do.	$1.50
AMONG THE GUERILLAS.— do. do.	$1.50
A BOOK ABOUT LAWYERS.—Bright and interesting.	$2.00
A BOOK ABOUT DOCTORS.— do. do.	$2.00
WOMAN, LOVE, AND MARRIAGE.—By Fred. Saunders.	$1.50
THE GAME FISH OF THE NORTH.—By R. B. Roosevelt.	$2.00
THE GAME BIRDS OF THE NORTH.— do. do.	$2.00
PRISON LIFE OF JEFFERSON DAVIS.—By J. J. Craven.	$1.50
POEMS BY L. G. THOMAS.—	$1.50
PASTIMES WITH MY LITTLE FRIENDS.—Mrs. Bennett.	$1.50
THE GREAT TRIBULATION.—By Dr. John Cumming.	$1.50
THE GREAT PREPARATION.— do. do.	$1.50
THE GREAT CONSUMMATION.— do. do.	$1.50
THE SQUIBOB PAPERS.—A comic book. John Phœnix.	$1.50
COUSIN PAUL.—A new American novel.	$1.75
JARGAL.—A novel from the French of Victor Hugo.	$1.75
CLAUDE GUEUX.— do. do. do.	$1.50
LIFE OF VICTOR HUGO.— do. do.	$2.00
THE PHILOSOPHERS OF FOUFOUVILLE.—A Satire.	$1.50
NEGROES IN NEGROLAND.—By Hinton Rowan Helper.	$1.00
ALABAMA AND SUMTER CRUISE.—Raphael Semmes.	$1.50
CHRISTMAS HOLLY.—By Marion Harland, Illustrated.	$1.50
THE RUSSIAN BALL.—An illustrated satirical Poem.	.25
THE SNOBLACE BALL.— do. do	.25
THE PRINCE OF KASHNA.—Edited by R. B. Kimball.	$1.75
THE LAST WARNING CRY.—By Rev. John Cumming.	$1.50

Miscellaneous Works.

A LOST LIFE.—A novel by Emily H. Moore $1.50
CROWN JEWELS.—   do.   Mrs. Emma L. Moffett. $1.75
ADRIFT WITH A VENGEANCE.—   Kinahan Cornwallis. . $1.50
THE FRANCO-PRUSSIAN WAR IN 1870.—By M. D. Landon. $2.00
DREAM MUSIC.—Poems by Frederic Rowland Marvin. . $1.50
RAMBLES IN CUBA.—By an American Lady. . . $1.50
BEHIND THE SCENES, in the White House.—Keckley. . $2.00
YACHTMAN'S PRIMER.—For Amateur Sailors.—Warren.   50
RURAL ARCHITECTURE.—By M. Field. With illustrations. $2.00
TREATISE ON DEAFNESS.—By Dr. E. B. Lighthill. . . $1.50
WOMEN AND THEATRES.—A new book, by Olive Logan. $1.50
WARWICK.—A new novel by Mansfield Tracy Walworth. $1.75
SIBYL HUNTINGTON.—A novel by Mrs. J. C. R. Dorr. . $1.75
LIVING WRITERS OF THE SOUTH.—By Prof. Davidson. . $2.00
STRANGE VISITORS.—A book from the Spirit World. . $1.50
UP BROADWAY, and its Sequel.—A story by Eleanor Kirk. $1.50
MILITARY RECORD, of Appointments in the U.S. Army. $5.00
HONOR BRIGHT.—A new American novel. . . . $1.50
MALBROOK.—   do.   do.   do. . . . $1.50
GUILTY OR NOT GUILTY.—   do.   do. . . . $1.75
ROBERT GREATHOUSE.—A new novel by John F. Swift . $2.00
THE GOLDEN CROSS, and poems by Irving Van Wart, jr. $1.50
ATHALIAH.—A new novel by Joseph H. Greene, jr. . $1.75
REGINA, and other poems.—By Eliza Cruger. . $1.50
THE WICKEDEST WOMAN IN NEW YORK.—By C. H. Webb.   50
MONTALBAN.—A new American novel. . . $1.75
MADEMOISELLE MERQUEM.—A novel by George Sand. . $1.75
THE IMPENDING CRISIS OF THE SOUTH.—By H. R. Helper. $2.00
NOJOQUE—A Question for a Continent.—   do. . $2.00
PARIS IN 1867.—By Henry Morford. . . . $1.75
THE BISHOP'S SON.—A novel by Alice Cary. . . $1.75
CRUISE OF THE ALABAMA AND SUMTER.—By Capt. Semmes. $1.50
HELEN COURTENAY.—A novel, author "Vernon Grove." $1.75
SOUVENIRS OF TRAVEL.—By Madame Octavia W. LeVert. $2.00
VANQUISHED.—A novel by Agnes Leonard. . . $1.75
WILL-O'-THE-WISP.—A child's book, from the German . $1.50
FOUR OAKS.—A novel by Kamba Thorpe. . . $1.75
THE CHRISTMAS FONT.—A child's book, by M. J. Holmes. $1.00
POEMS, BY SARAH T. BOLTON. $1.50
MARY BRANDEGEE—A novel by Cuyler Pine. . . $1.75
RENSHAWE.—   do.   do. . . $1.75
MOUNT CALVARY.—By Matthew Hale Smith. . . $2.00
PROMETHEUS IN ATLANTIS.—A prophecy. . . $2.00
TITAN AGONISTES.—An American novel. . . $2.00